Dance with the Desert

Julia Jaxsun

ISBN:9798998636318
Celestial Desert Media Publishing

Dedication

To the anonymous ladies I met in Truth or Consequences, New Mexico, in a hot spring, whose vibrant, joyful personalities and friendships inspired this novel.

That brief conversation reminded me of my own friendships, the power of quirky women and the magic of the desert, and I thought, *I'm going to write a book about this.* And here it is.

"Music gives a soul to the universe, wings to the mind, flight to the imagination, and life to everything." —Plato

Sliver in the Sky

heo sat in the warm spring water facing a cozy couple soaking up the minerals, though the man of the two appeared slightly perturbed to have a third person simmering with them. Just as she was debating getting up and out, she heard voices approaching that sliced the stillness of the desert night air. They were laugh-y and happy, liquid with intoxication, and their lightness drew nearer as three women's silhouettes lengthened across the dark night toward the tub.

"Hi!" said one of them at the end of a laugh, her movements fluid and soft. "Mind if we join you all?"

Her name would turn out to be Winona Ampeg, Winny, for short.

The woman Theo was sitting in the tub with, (Theo never did catch her name) responded, "Sure, join us!" to the surprising dismay of her male partner.

You'd think being in a hot spring tub with several nearly-naked women would be pure delight, but all he clearly wanted was alone time with his woman.

Man, now that is true love, thought Theo.

The three ladies clambered into the tub, drinks held aloft and cozied up next to the others in the small trough. Theo felt like she was getting drunk off them from osmosis. She wondered how old they were, but they looked to be in their late twenties, or thirties, like herself.

"Hey, so do y'all know why this town is called Truth or Consequences?" asked Winny.

Theo realized she reminded her of Veronica Lodges from those old-school Archie comics, but an edgier version, with short black bangs and tattoos covering her arms with hints of red and green. The other lobsters in the hot springs tank shook their heads, waiting for the answer.

Winny took another swig of her beer. "Well, it used to be aptly named Hot Springs, New Mexico, but in the fifties, there was a Radio Show called *Truth or Consequences*, a quiz game show, that announced they would air their tenth-year anniversary show from whatever town changed their name to Truth or Consequences first, and, well … *Voilà!*" She made a swoop of her hands across the water, exclaiming, "True story!"

Winny had a confident air to her, a quality Theo *wished* she could absorb, and a way of saying her words with rhythmic clarity. She had a kind smile that reminded you of a friend keeping your truth in confidence for you. The conversation soon switched to travel, abortion, and astrology, which she was delightedly unsurprised by, validating her original feelings that she would like these women. She herself wasn't much into horoscopes, but loved observing the conversations surrounding the topic.

It came to light the lady in the tub, the one Theo never caught the name of, was a Pisces. The attention turned to her, and one of the women, Jen Hernandez, rhetorically asked, "A Pisces, huh?!" to which the lady nodded again. "That's cool," Jen continued while flopping her dyed-blonde, grown-out mohawk to the other side like a mop. "I haven't met a Pisces in a long time." The light from a nearby campground streetlamp illuminated Jen's tan skin, her eyebrows attentive and thoughtful.

"A Pisces, I knew it," Winny concluded.

Theo thought it was funny when people said this. *Wouldn't you say that about any sign and adapt your perception of the person accordingly?*

"Pisces have an inert wisdom and are on the next plane of awareness," said Winny sagaciously.

"Well then, what would you all like to know about the universe?" the woman with no known name responded, further feeding into the mystique of the conversation with a smile.

The third woman in the group, tall and quiet, named Rain Westfield, adjusted the strap on her tie-dyed swimsuit as she swam closer to the woman, putting down her whiskey bottle. She looked captivated. "What does the rest of the year hold in store?"

The unnamed woman thought for a minute. "This coming year holds; hardship, water, fire and a long journey."

The ladies looked on, wide-eyed in anticipation of more. Theo thought this response was perfectly vague for any sort of interpretation.

Winny was now standing in the tub in her black, high waisted swim shorts and leopard-print swim top. She stared off into the distance, absentmindedly commenting on the woman's response, "Pisces are also known to be in their own world, if you know what I mean," which caused the smile to slide slightly from the woman's face.

"What's your sign?" Jen inquired, her mohawk tweaking to the side, switching gears and looking at Theo.

"Virgo," she responded without hesitation while kindly accepting a swig of whiskey passed to her by Jen.

As if right on cue, Winny responded that she 'knew it' and proceeded with some classic Virgo attributes which Theo nodded to, and made a *hmm* face, a neutral response which neither agreed nor disagreed, bemused.

"So what's your story?" said Jen looking towards Theo.

"My story?" Theo said, half choking, nervously playing with her thickly braided, brunette hair. *What was her story?* Images of needles, fluorescent lights, crisp cardboard-like linen and sterile smiles flashed before her eyes. More images. A slamming car door, loud exchanges and long days. Like fingernails on a chalkboard.

"Theo?" someone asked.

The three ladies and the couple were staring at her; Winny with her kind brown eyes, Jen with her shapely eyebrows raised and Rain with her frizzled hair, as well as the curious couple, all looked at her expectantly. She must have been lost in her thoughts for a minute.

The quiet man of the group took the moment's silence as an opportunity. "Well, I think we're going to head out," he said.

Theo had noticed they made that snapshot look at each other, the one where couples give each other, that says, *Ready to go?*

"Nice to meet you guys," he said, polite, ready to have alone time with his girlfriend.

His girl grinned, her face flushed with the hot spring warmth and the couple disappeared into the quiet night across the starry campground toward their yurt, never to be seen again by the other travelers.

Now it was just the four of them: Theo, Winny, Jen and Rain, stewing in the sorceresses' brew. Thankfully, they seemed to forget they'd asked Theo about her past. It was not something she wanted to dredge up. After all, she'd taken this solo trip aspiring to escape it.

The three of them chatted emphatically about something that sounded like an alcohol-free bar Winny managed in Albuquerque from afar, while Winny guzzled her Montucky beer with a touch of irony. Winny also ran the campground they were currently in.

What a go-getter, Theo thought, impressed. She stared up at the stars, vast and bright in the western sky. The desert was unique, like nothing she'd ever seen before, having never traveled outside the South. Never. But out here, currently in Truth or Consequences, New Mexico, the air was dry and crisp in the day, cold and firm at night. It was so otherworldly to Theo, it felt to her as though she were in a vivid dream. Jagged mountains turned pink at sunset and crackly dirt scuffed under your feet. Juniper and chamisa and cacti prickled the landscape. Roadrunners jutted across the mirage-laden highways.

Truth or Consequences was a sleepy adobe town dotted alongside the Rio Grande. Agave, 'Peach Pie' hard cactus, yucca and Opuntia phaeacantha or 'Desert Prickly Pear' dotted the landscape and trees lined the impressive Rio Grande which sauntered languidly toward the ocean. An occasional hawk could be spotted gliding through an updraft, enjoying its flight in the sun rays. Hot springs bubbled up naturally and formed pools alongside its river shore, offering healing minerals to the plants reaching their roots down into the soil, and for people too, looking to lay their own weary roots in water. Perhaps it was the geothermal energy wafting up from the earth's crust and core and into the hot spring healing waters that gave the town a feeling of subtle, albeit rundown, enchantment. Local indigenous people, mostly Chiricahua Apache, utilized the medicinal waters of the hot springs well before white settlers capitalized on the region and long before they dammed up Elephant Butte nearby. Geronimo himself was said to have lived there for a full year.

Theo lay in the healing waters of the springs, her new companions' muffled voices dancing off the waters, their sine waves echoing across the surface. She could just make out a slender sliver of moon above the dark mountains and imagined for a minute, what it would be like to see a flying saucer rise from above them. After all, wasn't it New Mexico where that UFO was spotted? Roswell?

For a moment, she saw a glimpse of light move oddly and disappear just behind the mountains. She paused. Was that … her imagination? The whiskey? Her thoughts were disrupted by a nudge to her elbow from Rain. "Hmm?"

"Would you like to partake, lovely lady and fellow friendly traveler?" Rain made a tip of her imaginary hat while holding out something in the palm of her hand. Rain wore a smiling, spacy expression as though she were on another planet. Theo got the sense she'd been to a lot of Grateful Dead concerts.

A sliver of something lay resting in her palm, like the moon peering overhead.

"What is it?" Theo wasn't big on drugs, she wasn't even much of a drinker and that whiskey must have really been getting to her head. But also, why not? Wasn't this trip about turning a new leaf, finding the joy that had mostly been sapped from her life, like a tap stabbed into a maple tree sucking out the juice? She was on a mission to restore joy. Joy she hadn't felt since she was a kid. Whatever it was, Theo put it on her tongue and it dissolved into nothingness in her mouth.

Within twenty minutes, the stars swirled into spirals and giggles from the ladies turned into harmonic melodies playing between her ears.

Waves of Color

Theo rubbed her temples and woke with a crumpled yawn. She felt a searing pain at the back of her head and winced. She rubbed the back of her skull, thinking her head was about to explode. *This is definitely the worst hangover I've ever had,* thought Theo. Images from the night before sprinkled into her mind.

Dust between her hands vibrated bright reds and blues, her footsteps gliding one by one along the dark earth. Waves of color washed across her. She felt like she was floating and the air was oddly still. These strangers, who Theo now knew by name at this point in the night, Winny, Jen and Rain, were walking in front of her along a path while the stars zoomed in ever closer. They walked along a valley laden with spiky desert trees. Where were they going? Theo couldn't remember. Jen walked in front of her, her jagged grown-out mohawk hair morphing into the trees, dotted lights of the barren city behind them sprinkling into earshot like chimes.

They arrived at the base of a mesa, its shadow looming

down upon them. It rose high up into the air, daunting. A saguaro cactus stood tall and out of place with six, spiny arms reaching to the sky. That was odd. Theo thought saguaros only grew in the Sonoran Desert. She then felt a terrible shooting pain jolt across the inside of her head. Streaks of white crossed her vision and she instinctively closed her eyes, holding the back of her head in her hands, squinting in pain. She took deep breaths, slowly, calmly before opening her eyes and feeling the pain ease as it passed, wondering if this was a side effect of the drugs. The pain departed and she took a step to catch up with the others, but stopped when she saw something.

A roadrunner sped across her path then stopped in front of her. It turned and looked at her, opening its beak as if to say something. Theo froze. Was it staring at her? Its beady eyes twinkled in the starry night. Theo stared back at it, amazed. It was beautiful. It had a red streak across its head and the sand-colored feathers were accented with dark dots. One marking stood out. Across its wing it had a dark blue patch resembling a tiny wave. Theo scratched her head at the oddity of this and found herself staring, her pupils wide. The wave marking seemed to be flowing, moving.

The roadrunner continued looking up at her. Theo leaned in closer. Its beak was opening and closing and it seemed to be whispering something. Theo crouched on the dirt on her hands and knees, leaning in close to hear what it was saying. Her friends faded into the dark ahead of her but she leaned closer, turning her ear to the side for the bird to whisper in her ear. The bird opened its beak and said—

Theo heard a sound. She was lying on an air mattress on the floor. She looked around and realized she must have fallen asleep last night in the gargantuan, old Airstream. It was a 1980s Excella Motorhome, the type where there is a driver's seat up front. Best friends Jen and Rain had been traveling in it for weeks and it showed. The third gal, Winny, lived in the Winnebago closest to the campground gate. It was the best location to run things. *But what was that sound?* She rolled over to see a man with an impressive hipster mustache standing in the camper kitchen grinding coffee beans.

"Sorry, did I wake you? I guess there's no way to grind coffee beans quietly," he said with a laugh.

More images from the previous night swam into view.

Jumping a fence into a manicured and rocky backyard. A lit up pool next to a boxy, modern, expensive-looking house, quite out of place for Truth or Consequences. Swimming around in that pool, floating. Laughing with her new lady friends and dunking each other in the water. The water turned hues of purple and red just as the sand had earlier in the night. The stars did that thing again where they zoomed in closer and closer.

A sound from the house and a jolting light from inside.

A man with a mustache, who looked to be about their age, walked out a sliding door, rubbing sleep from his eyes, mumbling, "Who's out there? Who's in my pool?"

Winny laughed as she had earlier in the night when she'd approached the hot spring tub. A full hearty laugh and went back under the water to move her black hair out of her eyes.

Theo remembers looking at the man. She swam closer to the side of the pool and propped her elbows on the concrete overhang, squinting as she inspected him. He had a good energy, albeit sleepy. Out of character, Theo heard herself say, "Wanna join us for a swim?" as though someone else had said it.

The man looked at Theo and raised an eyebrow. He looked surprised, maybe even taken aback. "In my own pool?"

"Yeah. Join us," Theo had said. "Join me."

The man had smiled and introduced himself.

Mark. It was Mark standing in the kitchen grinding coffee beans. He now offered her a mug while he sipped his own. "Coffee?" he said, handing her a cup.

There was the sound of laughter outside and Theo leaned over the kitchen counter to peek out the window. The three gals she had met last night were perched in mismatching dining chairs around a calm fire.

"Go ahead, I'll meet you out there. I'm finishing up this toast and scrambling these eggs for us," he said, pointing to the stove and what looked like almost fluffy eggs with some green and red pepper chopped up.

Theo was catching some feelings already for this dreamboat and she only just remembered they'd met last night. She gave him a smile and walked out into the crisp air.

Since her time in the desert just a few days ago, Theo was no longer surprised at how much the temperature dropped at night and how cool it remained in the morning. She walked down the steps of the camper and was greeted by a sweet, gentle dog, a mutt of some kind. She didn't remember there being a dog last night, *Whose was it?* Normally not the partying type, she wasn't used to gaps in memory like this and was undecided whether or not it was a positive new trend. Escaping the South's issues to discover vices and drugs in the desert wasn't exactly a positive trade. Certainly not in her mental state.

"Heyo! It's our girl Theo!" said Winny, cheers-ing her coffee to her in the air while the other girls followed suit.

Theo mirrored the gesture with her mug and took a seat in a turquoise-painted wooden chair that *creaked* as she sat beside the fire. The scene was comforting. Friends, a dog, the desert, a cutie in the camper and Winny strumming lightly on an acoustic Martin guitar.

"We didn't have breakfast sausages so we're roasting up some hotdogs," said Winny between chords, pointing to the sticks with hotdogs at the end, resting in the air near the coals.

"Looks like you roped yourself a keeper," said Rain softly, nodding toward the camper where Mark was still inside making toast and eggs.

Theo smiled and shrugged. "Not sure it's gonna last," she said, "after all, I'm leaving Truth or Consequences tomorrow." The ladies got quiet and then Theo broke the silence, "Wow, what a night huh? Did we take a midnight hike?" she asked.

"We sure did," said Jen, her face brightening. "Man, I was tripping pretty hard, what about you guys?"

The group laughed in agreement. Winny rubbed her elbow where a red abrasion was.

Theo began to speak, "Yeah I coulda sworn I saw—" but was

interrupted by the sound of the camper door swinging open and Mark holding a plate of a pile of eggs and toast.

"The chef has arrived!" whooped Jen.

The others did some whooping of their own as Theo looked at her temporary newfound crew with a smile. *What was this feeling, was this joy?*

They passed the big plate around and took turns eating, sharing the same fork. Theo didn't normally like to share germs but hell, Theo was just going for it at this point, retraining her mind to settle into relaxation.

The time passed and the sun spread its rays, lengthening the little Peach Pie cactus shadows and settling the morning birds in for a midday snooze. The desert had a different feel to it from yesterday, warm to the tongue and dry to the eyes. A wisp of something firm, but kind. Theo reminded herself to soak in the moment and enjoy her comforting present company. It was too bad her time here would be short-lived. She needed to hit the road tomorrow at the very latest, as she had something waiting for her down the road. Sometimes she could swear her tight back felt like a bundle of twigs ready to snap.

"You never did say what your story is," said Winny, looking at Theo as though she knew something turbulent was going on in her mind.

How could someone you knew for just one night, on acid, in the desert, know you so well?

Theo decided to vaguely lay it out on the table. She took a breath. "I'm running away from a failed career, a failed marriage and I need to hit the road because … something is waiting for me." *Did I say too much? Felt pretty good to say though,* she decided.

Winny, Jen, Rain and Mark, and even the dog looked at her, knowingly.

After a pause, Winny responded, "I feel that, sister. I've run the gauntlet myself. I escaped an abusive relationship just a year ago today, when I moved into that Winnebago camper over there and decided to run this campground. That's when my life got better though. You gotta know that things'll get better," she concluded, taking the plate of eggs, toast and hot dogs, and stuffing her mouth for a minute. "Oh and don't be hard on yourself. We all fail," she added with her mouth full. "I failed over and over again to get away from Joe but I finally did it, didn't I? I got away. You can always start again."

Jen chimed in, "I'm constantly in an identity crisis. I'm a straight, lesbian-looking Latina from Tucson who can't speak Spanish, whose Chilean-as-fuck parents named her Jennifer, *and* I'm hanging out with a bunch of loud-ass white girls."

They all laughed, almost a little nervously.

"I'm not white though, so I guess you don't mean me," winked Winny.

Mark decided to throw his two cents into the mix too, "Hey, don't forget me! I've been kidnapped by a bunch of tripping ladies, trespassing on my yard late at night and offering me a swim in my own damn pool, and I can't get enough of hanging out with them, and pretty sure I'm already falling for one of them," he said, looking warmly at Theo.

There was a collective *awww* in the group.

"Classic Stockholm Syndrome," Jen joked.

Theo felt lighter, like a weight had been lifted. "Mark, remind me what your last name is?" she asked shyly, very aware they had not exchanged last names yet.

"Gladden. Yours?"

"Hart," responded Theo.

"That fits," Mark smiled.

Theo didn't know what he meant. He then stood up and looked toward the dog, making a slight whistle to which the dog came over running obediently. *Ah, yes! The medium-sized mutt is Mark's.* Theo could still feel its tongue licking the chlorine from her face after it had jumped in the pool last night, dog paddling, joyfully herding the ladies.

"I've got to head to work. Pleasant meeting you all," he said, gesturing to everyone around the early morning fire, then looking at Theo, "Give me a call later. Maybe I can cook for you tonight before you leave?"

She smiled and nodded.

"Let's go, Bowzer," he said and the dog trotted off alongside him.

Winny continued the conversation where they had left off, "What about you, Rain, any interest in sharing your story?"

Curly-haired Rain seemed to think about it for a moment, then shook her head.

Theo was still getting to know everyone but she had already picked up that Rain was often quiet, more of an observer than an active talker.

Hardships and Later,
a Feathered Messenger

Later that afternoon, after spending the day with her newfound friends, Theo went back to her camping spot where she had parked her Subaru next to the tiny camper titled 'Blissa' that she had rented. She walked into the cozy RV space accentuated with built-out countertops and fifties-style diner aesthetics, black and white tile backsplash, velvet green curtains next to the bed jutting up to the low windows. She opened the bunched-up curtains and a massive spider launched out, causing a *yelp* of surprise. She grabbed a mug, scooped up the little creature and put it outside.

As she lay back down on the cushion she called a mattress, the place felt like home at this point. She'd been traveling for quite some time. Things had gotten so bad back home in the South, she just had to get away. She glanced at her phone: Five missed text messages and three voicemails. She turned it off and stared at the camper ceiling, exhausted. The previous evening had been a trip, literally and she thought back to last night.

There she was in that dark valley, the roadrunner getting ready to speak as she leaned in closely, trying to hear what it was saying.

"Look over there," it said, pointing its beak to the top of a mountain where a dim light flickered.

Then it had puttered off into the darkness, its soft, quick feet making a sifting sound on the sand, which seemed to echo in her ears as though in an acoustic dome. The stars zoomed in closer again and Theo looked into the distance toward the mountain, but the flickering light was gone. Her three new friends then noticed Theo wasn't behind them so they doubled back.

"What're you doing on the ground?" said Jen.

Theo looked up at them, perplexed, her pupils engorged. "I swear a roadrunner just talked to me."

The girls howled with laughter.

"I love vicariously experiencing someone's first time on acid!" Winny remarked.

"What did it say?" asked Rain inquisitively, a spark of genuine curiosity apparent on her soft face, her rainbow earrings swinging from her ears.

Theo gave a chuckle, knowing how ridiculous it was. "It pointed over there and said, 'Look over there.'"

The girls paused.

"Well then, there is where we must go!" shouted Winny, determined, with an exultant finger in the air, pointing to the top of the mesa.

Her words echoed, just as the roadrunner's had.

Tap, tap, tap. Someone was tapping at her window. Had she fallen asleep?

She went to look at the phone to see the time but remembered she had turned it off. As she brushed the curtain aside, she saw Rain waving her outside, so she lifted up the handle to the camper and climbed out.

"Come over, we have something to show you," Rain said.

They walked over to the Airstream where the other gals held out a homemade-looking Funfetti cake, the kind you get out of a box. Across the frosting were the words: 'Stay with us?!' and a heart scribbled on top.

"We didn't let the cake cool enough," Jen stated, her eyebrows quizzical, looking at the cake's disarray.

"It's beautiful! And I would love to," Theo started to say, "but, I'm so sorry, I can't stay. I have to leave tomorrow." The ladies looked dismayed, before she added, "I would love to hang out for one last fun night though."

"I thought you were going to Mark's, isn't he cooking you dinner later?" Jen asked.

Theo had been thinking about it. She really shouldn't get mixed up with a new love interest at this point. She needed to find herself, by herself, for herself. Plus, she didn't want to get him involved in her mess. "No, I don't think I should get mixed up with someone right now," she said. "Can we, uh, party?"

Winny nodded. "But how 'bout we enjoy each other's company, *sans* acid? We were only gettin' rowdy like that last night to celebrate Jen's birthday."

Oh yeah, it was Jen's birthday, that's why her newfound friends were hitting it hard. What else had she forgotten? The amnesiac feeling made her uneasy. Maybe she needed to clear her head. "Yes, let's just enjoy each other's company. I like that idea. Do y'all mind if I take a walk first?" she asked.

Theo punched in the code to go out the front gate from the hodge-podge camping spot in the middle of town where she was staying. With a clank, it began slowly sliding aside.

The sun was just about to set, the jagged mountains were illuminated in rays of gold and that desert pink hue she had come to look forward to so fondly. Something about this place was truly magical. She hated to go but of course, she had to. She meandered along the cracked paved road and through what town residents called downtown but which was more like an old Western movie town with a couple of hippy stores, several cannabis shops and green chile restaurants.

She rounded the corner of one shop closed for the day with overgrown philodendron plants encircling the window trim, with proudly displayed hand painted signs that stated one could both come to a free pottery class on Wednesdays and get their palms read here.

She walked past an auto body shop and noticed a guy polishing a car out front. He was clean-cut and wore sunglasses. He turned toward her, and Theo noticed a strange tattoo on the side of his buzz-cut head. It was a realistic looking eye. There was something odd about the way he looked at her. Theo often felt the weird sensation she was being followed, ever since leaving home in the South. But, despite the feeling, she turned away from the man and brushed it off. *Probably just paranoia,* she thought.

She walked past a music shop with a stage out back. It looked haunted and old, but had a few nice guitars in the window. She continued past another place with a coffee-cup-shaped sign saying, 'Truth or Coffee.' *Clever*, chuckled Theo. She liked this town, she decided. Strolling further brought her into a neighborhood while thinking about her life. She had gone to nursing school to become a nurse practitioner in obstetrics and gynecology, but the panic attacks had hit hard, even when she graduated and had officially became a nurse. The hours were rough, the pay wasn't great and the pressure was immense. Half the time she felt like she wasn't good enough to be a nurse and the other half she wasn't even sure she wanted to be a nurse. There she was, in a career she hated and had pushed herself to be in, because she'd thought it was the right thing to do; to give back to others; to be a good person. Abandoning her nursing career and her higher purpose in life made her feel like a failure, not to mention all the money she'd spent on nursing school. *If she wasn't a nurse, who was she?*

On top of that, there was the bad, too-young marriage and—well… the other situation. She sighed, reminding herself that she never regretted what she had done and knew she never would, as it was the right thing to do, but she acknowledged that some people wouldn't understand. So she'd had to run. And now, she was paying the price.

She meandered onward and up a dusty, dirty hill, lost in thought.

The moment she realized she needed to get out and run she had just clocked out from a graveyard shift when the nurse light came on for room 223. A patient who had just given birth to a baby while being a surrogate mother was undergoing respiratory failure. Theo was off the clock but ran in to help. The doctors were perplexed as the patient had seemed fine just a few minutes ago. Theo recognized the symptoms right away. It was eclampsia. But it had been too late. The patient had passed. It felt wrong and grossly unfair. This person had risked her life bringing life to another, for the sake of others and she had died doing it.

Theo remembered the panic attack she'd had in the car that morning. Had she done something wrong? Was this somehow her fault? And why, if there was a god, had this person died? She turned in her notice the next day and resolved that life was too short to continue suffering. She deserved to live a full and happy life. So she made a choice and left town as fast as possible, embarking into the unknown of the Southwest, as far from the South as she could get. She planned to be on the road, possibly forever.

Theo's feet had taken her to the top of a flat-topped mountain, a mesa, as she had learned it was called, and peered out across the valley. The little town lay stretched out before her, quiet and calm. She allowed her mind to mimic the peace of the scenery before her and let go of the thoughts that had pulled her into the past.

She sat down and picked up a handful of dry clay, letting it fall between her fingers. The desert felt soothing and surreal, healing, and she let a moment of gratitude settle. Gratitude for being out of that life-sucking career. She still had the utmost respect and appreciation for people who could stick with nursing, but she realized she just couldn't. She let gratitude seep into her bones for the fortitude to get out of her marriage and do what she had felt was right. Gratitude for her resilience and her will to transform. She felt like a failure but, like Winny had said, '*We all fail.*' We just needed to move on.

Never before had Theo done a trip like this, traveling on her own into the Wild West.

She sat at the top of the mesa now in silence, pondering the expansiveness of the land and sky and let herself breathe. *Wait, had she been here before?* Theo suddenly had that déjà-vu feeling and her thoughts brought her back to last night.

> *She and the three women were meandering up the hillside path to the mesa, singing an alt-country song Theo didn't know but was enjoying listening to. The stars seemed to be singing too. She couldn't explain how, it was more of a feeling. The trail got so steep they used their hands to pull themselves along until finally they got to the top.*
>
> *"Is this where the roadrunner pointed?" Winny said with a wink in her eye.*
>
> *Theo looked down into the dark from where they had come for a line of reference, where the out-of-place saguaro cactus and roadrunner had been. "Maybe a little over that way," she said pointing to a further point.*
>
> *A flickering orb of light then illuminated before them. It glistened and exuded a melodic humming sound, ethereal, like Buddhist monks humming in unison. It was the most beautiful sound Theo had ever heard. There was a shadowy figure behind it and Theo felt a sense of confusion at what she saw.*

Sitting on the mesa, looking behind her in the direction of where that light must have been last night, the sense of confusion returned. She walked over to what seemed to be the same prickly cactus and otherwise unfamiliar landscape. *What had omitted the orb of light?* Looking around and seeing nothing that could have been the source, she noticed an area of sand that had seen a scuffle and a few droplets of blood. *Odd*, she thought.

The sun slipped past the jagged mountains heralding the onset of dark. She needed to get off this mesa and ensure she could find her way back to the campground, back to her new, fleeting friends. She tucked the odd scene away in her mind and headed back to her Blissa home.

When she returned, the ladies had already set up a fire and food on a folding table. Taco fixings and ceramic plates.

"She returns!" Winny shouted as Theo approached.

The other girls whooped. Theo couldn't help but grin widely at being greeted this way. It warmed her heart. She hadn't felt friendship like this, in say—ever. *Could it last, after only a night, long distance?*

As she sat by the fire and enjoyed eating the food they had provided, she had texted Mark that it was lovely to meet him but that it didn't feel right leading him on when she was not in a good place to start up a new relationship. He hadn't yet texted back.

After eating, they shared a neatly rolled joint together, passing it around.

Jen said with a puff, "That'll take me to the moon!" and they all relished the Funfetti cake slices on their plates, and sang old country songs while Winny strummed the chords on her beloved Martin guitar.

In between songs, Theo frowned. "I'm going to miss this. I feel like I've known y'all forever."

"You don't have to go!" Jen pleaded.

"Yeah, stay here with us. Dance with the desert!" Winny

shouted, jumping to her feet and letting her guitar fall off her lap and onto the ground with a crunch.

Theo grimaced and laughed at the same time, and let Winny take her hands gently and give her a twirl to no music, just the crackling fire. Jen and Rain laughed and joined them in dancing. It could have been the weed, but it felt like they were all dancing for a long, long time.

When they finally sat down again, Winny reiterated that Theo should stay longer with them.

"I wish I could … I just can't," stated Theo with a sigh. "There's something I have to get away from. So I do need to hit the road."

Winny ignored that ominous sentence and said, "We could start a band! It's always been my dream to have an all-female alt-country band."

"So what makes it 'alt' country?" asked Rain.

Jen piped in "Alternative liberal country, baby!" and gave her friend a punch on the arm. "Imagine hipsters listening to country, and boom! You've got yourself alt-country."

Theo was glad to get an answer to this. She had been wondering the same thing.

"Ya know, here's a thought," Jen continued while scratching the buzzed side of her head, "we could be a metal band instead, called Face Orifice."

"Eww, Jen, why you gotta be gross?!" winced Winny.

"That's the thing! It's not gross. Orifice just means an opening in the body, like nostrils or something, so really, it's not gross, but it sounds disturbing doesn't it? Perfect for a metal band."

Winny moved past Jen's idea. "I could do guitar and vocals," she continued, "and Rain, you used to play the keyboard, right?"

Rain nodded, "Sure, I could play keys."

Jen jumped in, "Oooh and I could play bass! I've always wanted to play the bass."

"So that just leaves drums. You wanna be our drummer, Theo?"

Theo laughed. She'd never touched a set of drums before. She'd once played another instrument before in high school but it hadn't been drums. "Sorry to disappoint y'all but I don't know how to play the drums," she said.

"You could learn!" Winny said.

"Play. The. Drums. Play. The. Drums. Play. The. Drums," Jen chanted and Winny and Rain joined in.

The sound of the gate screeching to the side and slowly opening disrupted their chanting. An old beat-up truck glided in and parked by the hot springs tubs.

A guy and his dog got out. It was Mark.

A Discovery in Cardboard

Mark and Theo sat on the bumper of her Subaru, talking, with the flowers he'd brought sitting in a Nalgene water bottle and a candle he'd also brought, sitting next to it on the dirt.

"I don't know entirely what it is but last night was magical. Meeting you made me so happy," he said. "I, too, moved out here to escape some things. Maybe we're all just running from things but sooner or later they catch up to us and we have to try to let them go and move on, right? If you're afraid to find love again since your marriage failed, please know you can find love again, with me. Just maybe. I want to get to know you more. Can we give it a shot?"

Theo scratched Bowzer's ears, his tail wagging and tongue sticking out, to give herself time to respond. It did feel so comfortable with Mark. And Bowzer. "Why'd you name him *Bowzer*? What does it mean?" she said.

Mark gave her a look of incredulity. "You really don't know who Bowzer is?"

"What, is it some historical figure I'm supposed to know?"

Mark laughed. "No, I wish I were that smart. Remember, you're the smart one. No, he's a character from Super Mario. You know, the video game?"

"Oh, right! But isn't Bowzer the big tough one? This medium dog Bowzer is anything but."

"Exactly," Mark stated while patting his dog on the head. "It's ironic."

ΔΔΔ

Sometime later, Theo strolled back over to the fire where her lady friends were.

"So! How'd it go?" Rain asked.

"I'm just not ready, you guys," Theo answered.

"Boooooo!" hollered Jen. "That marriage must have been a bad breakup, huh? What was it about the guy?"

"I'd rather not say. I want that in the past," Theo said, ignoring her phone lighting up to another missed call.

ΔΔΔ

The next morning, she awoke from an odd dream.

The talking roadrunner and she were up on the mesa. The roadrunner was busy digging its long slender beak into a cactus flower, drinking the liquid within. It looked at her and this time, said nothing and resumed its drinking, stabbing its beak back into the flower.

Theo yawned and stretched. She did a little yoga as the sun rose, a habit she'd picked up along her travels. No one was awake yet over at Winny's Winnebago or Rain and Jen's giant motorhome. She made herself a cup of coffee in the tiny provided machine in her camper and snacked on some leftover cake while packing it up to go. She started up her Subaru's engine and began to drive away.

While approaching the gate, she heard a clunking sound coming from her car and realized she was absolutely driving on a slant. She got out to look and sure enough, a flat tire. She thought of the dream she'd had that morning and imagined the roadrunner digging its beak into the tire like it had into the cactus flower.

ΔΔΔ

The mechanic shop said they wouldn't be able to get to replacing her tire until the afternoon and Theo was embarrassed she couldn't do it on her own. To her relief, the odd clean-cut guy she had seen there previously was nowhere in sight.

While her tire was being replaced, she figured she'd make the most of it, grab a cup of coffee and meander around the sleepy town. 'Truth or Coffee' was a hole-in-the-wall spot with a few tables and a loft space above with more seating. She hoped she wouldn't run into Mark, even though she did like him. She ducked in and out, holding her paper cup as she stepped back into the clean air, past the music shop where she paused for a moment, thinking about her friends' dream of having a band. She looked up at the rickety sign with the flickering pink tube that read 'Bert's Bonanza: Basses and Guitars.' *How could she leave such intriguing new friends so soon?* The thought rolled around in her mind.

She continued on her journey past the quirky pottery shop again and onward to a new part of town she hadn't explored yet, all while deep in thought. Her feet carried her further until she came upon a thrift shop.

She walked the aisles, examining the discarded remnants of

people's lives, items ready to be invigorated by the next person who would rescue them from a landfill. She tried on a brimmed hat with an interesting symbol on the side, two seed-looking shapes nestled next to one another surrounded by a circle. Theo didn't know the meaning of it, yet decided she liked it anyway. At first, she felt slightly squeamish about wearing a previously-owned hat but then decided she didn't care and put it in her basket to buy.

As she headed to the counter to the checkout, she noticed a big coffin-sized box leaning against the corner. Curious, she opened it, and couldn't believe what she saw. Perfect condition, slightly used but authentic and gorgeous. It felt like a sign. The coincidence of finding something like this truly made her think, perhaps she should stay in Truth or Consequences after all. She thought about it for another moment. "When in Truth or Consequences," she said to herself and decided to buy it, too.

Donning her new hat and hefting the big box, she left the shop. *New leaf, new me.*

She returned to the campground later that afternoon, new hat, new box and new tire in tow. Winny was out front but the other two were nowhere in sight. Theo parked and walked over to her.

"We thought you left without saying goodbye," Winny said, her brown eyes slanting downward.

"I'm sorry, yeah I was about to leave. I don't like rufflin' feathers. Just thought it'd be easier without saying goodbye. I like y'all too much." Sometimes Theo noticed notes of a Southern accent in her own voice out here. Not much, just a bit. She'd never noticed it before she'd traveled out West and she'd only noticed it out this way since she rarely came across anyone with her kind of accent. Except she had noticed Winny and the others use the word 'y'all' sometimes too. "But then I got a flat tire so I had to get that fixed and I, well … I was thinkin'…" Theo trailed off then changed her thought process, "Hey, I wanna show you and the others something. Got a minute?"

Theo went back to her car and began lugging the large box back over to the big Airstream where all three ladies were now waiting outside. Winny, Jen and Rain stood in front of the Excella Motorhome, looking into the hot sun towards her. Winny's hand was resting on her hip, Jen's arms were comfortably crossed and Rain was shielding her eyes from the sun. They looked like a band photo to Theo. The sound of chimes could be heard in the distance. She set the big box on a picnic table and opened it up. The three ladies all peered in at the big box.

"A cello?" said Rain pushing a lock of curly hair out of her eyes. "None of us know how to play."

"Well, I know how to play," Theo said, running her hand along a pronounced scratch across the front of the instrument. "Kinda. It's been a while but I know all of you wanted to start a band, so I thought, why not? We'd still need a drummer but—" Theo shrugged and squinted. "But you'd have me."

"Does this mean you're staying?!" Winny practically yelled.

"Yes ma'am, if y'all will have me," said Theo, hastily adding, "Maybe a month or two, but after that, I'd better hit the road."

"Yes, yes, to this mysterious thing you have to do *down the road*," finished Winny. "Ok! This means we've got a month to get good and a month to play and perform at a venue, hell yeah!" she exclaimed.

What a goof, thought Theo with a big grin on her face. Theo thought Winny's goals were lofty but liked them. "Oh, but don't tell Mark I'm staying. I'm still not ready yet."

ΔΔΔ

The next day, they all walked to Bert's Bonanza: Basses and Guitars down the street to see if they had an affordable bass guitar for Jen and a keyboard for Rain. When they walked in it was oddly quiet for a music shop, empty of anyone except the four of them. The bell above the door clanged as they walked in, breaking the silence. It was mostly old electric basses and acoustic guitars on hangers on the walls, instruments jutting out from all angles, with high up windows shining light through the dusty wooden rafters.

Theo stumbled upon a cello. *Hmm guess I could've gotten one here too*, she thought, but then flipped the tag over. $1,500 dollars, used. *Or not.*

They walked around, boots and shoes clunking loudly on the floor but still no employee appeared.

"Hey, check it out!" whispered Rain around the corner.

There was a dust-laden bass next to a small amp. None of them knew the first thing about basses but the tag said Ibanez BTB865sc, weathered black. It had five strings but Theo thought basses usually only had four. With the wooden trim and red color on the back, natural wood and black lacquer on the front, it was absolutely beautiful.

"Ain't it a beaut?" someone said from behind, making all four of them jump out of their boots.

The man was tall and crotchety-looking, with thick glasses like coke bottles.

"It's maple and walnut with an ash top," he continued. "Plays real nice. Strong, bright tone with a punchy mid range and great low end too. Warm and smooth response. After all, that's what you want in a bass, right?" he said.

The four nodded, trying to give an impression they knew what the hell he had just said.

"Ibanez, as you might know, has been a pioneer of basses for over forty years. But they're not your usual bass, no, no. Not your Fender or your Music Man, no. They're special. Unique, boutique even," he said, giving a nod to his shop. "Whattaya say, you wanna plug it in, see how it plays?"

Jen looked slightly frightened, but nodded.

"The name's Bert by the way," he said, outstretching a wise hand to all four of them. *Bert, the namesake of the shop*, Theo surmised. His bushy eyebrows were like caterpillars ready to crawl off his forehead.

Bert set them up with a cable and an amp and walked back toward the counter around the corner. He was the first person Theo had come across in the Southwest with a lilting twang to his voice, more pronounced than hers. She felt a fondness towards the old man just from that.

Winny threw out a few instructions, given she was a guitar player and knew a fair amount about the bass just from that. Jen listened and plucked the lowest string (confusingly on the top but, as Winny explained, it was the lowest in tone). When she did, the bass guitar reverberated around the shop and vibrated everything around them with an extended sympathetic resonance in each instrument.

"Raaaaaaad," said Jen with a gleam in her eye, clearly hooked after playing one note.

You could tell she felt its power. Winny instructed her to push her finger down on the fourth fret and pluck and then do the same on the fifth fret. Also known as notes E, A, and B. They would come to learn that particular pattern could be moved along the fretboard and was called a 1, 4, 5 progression, something very common in music. And for whatever reason, it did indeed sound good. Winny said there were all sorts of patterns in music like that. Magical-seeming patterns and mathematical ones. Music theory. When Theo played the cello back in the day, they'd never taught her that.

Jen turned the tag around. $650. *Used.* "Used? What would it go for new?" exclaimed Jen.

Rain raised her eyebrows, quietly agreeing with her friends surprise.

Bert appeared out of nowhere and piped in, "$1,149.99 new. So that's a helluva deal!" before once again, disappearing around the corner.

"Well, I still can't afford $650 right now," Jen said to her friends, her posture wilting, "I just moved to T or C and only just got that waitress job. And Rain still hasn't found a job. What about you, Winny? You got some secret money from running the campground or that alcohol-free bar, what is it called, Bar None, in Albuquerque you're miraculously managing from afar? You wanna donate to the music cause?"

"Well I certainly have some, but not much," said Winny.

They all looked at Theo.

"Don't look at me, I still have nursing school debt. But, maybe …" she lowered her voice. "Maybe we could talk to the owner, see if he'd cut us a deal."

They walked around the corner to the counter where Bert seemed to be doing his taxes by hand, on paper.

"S'cuse us, sir. But this here lady," she said, pointing to Jen, "is terminally ill and," all three ladies raised their eyebrows and looked at Theo as she continued, "and it is her dying wish to play the bass. Could you cut us a deal?"

The man set down the paper he was working on and looked at her over his glasses.

"Okay, okay, I'm so sorry, that was a terrible lie." Theo was sweating bullets. "Honestly, we're just four women who've never played in a band who want to give it a go. Would you cut us a deal?"

"You're starting a band, huh? T or C could use a band." He looked at the four anxious people in front of him, a kindness to his eyes behind his thick glasses. "Tell you what. I cannot cut you a deal on that bass, but I can give you one of my old ones for free. My wife has been asking me to get rid of a few instruments for years, it'll spark joy for her like Marie Kondo getting rid of it. C'mon next door for some tamales with me and my wife, we're bored to death in retirement. Share a story or two with us and we'll call it even."

The ladies agreed and ambled with him next door where a small house with turquoise trim and a red ristra hung out front. Turquoise certainly seemed to be a theme out here. They walked through the front yard past tomatoes growing perky and zucchinis slouching flaccidly.

A woman about the age of Bert opened the door, making Theo think of Joan Baez in her older years. She looked as though she'd been a folk-rocker in her heyday, headstrong and sweet, just like, well, Joan Baez.

"Who've you got here Bert?" she said.

"These four ladies say they're looking to start a band!" Bert said, introducing his wife Jane.

"'It's about damn time we had some more women rockers out here!" she said with a warm smile as she opened the door wider and went in to hug each of them.

"Do you play music too?" asked Rain.

Bert answered for her. "She sure does. Best tambourine player west of the Mississippi," he joked.

Jane gave Bert a fake punch to his side and he laughed. She put a hand on her hip and retorted, "I play the drums, dammit, and I'm good."

Theo's jaw dropped. "I knew you looked familiar! At first, I thought you looked like Joan Baez but now I realize you look like Jane Harper, the drummer from the Semi Hollow Bodies!"

The three others looked on, amazed. Winny was smiling at Theo, seemingly impressed she knew about the Semi Hollow Bodies. Jane Harper, for it was she, looked elated that someone had recognized her. And her husband looked proud.

"Yep, she's the one and only," Bert said, pulling his wife close to him by the waist. "Coming in for some tamales, ladies?"

The Old Rockers

"**W**ow, I can't believe I'm sitting in Jane Harper's kitchen," Theo said, looking around.

The kitchen had clearly been remodeled but with vintage-looking appliances put back in. It seemed out of place in Truth or Consequences where everything seemed to have been built in the classic adobe Pueblo style, including the outsides of everyone's houses. But inside, it looked completely different. It was modern and cozy, with a fifties ranch feel and nothing like the dusty, disorganized music shop next door.

Onward into the living room, you could see an upright piano and a wall full of guitars and music memorabilia. They'd certainly stumbled into the right situation here.

Maybe Jane could be our drummer, Theo thought. The living room seemed to have everything except ... where were the— "Drums?" sputtered Theo. "Where are the drums?"

"Oh, I don't play anymore," said Jane. "Arthritis got me down."

Damn. So maybe she wouldn't be our drummer.

"Hey, so who's got a fun story for us?" said Bert, changing the subject quickly.

Everyone looked around at each other.

Theo thought for a moment. She wanted to offer the retired couple some entertainment. Plus, she was really enjoying hanging out with them. "Well, the other night we walked to the top of a mountain, that mountain," she said, pointing at the sliver visible through the kitchen window.

"The mesa?" Bert interrupted. "That mountain has some lore to it, I'll tell ya that. What happened up there?"

"Well," Theo continued, looking at the three of her friends, imploringly, trying to get a feel from them if it was okay to tell. She saw a couple smiles and continued, "We hiked to the top of that mesa in the middle of the night while we were tripping on acid and damn, were we tripping."

The elderly couple chuckled and Jane added to the recollection, "I remember my first time on acid! I could have sworn a cactus was talking to me!"

"Well, that's just it!" continued Theo. "The reason we went to the top was because a talking roadrunner told me to, *'Look over there,'* and there was a dot of glowing light up on the mesa. So we hiked up."

"And?" asked Jane Harper. "What was there?"

"Well, it was weird," Jen started to say, leaving off where Theo had begun. "When we got to the top, the air felt extra still and quiet. No crickets chirping like they usually do here, no rustle of the wind, nada. Nothing. It felt like the time I went caving underground in Arizona when I was a kid and everything was dead still, like the world had been put on mute. And I could have sworn the city lights down below flickered out and then back on again."

"That would be the acid," said Winny and nodded sagely.

"Well," continued Theo. "I saw that happen too. And then I saw a flicker of light near us; the same weird light the roadrunner told me to look at. It was glowing. It was like this giant orb of light. And well—" Theo wasn't actually sure how to proceed next. The four of them hadn't talked about this part together yet. Had they seen what she had seen? Was it just the acid? Or her imagination?

"Yeah, I saw the floating orb too," Jen added, flopping her mohawk to the other side of her head.

"To be honest, I saw it too," said Winny. "It completely took me by surprise so I stumbled on a rock in front of me and fell."

Theo put a soft hand on Winny's elbow. That explained the gash and the blood in the dirt the next day when Theo had hiked up there. Winny looked into Theo's eyes at the touch. Theo returned Winny's gaze but was distracted by a pulsing pain in the back of her head. She brought her hand up to the back of her head and felt something cold, tender to the touch. Had she fallen at some point too? She couldn't remember. But she did remember seeing something very odd. So she continued her story, "And I know it's strange, and maybe I imagined it but I have this vivid recollection of what happened next. It's dreamlike and I know I was on acid for the first time but I swear I saw—" Theo's mind wandered back to that night.

It was so clear. They helped Winny off the ground and started walking toward the glowing orb. A tall, lanky figure came into view. It was holding the orb but floated above them. They weren't sure at first whether to be scared or enlightened. Their mouths were agape, frozen in time and there was that sound; both transfixing and ethereal. Theo couldn't help herself. She found her feet stepping one in front of the other, getting closer and closer to the figure and orb. The orb, or the figure, or both, were drawing her in. Rain walked forward too with Theo leading. The figure came into view and it was strange and clearly not human. It had glowing big green eyes, the city lights illuminated in them. It seemed to be—

"An alien," stated Theo to the group, huddled around the table, as the elderly couple listened rapt, clutching their forks, mouths slightly ajar.

The other three ladies listened intently as well, as though this were a new part of the story, except for Rain who added, "Yeah I saw it too. It was really tall."

"Even taller than you?!" added Jen, jabbing Rain slightly, clearly not on the same page.

"Yeah. Strangely tall. Nonhuman," said Rain assuredly, unbothered by her friend's apparent doubt, "and it had big eyes and … and it gave me this strange feeling. Not bad, but strange. Different. Unique. It's hard to explain …" Rain looked around at the others.

Theo hadn't heard Rain speak this much since she'd arrived in Truth or Consequences. "Yes ma'am," she continued where Rain left off, "It was kinda like those aliens from that documentary. You know the one about the alien encounter in Zimbabwe?" Theo surprised herself again. She knew she was more open-minded than her friends and family in the South about this sci-fi kind of stuff but she'd never paid it much attention. She'd never been an alien believer, but, like horoscopes, found them intriguing. It was beginning to look like she was even more open-minded than the hippies she'd run into out here, clearly more so than Winny or Jen who looked surprised at the words coming out of her mouth. Like they were seeing a whole other side of her.

"I saw that documentary," Rain said clearly and quietly, while taking a bite of an avocado like an apple. "Most aliens communicate telepathically. You know, they speak to you directly into your thoughts, instead of formulating words."

"Yeah." Theo paused, then continued, "It was … eerie. But transfixing."

"What did it say?" asked Jane Harper, steadying herself as she took a sip of water.

Theo shook her head. "I don't remember."

Silence. Then, Bert scoffed, breaking the quiet, "That sounds about right. Honestly we've seen and heard some crazy stuff going on up there for the three decades we've been living here," he said, looking at Jane, who gave an unnerving nod.

"Really?" said Theo, feeling slightly relieved.

"Oh yeah. I've seen flying saucers come and go. Don't know what it is about that mesa," Bert said.

Theo wondered herself, looking out the window at the flat-topped ridge, the dark blue clouds bubbling and threatening rain. *So maybe she wasn't crazy.* "And you guys saw it too?" she implored, asking Winny and Jen. They seemed unsure.

"Well, I saw some sort of orb … But no alien, to be honest," shrugged Winny.

"You gringas are crazy," Jen said.

"C'mon, you didn't see it?" asked Theo, a little stubbornly. She was beginning to wonder if maybe it really had just been the acid.

"What's your band going to be called?" asked Jane Harper, clearly sensing the conversation direction needed a diversion.

But Theo wanted to talk about the alien. It was the weirdest thing she had ever experienced.

It had made her feel odd. Not necessarily in a bad way, just strange. Just like Rain had said. That sound from the orb got into your bones. A transfixing and palatable sound, or warmth, radiating from it. In a way, it seemed to suck you in toward it. And Theo was positive she'd seen the alien. Then again, maybe not. Maybe she was crazy? But Rain had seen it too. Theo vowed to herself to never do acid again, either way.

Theo was afraid perhaps she was going off the deep end. Was this a good idea being out here so far from home? She felt the silent burning of her phone in her pocket calling her, ensnaring her back home to what used to be her placid life and monotone existence. Before *it* all happened, at least. She zoned back into the conversation, attempting to get her mind off her phone.

"Sorry, can you repeat that," Jane Harper was saying. "What did you say your band name is?"

"Face Orifice," Jen replied, to the slightly disgusted faces of the elderly couple.

"That is *NOT* our name," Winny immediately responded.

"Yes it is!" said Jen with a gleam in her eye. "We're a stoner metal band inspired by King Bong Kong."

"No, we most certainly are not," stated Winny while the others laughed and the old rocker couple looked onward, confused.

"Well, I'm just glad you ladies are starting out on a musical journey," Bert said, taking a bite of tamale. "Music has certainly brought me endless joy."

Jane nodded in agreement, then added, "The great late jazz genius Duke Ellington once said, 'Music is the oldest entity. The scope of music is immense and infinite … What would you be without music?'"

They continued the afternoon there, Jane and Bert showing them around their house and their special pieces of music memorabilia. Jane Harper took them to their garage and said once they 'got their shit together' they could use the space to practice. Maybe even perform on the old stage out back. And she would rustle up a drum kit from the attic for whoever would be their drummer. Bert said he was all on board with the chick band from the campground. Band name pending.

He then stood up from the kitchen table and walked into the living room to pull an instrument case out from beside a densely-packed bookshelf. Inside it was an Ibanez bass, different and older than the one they had seen in the shop. Bert had said it was his first instrument ever. The bass glimmered slightly purple and had a couple of dings on it but, as Bert demonstrated, it played beautifully.

Jen's eyes gleamed. "Are you sure? Your first instrument ever?"

Bert said he was sure and Jen gave him a big hug. Theo could have sworn she saw a tear on the side of her eye before she looked away.

So it was settled. They had a space to practice, they just had to find a keyboard for Rain, and, potentially the hardest part, a drummer.

The Wild West of
Music Stores

The next day they all piled into Jen's Excella Airstream and made the trek to Albuquerque to go to the city's largest music store, wondering why they hadn't taken someone's smaller vehicle, to get a keyboard for Rain.

Theo sat in a seat at the motorhome table and watched the landscape slide by, while Winny snoozed beside her, her head gently resting on Theo's shoulder. She looked so peaceful, her head nestled between Theo's neck and shoulder. Theo liked the rhythm of her breathing and noticed for the first time how olive-y Winny's skin was, the tattoos popping with color from her arms, and liked how jet-black her bangs were. Theo found her beautiful and unconsciously fiddled with her own bulky, brunette braid.

Rain and Jen's conversations up front were muffled musically among the white noise of travel and Theo admired the Airstream which, clearly, Jen and Rain had cleaned. There was a questionably refurbished kitchenette, most likely Jen's work, and an untouched eighties carpeted floor. The domed walls and ceiling had recently been freshly painted. The view to the driver and passenger seat felt faraway, but with Jen's booming voice, the distance was easily closed like a Slinky, when necessary.

It had rained all night, so the earth smelled fresh and sweet, wafting in through the open window, yellow grass stretching onward against a deep blue sky, and drops of rain satiating the distance in moisture. The water sprinkled rhythmically on the windshield offering a hint of what was to come.

When they arrived at Guitar Mart, the Wild West, big box store of music stores, the four women's mouths dropped open. From floor to ceiling were electric guitars covering what seemed like the length of a football field. There was a blaring of cacophonous music coming from every which way: A guy who surely needed lessons on the bass (Jen hoped she wouldn't sound that bad), another guy playing *Master of Puppets* (probably for the third time that hour), and another playing, what Theo would later learn was, a semi-hollow body Gretsch, through a tube amp and a silky smooth pedal adding texture. The melodies emitted from that Gretsch sounded positively delicious: Reverby rich tones and quality pick work. Theo hoped their music would sound like that. It also had a twangy lilt of country, the type of music Theo assumed Winny would want them to play together. Theo was beginning to feel as though she'd known Winny for years.

The place was busy. It looked like a bustling bus station of people walking around, coming and going, lugging large equipment and instruments about.

"Hey! Hey, sir!" an employee was shouting near them.

Jen pointed to herself with an eyebrow raised. "Sir?" Jen

whispered, clearly confused, then visibly relieved to see the employee was hollering at someone else.

A man with sunglasses and a hat picked up his pace with a guitar in hand, tag swinging, and briskly walked out the store, never to be seen again. Clearly he had not paid.

The employee muttered to himself, "Sunnava bitch, another one."

An employee next to him with patches on his pants was looking at his phone and muttered something about capitalism and shrugged. The retail musicians had not taken any note of the four women whose expressions looked like they'd just walked into Narnia.

Winny's eyes were lit up like stars. "I love this place. I used to come here all the time when I lived here."

Theo felt out of place. There were probably thirty some people, including customers and employees in this big busy store, and not one of them looked like them. They were all guys. *Mostly white too*, she thought, thinking of Jen and wondering how she must feel.

She looked at Jen to see her reaction but Jen was facing the other direction, watching the guy who had stolen the guitar walk to the bus stop. Rain appeared to be absorbing the scene in her usual transcendental state.

Seeing how little they were represented at this store reminded Theo of how few women bands she knew of, and frankly how few female musicians were out there in general. *If we did this band thing*, she thought, *we would be doing something unique, just by sheer fact it was us women doing it.*

They meandered around, tinkered on instruments and

drooled over interesting machinery, all foreign to Theo. But to Winny, they were knowable magic.

"See this, here?!" she said, pointing to a case full of what Theo had learned were guitar pedals. "This is the Oceans 11 Reverb Pedal. It's called that because it has eleven different reverb settings. Oh man, the Shimmer setting is heavenly."

"So let's buy it," said Rain, blue eyes bright as buttons.

Winny scoffed. "Nah it's two hundred bucks. Not today, cowgirls, not today."

They made their way to the keyboard section. In the corner, someone was playing Chopin Nocturne No 8 in D flat. It was one of Theo's favorites. She used to accompany her aunt on the keyboard with her cello.

Theo took a deep breath and was lost in the piano keys for a moment as the player went into the part of the piece where it gently sways from major to minor and back to major again. The cacophony of poorly-played rock instruments in the guitar section faded into the background as the piano music came to life between her ears. Chopin had been a genius in sentiment at conveying the human repertoire for feeling. Schumann, another famous composer of the same era, and a renowned music critic, had said of his contemporary, Chopin, 'Hats off gentlemen, a genius.' Clara Schumann, wife to Robert Schumann, had been a respected composer in her own right, too. She had written sixty-six profound pieces herself. But, Theo mused, we didn't hear much about her.

Theo's thoughts were propelled back into the present when a toddler plunked the keys of another keyboard before his mom pulled him away. Then Rain swooped in, looking at the piano the child had just played and picked at the sticker letters that were peeling off its keys.

Used. 100 dollars, the tag read.

"Why is this keyboard so cheap?" she asked an employee who was rushing past to help another customer.

"Came from our lessons department. Got a whole lotta use," the guy said before disappearing behind some giant subwoofers.

Rain sat down and examined the buttons, made a few adjustments and played a jazzy riff, then another, then another.

"Damn, Rain, I didn't know you crushed piano so hard!" exclaimed Jen.

Sure enough, Rain was quite good. With Winny's guitar skills and eclectic vocals, Jen's enthusiasm, and Rain's clearly just-demonstrated piano abilities, Theo was beginning to think they might really have something. She wondered though what she would really add with her cello, if anything and squirmed a little.

"I'll take it," Rain said and they brought the keyboard to the counter.

Once more, Theo felt the sensation of being watched. She saw someone peering at her from behind the music books. He was clean-cut and wore sunglasses. Odd to wear sunglasses indoors. He immediately looked away when she noticed him.

For a second, Theo thought she recognized him but couldn't place him. Just before he disappeared through a pair of wooden doors into the acoustic guitar room, she caught a glimpse of a unique tattoo on the side of the man's head. A piercing, real-looking, eye. Then it dawned on her. *The man from the mechanic's shop.* Was it a coincidence that this stranger was here too? Theo wondered if they should leave. But they still had to buy the keyboard. *Should I tell them?* she wondered.

As they were checking out with their keyboard they were distracted hearing someone on the drums. Whoever they were, they sounded damn good. The person could *play.* Probably needed a little refinement but the unique drum beats certainly caught all four women's attention.

Keyboard in tow, they followed their ears to the drum section where they saw a woman with long flowing-to-the-beat hair, head down, lost in the rhythm, her dark-rimmed glasses at the very end of her nose, threatening to fall off.

Theo found herself transported by the beat, bobbing her head and closing her eyes.

"Let's ask her to be our drummer!" Winny said, excitement flaring in her eyes.

"Pshhh, sure Win," said Jen. "Hey random person, wanna join a bunch of psycho gals who can't play their own instruments in a band several hours from here? Uh, yeah, ok."

Winny looked dead serious. "Yeah. Why not?"

They talked among themselves briefly then waited for a moment's opportunity to talk to the drumming woman. But she kept playing and took no notice of her surroundings. She was so lost in the music, and tangled in her own wild red hair that she didn't notice four vultures surrounding her, ready to recruit her to their fledgling band in Truth or Consequences. She played with such ease, like she'd been doing it her whole life and moved so fast it was like she had extra limbs in order to hit all those drums.

It seemed Winny was thinking the same thing because she leaned toward Theo's ear and added some musical pop culture reference, "No wonder people like to allude to drummers being like octopuses, huh?"

Theo nodded in agreement.

"Uh, hello, s'cuse me," said Winny politely, trying to grab the woman's attention. "Um, hi, we—"

"Yo, octopus drummer lady!" shouted Jen.

But nothing.

So Theo tried. Not normally one to interject, she gave it a shot nonetheless and stepped in front of the woman's line of sight. "Hey, pardon me!" she shouted.

The woman put down the sticks. The halt to the music was jolting.

"Would you like to be in our alt-country woman's band, in Truth or Consequences?" Theo asked.

Water

On the car ride back they discussed the drummer, Maria Morales, as they learned her name was, and her reaction to their proposal. She didn't seem very interested, to be honest. But she had said she'd think about it. Theo had handed her a piece of paper with her number and 'Crazy ladies from Truth or Consequences' on it.

The rain was now coming down in sheets. Monsoon season out in the desert. Jen's windshield wipers worked hard to push aside the water and the land soaked it up like an eager sponge. Theo found her thoughts drifting to that night on the mesa. The orb, the figure, the weird, indescribable feeling from it all.

Her phone lit up next to her on the Airstream sofa. There were plenty of missed calls and text messages, but none from Maria Morales. She was beginning to get really invested in this band.

"When're you gonna answer those texts?" said Winny, peering over her shoulder and pointing to the fourteen missed messages.

Clunk, clunk, clunk.

"Oh damn, not right now!" said Jen slamming her fists on the steering wheel.

They pulled over, as their car sputtered and smoked.

Jen hopped out with a wrench, and opened the hood to a wave of smoke as though she were opening a barbecue. Rain got out to help too.

About a minute later, both returned to the car, sopping wet.

Jen turned around to face Winny and Theo, grimacing. "It's a no-go situation."

Time passed as they waited for the tow truck. Meanwhile, they passed a joint around, sitting on the back couch and floor in a circle, smoke clouding the Airstream, the rain pounding the steel ceiling.

"Ok, here's a little game I like to call 'Truth or Consequences,'" Winny said. "It's like two truths and a lie but if you don't guess the lie right, there's a consequence."

"Where'd you pick up that game?" Jen asked.

Winny shrugged. "I made it up."

"What's the consequence if you don't guess which one's the lie?" asked Rain.

"That's the thing, you don't know yet. Until you get it wrong and the person whose lie it is decides what the consequence is," Winny responded with another puff and cough from the joint.

"I like it!" shouted Jen. "Who's going to go first? Rain! Wanna go first?"

"Sure," Rain acknowledged. "One," she said and held up her pointer finger, "I've never had Taco Bell. Two, I've climbed to the top of K2, you know, that mountain in Pakistan, annnnnd three, it was me who slashed Theo's tire."

Theo's eyes went wide.

"Great goddess, Rain that's easy as fuck!" said Winny. "You

have Taco Bell every week and you've never been to Pakistan. You slashed Theo's tires? Why?"

Rain smiled and laughed gently just as smoke came out her mouth like puffs of air from a laundry vent. "Tire! Singular! I did it so she would stay. Duh!" Then turning to Theo, "Aren't you glad I did it?"

Theo was shocked. But, when she thought about it, she *was* glad. "I am actually," she admitted. "Otherwise we all never would have gotten to know each other." She had grown to feel so close to these women in such a short amount of time. She paused as she thought of something interesting, then added, "Ya know, I had a dream the night beforehand that the talking roadrunner I saw when I was tripping was the one that slashed my tires."

That really made them all howl.

"What?!" Theo exclaimed.

"What is it with you and this talking roadrunner?" Winny chuckled.

"Okay, my turn!" Theo added, sidestepping the rhetorical question, because she too was not sure what the recurring talking roadrunner was about. *Real or just a hallucination?* She shook off the thought and allowed the weed to melt her brain, instead focusing on the game. "Uuuuuuuh, Okay, here goes. Sooooo," she said, massaging her temples. "One, I used to be a nurse and that crashed and burned … Two, the calls I've been ignoring are from the cops, and threeeeee, I'm a Virgo."

They looked at her blankly for a minute.

Winny dissected her statement, scrunching up her face exaggeratedly, her finely shaped eyebrows raising under her straight bangs. "Okay, well, we know you're a Virgo, you said that the first night we met. I seem to remember your career did crash and burn. And, I think I remember you saying you were a nurse." She thought for another pause. "The cop thing?"

"Bzzzzzzt" Theo made the sound of a buzzer, "Nope, that's real," inhaling from the joint, "I'm not a Virgo."

Winny looked betrayed. "What? Yes you are. You're a classic Virgo!"

Theo laughed so hard her eyes started watering.

Winny looked betrayed. "Why would you lie like that?"

Theo continued laughing. She would have thought the fact that the cops were trying to reach her would have been more of a bombshell than the fact she lied, *no, gently pretended*, to have a different horoscope sign. When she realized Winny truly looked heartbroken, like her belief system had been shattered, she stopped laughing and said, "I'm sorry, I didn't think we'd know each other longer than an hour! And it was an experiment. I wondered what you'd say or how you'd perceive me based on being convinced I was a Virgo."

Winny stared out the rain-soaked window, the sound of drops pounding the roof and didn't answer.

As suddenly as it had come on, Theo felt her laughter drain, replaced by guilt over lying to her friend. She wanted to make amends. *But how?*

"Well then what *is* your sign?" Winny said, turning to face Theo.

Theo said nothing.

"I'll figure it out," Winny said, clearly shaking off the betrayed feeling and returning to her usual jovial self. "You may have fooled me, Theodora Consuela Folsom-Hart," she said, completely making up Theo's full first, middle and hyphenated last name, but for which she would forever be known, from that point on. Winny's sing-songy voice continued, "Welp, yeah I guessed wrong! You decide what my consequence is. Oh! And most importantly—Why the hell are the cops trying to get ahold of you?"

Theo shook her head, realizing she wasn't ready to divulge this yet. "Nope, don't wanna talk about that. Okay, um your consequence for getting it wrong iiiiiiis ..." She thought for a moment, looking around the Airstream. An image of an old music video with an Airstream and someone speaking of a journey into the desert swam to mind. So Theo described what it was that Winny must do.

Winny stepped out into the rain into the brambly weeds that brushed against her skirt. She was so high she forgot to take the joint out of her mouth and it got immediately wet and useless.

She spun around, drenching herself, singing Cyndi Lauper's chorus from *Time After Time*, the droopy joint falling out of her mouth.

"Louder!" laughed Theo from the airstream steps. "Spin faster!"

Winny shouted, singing, obliging, spinning and clearly getting dizzy.

Jen and Rain whooped, leaning out the windows.

There was more lyrical shouting in the rain and then Winny slowed down, taking a moment to catch her breath, the laughter and weed taking over. She looked up, steadying her gaze and smiled at Theo leaning against the stairwell of the Airstream who was clearly admiring her goofy friend. Theo returned the smile and noticed Winny's bangs clung to her forehead like helmet hair, and still she looked beautiful. Theo noticed Winny looking back at her as though she thought she was beautiful too.

Before Theo could stop her, Winny had grabbed her out from the dry stairwell and pulled her into the rain which drenched Theo's curls almost immediately. They laughed, looking at each other.

"Your hair," Winny observed, touching Theo's curls. "The rain is making your hair even more curly."

Water streamed down Theo's heart-shaped face. "Yeah sometimes it's curly, sometimes it's straight."

"Like me." Winny winked.

Theo's heart fluttered into her throat. She couldn't help the excitement and ease she felt. What was this? Then the sound of crinkling gravel underfoot interrupted both their gazes.

Someone was pulling up in a truck near them. *Was it the tow truck finally?*

Winny steadied herself, her dark hair flattened to her forehead. She and Theo both squinted at the person in the truck.

"Need a lift?" said the woman behind the wheel.

It was not the tow truck.

It was none other than the drummer, Maria Morales, leaning out of the window of a heavy-duty pickup truck with a hitch on the back.

Alien Strata

The days trickled onward, and were filled with music in Jane Harper and Bert's garage most days. On Sundays, Maria would make the trek from southern Albuquerque to Truth or Consequences to play the drums with them. They weren't entirely sure how she got there most days, considering the truck she drove that rainy day had been borrowed—she'd said, though never mentioned from whom, but either way, they were always happy to see her.

During practices, Jane Harper couldn't help coaching Maria to reel in her crazy nature just a little bit. But Maria was often wide-eyed, like a traveler in a foreign space, pure joy radiating from her smile behind the drums and Bert would offer up tips and tricks to Jen on the bass. Jen looked so cool behind the giant instrument which seemed to dwarf her small figure, her posture straight, muscle shirt arms wrapped around the instrument, her forearm resting cooly on the body while her forefingers plucked each string casually. Jen often swayed to the beat, and closed her eyes, clearly lost in the music bobbing her head. One thing Theo loved about Jen was how she defied category. Jen looked so gay and yet was so straight, something Jen rather embraced, as did the occasional sweet male lover.

Between boisterously waiting tables at the chile restaurant in town, getting really good at playing the bass, and hosting an occasional attractive guy at her Airstream when Rain was away, Jen seemed to have a vibrance to life that was unmatched. She had spent a stint studying business at the University of Washington in Seattle and decided to take a year off to enjoy the finer things in life, like returning to her roots. For Jen, that was visiting the Southwest again. She also worked hard at renovating the Airstream interior, a task she rather enjoyed. Her most recent additions were intricately carved cabinets she had made herself, using a questionable table-saw setup and a few tools, including a chisel. Jen liked to stay in touch via FaceTime with her older brother Hector in Tucson and show off her new adjustments to the Airstream while he poked fun at her punk-rocker hair.

Jen and Rain had become friends when Rain attended a rally on the quad at the University of Washington to protect the Pinewood Poodle Beetle (A beetle Theo didn't even know existed) and Rain had approached Jen to borrow her Sharpie so she could write on her big sign. Jen had said 'Sure,' and Rain used her table to write. When Jen commented that Rain's handwriting made it look like it said, "Protect the Pipe Wool Poodle Beefle," they laughed and became instant friends. Now, in Truth or Consequences, Rain either slept in one of the bunks in the Airstream or, apparently, under the stars in a hammock, bundled up in a wool blanket. That sounded just like Rain. As her name would suggest, she was constantly in touch with nature. She grew up in Montana, with her aunt and uncle, fishing in the summer and snow-shoeing in the winter. As soon as Rain graduated from high school, she took to the road with fellow ecowarriors to fight for environmental justice.

Rain hardly looked at the keyboard when she played: her grinning expression gave the impression she was staring absentmindedly into a portal just beyond sight on the horizon. A seemingly perpetual attendee of a Grateful Dead concert who just got passed the peace pipe. Indeed, Rain had mentioned she'd followed the Dead around in a van for a year or two. Theo imagined Rain must have floated away with the wind after that. Rain herself never did seem to hold down a job, but rather got by on others' kindness, particularly Jen's. This was something Theo didn't hold against her and instead, embraced.

And Winny ... Theo thought Winny was ... wow. She seemed to radiate a genuine joy from her body and her guitar. Her electric guitar was a D'Angelico Premier Bedford edition with Southwestern-looking opal inlays. Winny told her it had both a humbucker pickup and two single coil pickups, gibberish to Theo, but she remembered the tidbit nonetheless, as she remembered anything that came from Winny's mouth. Her resonating, reverbing guitar strides and harmonious vocals made Theo melt and want to put her cello bow down to just watch adoringly. Winny was wild. She was free and light as a feather and Theo only knew small details about her life. She'd grown up in the Northwest, went to college for a few years in Portland before dropping out to focus on art and the guitar, sleeping on friends' couches and doing her best to avoid too many drugs and complicated relationships. She had said escaping that life via her Winnebago and finding solace in the desert was the best thing she'd ever done for herself.

Theo felt that maybe this was the case for her too.

Everyone seemed to find their place in their music beautifully. Except Theo. She was still working on it. She would stumble around with her cello and was conscious of being the worst one in the band. Once in a while, she caught glimpses of her bandmates' subtle, politely disguised winces when she made a wrong note with the bow. Nothing was worse than the sound of a bow instrument hitting a wrong note. Theo remembered playing in her ninth grade orchestra and how she'd mostly faked it in the back row, pretending to slide the bow across the strings but not really making a sound.

She had been especially quiet back then, the type who preferred not to stand out, which worked out in her high school orchestra, because the other cellists next to her would drown her out anyway. Mr. Tribianni conducting at the front didn't seem to notice, or if he did, he didn't care. His salary wasn't enough to care, he was just there for the stable paycheck. His gigs with his traveling jazz band were his real dream. Theo had only picked up the instrument to quell her mother's concerns that she wasn't involved in enough activities, or that she wasn't lady-like enough. Sure, lugging that cello around was less than ideal. But if it kept her mom from asking her to be in those pompous debutante balls, the ones with the full length gowns and white gloves, then the instrument was doing its job as far as ninth grader Theo was concerned. Cello offered her an escape, a way to be herself, even if she wasn't any good at the thing.

When she was growing up, she imagined herself as a wild and free woman in the forest, tending a thriving garden and taking care of her wildcat pet. Sometimes, she still looked back on that mental escape with a smile. Her creative mind had always been a good escape from an overbearing mom and a military father, who, thinking about it now with a smirk, would most certainly disagree with everything about her lifestyle now. She once considered them close, but mostly because she successfully kept her mouth shut around them. She hadn't talked to them since she'd left the South to adventure out West to the desert. They'd barely even called her anyway. Did they even care where she'd disappeared to? Theo couldn't help the pang of hurt that thought provided. So instead, she turned back to the cello.

This time was different. No more faking it on the cello. She wanted to get good at it, wanted the instrument to take her to the next level of being herself and to serve as a tool to come out of her cave, out of her shell, and show the world this time who she, Theodora Consuela Folsom-Hart was. But it was tough. She found herself stuck in between bookends wanting to show herself to the world and needing to hide from it, due to circumstances from back home. Nonetheless, cello was becoming her outlet and music, the desert and companionship with her new friends was becoming her source of joy. A side of herself she hadn't shown anyone before was beginning to emerge, and it was a part of herself she previously hadn't allowed herself to be.

The days sauntered onward. Theo enjoyed meandering around the town of Truth or Consequences and frequently admired the cactus blossoms bursting with reds against dark green prickly cacti, finding a way through the confines of the cement cracks, to grow and bathe in the sunlight. She practiced cello on late nights in Jane and Bert's garage who had shown her where the hide-a-key was for such occasions and, over time, she found herself getting better and better, finding a stride with a little patience with herself and a bit of practice.

Hours seemed to slip by when they were all playing music together on the weekends, a type of euphoria you only got from playing your own instruments together. Sometimes Maria would sleep overnight in the Airstream, or the Winnebago on the couch or sleep in Jane and Bert's extra room before making the trek back the next morning, somehow, to Albuquerque before going to work. The five ladies would stay up late most nights cracking jokes and smoking weed by the fire or taking the occasional dip in the hot springs, absorbing the healing minerals, while often reminiscing about the alien they may or may not have seen that night on the mesa.

Maria made it clear she agreed with Winny and Jen, and that she thought the idea was crazy. "I personally am not a believer in aliens," she had said.

But she wasn't much of a talker, more of a listener. Theo thought Rain was quiet, but *damn*, Rain was a blubbering auctioneer compared to Maria who certainly was more of an observer. Rain was a complete believer that they had seen a lanky, long alien that night with big bug-like eyes. Whereas, by that point, Theo had mostly talked herself out of it. She was feeling fifty-fifty on what she'd seen. *Memory was weird like that, wasn't it?*

But Rain stuck to her guns and one night, said portentously, "It absolutely *was* an alien. And I bet we'll see it again, too."

This certainly got everyone quiet. Rain had a way of convincing you she knew the truth with her matter-of-fact-unblinking face. Like she was hiding the truth in plain sight for some reason, waiting for the right moment to spill her thoughts.

Or, like a gambler waiting for the right moment to reveal a royal flush.

Whether or not they saw an alien that night, to commemorate the evening they'd first met and embarked on that fateful, acid-drenched adventure up on the mountain, they decided on a band name: Alien Strata, referring to the encounter they may or may not have had with an alien and to rocks, or—more broadly—to Earth. Aliens on Earth.

They also liked the name because it got to the root of a feeling they all shared—they all felt out of place in this world, and yet, felt they belonged when they were making music together; or when they were laughing and passing a joint around a fire together; or when they were hiking to the top of the mesa together. For some reason, Maria was not a big fan of the band name, perhaps because she didn't believe in aliens, or perhaps because she hadn't been there that night. Nonetheless, she was accommodating and went along with it.

Days passed and the flat-top ridge of the mesa looked down on the town, knowing, impressive and influential. An enclave of vibrant energy and natural history seemed to watch over them as they practiced music, progressively getting better and better.

Theo postponed whatever it was that waited down the road for her. Each night, each of them would return to their new home, the glamping campground, and cozy up into Winny's Winnebego, or in Jen's giant vintage Airstream, where Rain also lived for the time being, or into Theo's tiny Blissa camper, which was cozy and certainly cramped.

Theo was beginning to love her little home. At first, she merely tolerated its tiny spaces and less-than-ideal mattress, if you could even call it that, but it was now officially home. Turquoise trim, fifties diner kitchen, spider-hiding home.

The moon had been through many phases since that first night soaking in the hot springs and it now turned from a subtle sliver to a voluptuous full circle, crisp and clean at the edges. In the desert, you didn't notice the shift into autumn quite the way you did in other parts of the world. There weren't as many trees that vibrantly shouted their changing colors. Only along the Rio Grande did they wisp into colors of yellows and brief oranges before they shed their leaves. This far southwest rarely got snow, but it did happen. But not yet.

Theo mostly noticed the change into autumn from the feel of the air. A chill set in and hardened along the edges of the sifting dirt and adobe and along the pin of needles rising from yuccas. The sage brush seemed to soften their pollen and their aroma, bees gently hunkered down and started to make fewer trips back and forth from the lavender to their honeycomb, their hive-building and nectar collecting accomplished for the season.

One afternoon, while the five ladies were running through a cover of 'Jolene,' Theo pulled out a leatherbound notebook from her bag, exclaiming, "I wrote a song and thought maybe we could try it?" She had been practicing in secret, doing vocals alongside her cello during the day when the others were at work, and when Winny was in Albuquerque managing the dry-bar. "It's called, 'Dance with the Desert,'" she said, putting rosin on her bow.

Winny smiled, apparently knowing the reference.

Theo ran her bow along the strings in an uncharacteristically seamless and beautiful note, then onto another, then an illuminating chord. When she began her vocals accompanying the cello, the ladies looked surprised by the strength and assuredness of her voice. They seemed to like it.

Theo thought her cello, despite having some good notes, still needed some work. "What did y'all think?" she asked shyly.

"That was beautiful, Theodora. Haunting, strange, and beautiful," Winny said with converging approval.

Theo loved the way Winny looked at her.

Jen, Rain, and Maria also liked it.

Maria had one suggestion, "I like your cello ..." she said, peering out at her from behind the drum set. "I just do not think you need so many notes."

Theo laughed nervously, embarrassed, knowing she wasn't very good.

"No, no, I mean that as a good thing!" Maria added, pushing her glasses closer to the bridge of her nose. "Sometimes music does not have to be complicated to be good. Do you agree? Those first few notes and chords you played were tremendous. Just focus on less, to expand the music more."

Maria, when she rarely spoke, sounded professorial in her suggestions, and Theo took them to heart. She agreed, working on the new leaf she was turning by accepting feedback and not taking it personally. She nodded.

They ran through it again, this time together, Theo finding relief in doing more with less, finding comfort in her own music. She found she loved Maria's suggestions and felt herself relax into the music. This round of the song, each added in their own instruments and flourishes: Maria on the drums, Rain on keys, Jen on the bass, and Winny, their confident leader, on the electric guitar. The music came together seamlessly, like magic.

The very same magic Winny had mentioned that day they'd first browsed Bert's Bonanza music shop.

For hours, they were lost in the music.

That night, Theo had stayed back to practice more cello by herself in Jane and Bert's garage and before she knew it, it was nearly midnight. She had grown more and more fond of the way the instrument reverberated in her lungs. She carefully tucked the cello back into its unceremonious box, noticing the notches and dings along its side, the scratch across the front, the wear and tear of its musical instrument life, present in the polish of its wood.

Bert poked his head around the corner, scuffing the floor in slippers and carrying a cup of water and a rectangular box of Monday-Sunday pills, clearly on his way to bed.

"Cello is sounding good, kid. Proud of ye," he said before he turned, heading upstairs.

Theo smiled. She'd never heard those words before.

Walking back to the campground, she passed the pottery studio with the solo light on inside and saw a hand drawn sign saying, *Help Wanted: Inquire Within*. Theo tucked the thought away for later and vowed to go back the next day.

ΔΔΔ

As it turned out, Theo found out the following day that the studio was pretty desperate for someone, *anyone*, to work. When she had gone back a few days later, they accepted her on the spot. So she began working part-time at the studio, selling locally-made pottery and learning how to throw on a wheel Wednesday evenings, as well as practicing music whenever possible.

Time sauntered onward like the waves of the Rio Grande, or sometimes felt pleasantly motionless like the gently simmering hot springs. The autumn air grew colder and the sentiment homier, desert life returning to nests or hovels and holes in the ground.

The ladies played a few open mic nights in Bert's backyard stage behind his music shop and the local audiences seemed to like their vibe. They took videos and shared them on social media, tagging their band name, Alien Strata, even though they didn't yet have a single social media page.

Just before falling asleep at night, Theo loved to think of those open mic nights they would do. The spattering of people swaying to the beat of their music, *her* music, spectators with beers casually in hand under the autumn sky and backyard lights, bobbing their heads as though they were listening to a *real* band. Theo had to correct herself sometimes. They *were* a real band. Before her journey to the desert, she had no idea how much she would like the feeling of playing music for people who enjoyed it.

During their first show, the five of them certainly had the jitters but Winny had turned around before each song to face them with a gentle, zen-like smile that would ease the band's tense nerves and somehow, each time, they would pull it off. It seemed everything was falling into place.

But, little did they know, things were about to get weird.

One of them was not who they said they were.

One of them had a strange and bizarre secret that would threaten each of their own individual understandings of reality and the universe. Yes, *that* sort of weird.

One of them planned to hide their true self to get closer to them, for purposes they wouldn't understand. This person was Maria.

Unbeknownst to the others, Maria was an alien. In fact, she was *the* alien they'd seen and not seen that night on the mesa.

Science, Aliens and Other Musings

One morning, as a cold gust caused her to button up her flannel a little closer, Theo walked to Truth or Coffee and approached the wooden countertop to order her usual dark coffee, when she saw a cute dog sitting in the corner politely and felt a pair of eyes dart toward her from a table by the window.

Theo locked eyes with Mark who tilted his head toward her with a shy smile.

She fumbled for her change as the barista passed her the coffee cup, which Theo then promptly spilled across the counter, onto her boots and over to the barista in a single swift movement of klutzy blunder that could easily be heard over the grinding of coffee beans.

Mark grimaced and made his way over to her after grabbing a towel at the bussing table and helpfully mopped up some of the mess. "Hi, I'm Mark," he said jokingly. "New here? I could have sworn I saw someone that looked like you a few months ago."

Theo smiled, "Hi."

Theo joined Mark and Bowzer at a table and sat down with a second cup of coffee, catching up over what the last few months had looked like. Bowzer apparently had stepped on a cactus on a recent hike, Mark had gotten a promotion at his work-from-home tech job, though he'd rather be traveling and blogging, and she told him all about the close friendships she'd formed with the gals of the desert and their blossoming band and addiction to weed.

"Sounds amazing," Mark said, "What is your band called?"

"Alien Strata."

"Why is that?"

"Well, we—" Theo began, the night on the mesa springing to mind. "No reason, just because it's kinda fun," she said with a shrug, not wanting to come across crazy.

"What does your music sound like?"

Theo thought about it for a minute, unable to pinpoint their exact sound. "I guess we are liberal cosmic country indie folk rock."

Mark chuckled, "That's a lot of genres. Er, well it sounds awesome."

"Thanks," Theo said, appreciating his company and patting Bowzer. "This is nice."

"So tell me again why you don't want to be in a relationship with me?"

"It's complicated."

"Yes, it always is …" he said. "… and it never is."

ΔΔΔ

That evening, the ladies—Maria included—were frying up zucchinis from Winny's garden behind her camper and making spaghetti and meatballs in Jen's Airstream kitchen. Winny turned the zucchinis with a spatula and Rain stood chopping some garlic at the counter, while Maria, Jen and Theo reclined on the couch. Offhand, Theo mentioned she'd run into Mark.

"Yeah? Remind me, why aren't you guys together?" Jen said sitting next to her, eyebrows raised.

"I don't know. I need to heal from my broken marriage, broken career, and, well, as you've all heard me say, I need to figure something out from back home. I want to resolve it first before I get involved with anyone," Theo said.

Theo would mention this topic shrouded in secrecy once in a while, then brush it aside. As though she wanted to talk about it, but at the same time, not. Winny clearly didn't know how to handle this, so instead, she appeared to think on it and stirred the pot of spaghetti, sliding the slices of zucchini into the sauce with the dull side of the knife and snagging the chopped garlic from Rain before adding it to the mix.

"You know," she began, thinking out loud, "you've got some soul searching to do, Theo. That's something Truth or Consequences can help with. This rundown town has a way of bringing your truth to the surface. And if you fight it, there are consequences. Trust me from experience. Fixing a broken heart, whether it's due to a broken career or failed marriage, is a mysterious thing. No human can figure out the perfect way to do that."

"Maybe an alien could help you figure it out," said Rain in her odd, random way, quietly sitting and listening, while fiddling with her nose ring.

This was seemingly out of nowhere and everybody laughed, except Maria, whose eyes shifted.

"I have an idea," Winny said, grabbing bowls out from the cabinet for all of them. "Doesn't the ceramics studio do tarot cards every First Friday?" she asked, looking at Theo.

Theo nodded, hoping this wasn't going where she thought it was.

"What's today?" Winny asked, looking at the group, but it was Maria who responded, anxious to make sure the subject stayed away from aliens and as normal as possible.

"It is the third Thursday of October, the moon is a waning crescent, the rotation of the earth is about a quarter amount complete on its rotation around the sun and it is currently the season referred to as autumn."

The others stared at her with raised eyebrows.

The other four had noticed Maria's behavior got weirder and weirder the more she talked and the longer they got to know her. Weirder even, than Rain.

"Sooooo, yeah. Um, right," said Winny, shaking off Maria's oddness and pulling out her phone to see what the date was. "It's the first Friday of the month. Let's go get some truth from a tarot card reader!"

Theo rolled her eyes. It had gone exactly where she was afraid it would go: To more *woo-woo* stuff. "I don't need my cards read, you guys. I need to figure out my life. I need to heal from this, well, this thing that happened and—"

"Oh, geeze, Theodora, give it a rest with your mysterious thing you have to do back home! Either spill the beans or don't," said Winny, giving her a hard time and a playful arm squeeze. "If not for the truth, let's go for the fun."

Jen piped in, "Yeah! Let's get your cards read tonight and let the desert give you answers!"

"Let's do something wild too," said Rain. "Let's go find that alien!"

Four of them froze, looking at Rain. *Again with the alien thing.*

Maria's eyes shifted. "What alien? Ha ha, there are no such things as aliens."

"Yes, there are," Rain stated. "We saw one." She pointed to Theo and herself.

Theo remained unclear on the subject. And she didn't like the idea of being lumped in with Rain's type. She loved Rain, but she was a hippy. Hippy, spacey, probably did too many drugs-type. But ... wasn't that how she herself was acting, too? And didn't she sorta, kinda, like it? Nonetheless, Theo resolved it had been, must have been, imagination. Being on acid had likely been the main ingredient in the whole alien situation. Most likely.

The conversation waxed and waned over dinner and went back and forth about the idea of aliens and what it could all mean, while they ate spaghetti sitting on the couch, at the table, and, in Rain's case, cross-legged on the floor.

Then, Rain straightened her back and dove into an uncharacteristically long monologue, letting her spaghetti go cold, "For centuries, it has been widely accepted as fact that humans are likely alone in the universe and that it'd be crazy to think life exists elsewhere." She pointed a spaghetti-full fork in the air. "It's only recently that broader society has begun to dream a little bigger; to entertain curiosities about the idea of life elsewhere. No other planet in the known universe contains the finite needed ingredients to sustain life, *as we know it*, most essentially water, but also carbon, hydrogen, nitrogen, oxygen, phosphorus and sulfur. But sometimes," Rain waved her fork again in the air, sauce landing on Maria's cheek, who squinted and wiped it off, "*Sometimes*, we don't know *what we don't know*," she said mysteriously.

Theo chewed, transfixed. It was possibly also the simplest mechanism of not leaving her mouth open.

"Wise cultures have alluded to the existence of extraterrestrial beings for a very long time," Rain continued knowledgeably, "Some cultures regard these beings as star people who travel across the universe. And there was a congressional hearing recently, where a respected military-guy, under oath, said they had found remnants of an unidentified object that had crashed on Earth, which they had determined contained 'non-human biologics.'" She helped emphasize the last phrase with air quotes.

Theo and her friends looked on, absorbing every word of Rain's, her own eyes glazed, lost in her diatribe of a topic she had clearly given much thought and also devoted a fair amount of internet rabbit-hole research to. Theo didn't know that someone in the military had found 'non-human biologics' in a wrecked aircraft. That gave her chills. She looked around at her friends. Maria looked uneasy at the conversation too.

Rain continued, summarizing her preliminary ideas with so-far unanswerable questions, "Would answering the question of the existence of aliens bring us closer to understanding the fundamental existential questions we've always pondered as humans, such as what is the meaning of life or what happens after death? If there is an advanced race of creatures or aliens out there, do they have such answers? What would it mean if there really were other creatures from other planets coming to visit us? Would they be visiting out of curiosity? Would they be peaceful? Or visiting with intent to harm?"

Her questions lingered in the air.

Maria shifted in her seat at the table and tried to change the subject, "Hey, let's get these dishes done before this sauce gets *caked* on the bowls?"

But Rain ignored her and plowed on, "Fighter pilots who conduct flight drills over the vast oceans have seen Unidentified Aerial Phenomena, ya know, UAPs, or UFOs, several times a day, for years on end, but have only recently come out to talk about it. New technology thingies, you know, the ones that show where another craft is?"

"Radar?" asked Winny.

"Yeah! New radar tech can now lock onto an object, where in the past, someone would see a flying dot that disappeared so fast fighter pilots couldn't register what it was. With new radar, it can lock onto a target to view it and determine that there is something flying in the air near them that defies our current understanding of physics. The Pentagon stated, under public pressure, that three, now famous, videos indeed were Unidentified Aerial Phenomena. It has opened the door to entire reports and government investigations n' stuff into UAPs and given more legitimacy to the idea. So, so, I think they're definitely real, and I think they're among us." Rain punctuated her soliloquy with a single nod as if to say, *And that's that!*

Maria got up awkwardly from her chair, collecting the bowls and slinking off to the kitchen.

Winny appeared to think for a moment. "I mean, I feel like there's usually an explanation for UFO sightings, or, umm, UAP sightings. Have you ever heard of the motion parallax illusion? It explains why people make mistakes and think they're seeing a UFO."

The others looked at her inquisitively, blinking.

So she continued, "Take pilots for example. Pilots are just people who make mistakes, too. When pilots see an object in the distance, it could just be another plane in strange lighting but because they themselves are moving very fast—due to the motion parallax illusion—it might make it look like the other object is moving even faster than they are, making the pilot presume the object is moving faster than the speed of light...or something."

The other ladies just stared.

So Winny elaborated, "Say a ping pong ball was hanging from a string in a tree. If you're moving, it might make the ping pong ball look like it's moving through the air, but it's not."

There were nods of understanding from the others.

So Winny summed up, "That illusion often explains away UFOs. It's why some people think they see a bright light moving, but it's just Venus in the sky. Also, I've heard about people who are having some sort of near death experience say they hallucinated aliens or beings or... whatnot. So maybe that's a thing, too. I think science can often explain these things." She shrugged in summary.

"Yeah, I agree," Jen piped in, "Plenty of experts are skeptical. Like, that guy, that scientist, Steel Grassy Bison,"

"Neil deGrasse Tyson," Winny corrected.

"Ya, that guy," Jen continued, "He doesn't believe in the existence of aliens and he's an astrophysicist. So, uh, I believe that guy."

Winny nodded earnestly. "Do you gals know about that new telescope NASA put into space? It's called the James Webb Space Telescope, I think. It's insanely advanced technology! It can take quality photographs of the edges of the known universe right after it came to existence, billions of years into the past, light years away, and we get these super clear images of tons of galaxies. If we have technology like that, why hasn't it captured signs of life elsewhere?"

"That's a really good point, Winny," said Maria, running water over the dishes at the sink. "Hey, why don't we, um, go to the hot springs!?"

The suggestion was, unfortunately for Maria, summarily ignored.

"Okay, but the James Webb Space Telescope is just designed to look into the past and to try to figure out how the universe made the stars and galaxies, not designed to look for life elsewhere. So the question still stands," continued Rain, to Maria's clear discomfort. "Would it become possible to see planets with life elsewhere, if we actually took the subject seriously, and looked for life elsewhere? Ya know, if we build instruments and technology designed specifically to figure this out? Possibly."

Winny stood up from the table, walking over to the sink and reached up to wrap a friendly arm around Maria's shoulders, settling at the last minute for an arm around her unusually tall friend's waist. "I'm just not sure aliens exist," she said, looking at where the rest of her friends were. "If Neil deGrasse Tyson thinks they aren't real, then neither do I."

Theo had sat mostly quiet during the conversation. Frankly, all the ideas made her head spin and gave her a headache. She rubbed her temples and slurped the last bit of her spaghetti noodles then turned to face Winny in the kitchen. "I'm so surprised you don't think aliens are real. You're so into, well, ya know, *woo-woo* stuff."

Winny shook her head and shrugged, "Maybe I just don't want them to be real."

Maria visibly grimaced a little upon hearing this, which Winny noticed. "What, Maria, I thought you didn't think aliens were real either?"

"I don't! No, no, no, nooooo! Uh-uh. Nope. Aliens certainly are NOT real and they most certainly are NOT among you on Earth studying you, pff, that's for sure," she concluded, attempting casual and failing. "I mean, who in their right mind would think aliens are real?"

"Apparently these two," Winny said, pointing to Theo and Rain. "Did we ever tell you the full story about that night on the mesa?" she asked Maria who towered over her.

Winny then proceeded to bring Maria up to speed, not knowing how well aware Maria already was.

ΔΔΔ

It had been the night she'd met the most fascinating creatures.

Four female humans who seemed so similar to her. She too adored music and its transcendental nature. They felt impelled to share their music like a language, their menial piece of existence in the vastness of space and the universe. These humans were odd. Like her. Certainly not like any creatures she'd ever encountered on her planet, Gazibnon 3000. She had come to Planet Earth to quietly, and discreetly, study humans. Her PhD was in Human Studies. She had received an incredible grant to come here and observe such fascinating specimens in real time. Only one in four billion Gazibnonians got such a chance. But it was more than that, she had felt an immediate sense of kinship to these ladies and was dying to know more about them. To study them, be friends, even! But she knew it was prohibited. To interact with humans at all was a major crime. To let them see you in your alien form was even worse! So she had to keep an itchy, uncomfortable human suit on for days on end. Yet, to her, it was worth it and the humans were very convinced. The only thing it didn't hide was her height. And maybe her eyes.

She had been so curious, that night on the mesa, she couldn't help getting just a little closer. Then closer. So excited to learn from them. There was something special and yet profoundly recognizable about each one of them. So she'd decided she would find a way to meet them.

Plus, she had one additional idea, one that was beyond crazy.

ΔΔΔ

After Winny was done retelling the story, Rain reiterated her interest in going back up to the mesa, "Well, if y'all're so sure aliens aren't real, why not go back to the mesa and try to find out, once and for all?" she said.

Maria looked nervous.

"Meh, why not?" said Winny, ignoring Maria's expression of concern and dropping her arm. "After tarot cards, let's go look for an alien!"

Maria choked on her own spit, worried that there might be something up there her new human friends were not supposed to see.

The Answers are
in the Cards

After dinner they headed to the pottery studio on the corner in town and mingled with the other couple dozen people there for the night, listening to the acoustic guitar a man was playing in the corner.

"Theo, we should play a show here!" said Jen.

Theo nodded distractedly, her mind on the past.

They waited their turn in line, sipping wine, while other attendees received tarot readings. While they waited, they ran into Jane Harper and Bert who gave them all big hugs.

"Fun event, isn't it!?" said Bert, slugging a little free wine, some of which dribbled down his chin. "You guys should play here!"

Jen shouted, "Hell yeah, that's what I said!"

Bert continued, nodding at his wife, "Jane has some exciting news for you."

The five ladies leaned in, anxious to hear.

"Yes, indeed ladies. I have a surprise for you," Jane beamed, clearly letting the suspense build.

They waited anxiously as she searched for something on her phone, the tarot line not moving. Once she found it, the five ladies huddled around the bright shining brick of Jane's mobile device. It was a music poster of bands playing a festival titled *Alt-Cuntry-Fest* with the subtitle: *The West's Best Feminist Country Music Fest.* The poster had majestic red rustic rocks in the background and a pastel sunset shining over band names. At the very bottom, in fine print was the name, *Alien Strata*, in sci-fi bold.

Theo's eyes widened and her stomach somersaulted into what felt like a very aerobic pretzel. This was a big show. Winny and the others looked excited fit to bust. Except Maria. She had a perplexed look on her face that Theo couldn't interpret. Winny was ecstatic.

Looking at Jane, Winny asked rhetorically, "You booked us a show at Red Rocks just outside Denver?! How? And we're opening up for—" she squinted at the name "Aurelia Olsen?! I love her!"

Jane grinned, running a hand through her old rocker gray hair behind her studded ears, clearly proud of her girls, her budding side project of a new ladies band. "Yep. I talked to some people in the industry and pulled a few strings. Plus, I sent in a couple recordings of your open mic nights directly to Aurelia Olsen and she just loved your energy. Y'all have something special."

"It's true," said Bert, now pounding a handful of free crackers and talking between bites while adjusting his thick bifocals, "You can't let that talent go to waste."

"It's true, y'all are magic! Pure, cosmic country magic!" Jane added.

"Why is it spelled, Cuntry, not country?" Theo wondered out loud, spotting Jen's eyebrow raising as though pulled by a fish hook.

"You've never read the classic feminist manifesto, *Cunt: A Declaration of Independence* where they reclaim the word?!" Jane grilled to a shaking Theo head. "Great book. They talk about the Lilith Fair in it, you know, a festival that's all women-fronted bands. This festival is like that, but more diverse, with women from all backgrounds, cis and trans alike. It'll be great!"

"Cunt comes from the goddess Cunti or Kunda, two goddesses who were the source of the universe," Jen added for Theo's benefit, taking a slug of wine. "The word basically means divine feminine power. Well, at least originally that's what it meant."

"Precisely!" Jane acclaimed.

A car pulled up outside and Jane glanced at it.

"We've gotta jet though, but let's meet tomorrow for dinner at my house and talk details. I think it'd be in your interest to do a whole tour traveling up to the show near Denver, while you're at it. Strike while the iron is hot!"

Jane Harper, their mentor, was full of phrases these days.

"But the show is only," Theo nervously looked at the date on her phone, "seven days away."

"Woah, that is a short amount of time …" Jen added. "I mean I've seen some badass shows that were haphazardly thrown together, don't get me wrong, but even for us, this is a little ridiculous."

Rain put an arm around her friend Jen, nodding in agreement.

"Oh, c'mon ladies! We can do it!" Winny whimpered.

"Yeah, you can do it!" Jane echoed. "It's now or never. To be honest, a band bailed last minute for the festival, and that's where you come in. Plus, I can't let my people in the industry down. So you've gotta do the show. And you might as well find a couple places to play while you're driving up there, no?"

The ladies seemed to think about it. Winny's brown eyes remained illuminated just waiting for the conclusion she most likely was hoping for; that they would do the tour and the show.

"Are we going to have time for a tour?" Theo asked. "And are we even good enough yet?"

"Inquire within girl!" said Jane, saying another inspirational phrase, like a poster with a cat hanging from a branch: *Hang in there!* Pulling at Bert's arm as he snagged more free crackers to go, Jane added, "You all have talent, let it blossom! Jump the gun! Go before you're ready! Insert more inspirational phrases!" she quirked, almost out the door to catch their ride, before stepping back in the shop to say, "I'll see you all tomorrow night. Here is a list of venues along the way you could try if you wanna get started on some calls," she said, handing a folded piece of paper to Winny. "They're more old connections of mine and they just might book you last minute as an old favor to me!"

With that, the old rockers were out the door, stumbling into their Lyft ride, drinks held aloft.

The music and clashing of voices in the pottery studio faded into the background and while Theo's friends chatted excitedly, she felt herself retreating into her thoughts, the sounds around her simmering, becoming a distant murmur in her mind. She was nervous about what this might mean. She really should get back to her home state and just face her fate before things got worse, or before she roped her friends further into her mess. *That or get out of town fast*, she thought. *I've already been in one place too long.* But how could she let them all down? They would be crushed if she bailed on the show and the possibility of a tour.

Theo was also concerned that they, as a band, weren't all that good yet. She felt she had improved drastically on the cello since the night she'd introduced her song *Dance With the Desert* to the rest of the band and received some advice from Maria, but she felt certain they still weren't good enough to play at Red Rocks. Playing for a couple dozen people outside Bert's music shop was one thing, but playing in front of a couple thousand people at one of the most iconic venues in the country? Well that was entirely something else. But, she reminded herself, this is what this trip was about: Getting away from her past, growing and becoming the person she wanted to be. If her current level of happiness was any indication, then she had to be on the right track.

The line started moving toward the woman reading tarot cards. When Theo's turn came, the woman doing the readings waved her forward. She had large hoop earrings and was dressed as though she were about to attend a Renaissance festival with a corset tied so tight Theo wondered how she could breathe and if she just might end their session by inviting her out for a goblet of mead and a turkey leg. Theo resisted the urge to roll her eyes.

"I like your hat," the tarot reader said, to Theo's surprise, with a wink, pointing at the symbol on the side of her hat.

"Thanks," Theo responded, fidgeting with the brim and adjusting it on her head. She was still curious about what the symbol with the two seed shapes nestled next to one another meant, but was too shy to ask the card reader if she knew. Plus, she wouldn't trust the woman's response anyway.

The woman explained she would turn three cards: one for the past, one for the present, and one for the future. The cards were some sort of Southwest tarot, Theo learned, not your average deck. More like oracle cards.

The first card was titled *Hardship*, and was decorated with geometric shapes arranged in an optical illusion. *Well, that one was spot on,* Theo thought. She had most certainly faced hardships recently. The ex, the specific obstacle she faced, the broken career. Despite her unbelieving nature in tarot and most other witchy-woo-woo stuff, she found herself leaning in, just a little, crossing her fingers, and hoping the next card, the present card, would be better.

And it was. The second card was titled *Water*, embodied by a vase pouring out into a river, the card brimming with Southwestern colors and shapes, perfectly on-brand with cacti in the background. The card meant cleansing healing waters, and signified 'bringing your truth to the water to let it flow into being,' according to the woman. Theo gulped and found herself feeling the truth of this card too. She thought, maybe this card signified when she was sitting in the healing hot waters that night she had met her new friends. The truth part, as Theo surmised, could mean it was time to tell her friends what she was running from. The idea of telling them this felt like a held breath, desperately needing exhale. She kept her fingers crossed under the table, to see what the future card would say.

The third card was titled *Fire*, represented by a woman holding a burning chalice. This card meant passion, friendship, and a burning of the past. It meant regeneration and life anew. Theo wondered if this card could designate her new passion for music and the comfort of her desert-dweller friends. She hoped it meant creating a new life for herself. A new self but maybe something else entirely. The card was meant to represent the future, after all, so there was no way of knowing for sure. She was curious and more than a little surprised to find herself reading too much into it. She straightened awkwardly —this was just a bunch of mumbo-jumbo.

As the woman described each card, Theo caught herself off guard, feeling they were all too spot on. Her four friends gathered round on stools next to her, eyes wide, while Maria muttered something strange about planetary shifts and alignments in dark matter and in space. That was odd. But Maria was an odd character, they had learned, even more so than Rain. So the ladies had learned to brush it off. Yet, there was something about these cards that reminded Theo of something else too …

Winny leaned in close to Theo to whisper in her ear, "Hardship, water and fire! Just like what the woman from the hot springs tub said the night we all met!"

Theo's eyes widened. That was indeed exactly what the words on the cards reminded her of. In fact, the whole thing was feeling kinda spooky to Theo. But it wasn't *that* spot on because the mysterious woman in the tub had said four things and clearly this whole thing was set up to only have three cards: the past, present and future.

The card reader stared at the cards, without a word to the others yet. Her brow was furrowed, deep in concentration, the headscarf sliding down her forehead. She closed her eyes, inhaled calmly and exhaled loudly, and awkwardly, like that person in yoga who breathes excessively loudly. Then she fumbled with the deck of cards in her hands and pressed a palm against them as if they were whispering to her through her palms.

"Hmm, interesting," she said, opening her eyes and tapping at the deck of cards with a ringed finger. "Normally I just do three cards but something is telling me I need to pull a fourth. Is that all right with you?"

Theo could hear Winny inhale sharply, and she herself held her breath too. At this point, nothing would surprise her. She was wrong.

The woman turned the card over. It was a roadrunner.

Her friends whooped and hollered.

You've got to be fucking kidding me, thought Theo.

"Ohhhhhh! It's the talking roadrunner again!" Jen shouted, alarming the man behind them as she spilled wine on his coat. Jen took no notice and continued shouting all-too-closely into the tarot card reader's ear, "She met a talking roadrunner one time while we were tripping balls!"

At this point, all eyes at the ceramic studio were on the group of ladies.

The card reader seemed unfazed as the mohawked woman jostled her excitedly, knocking her headscarf loose, hoop earrings swinging.

"What does it mean? The card?" Rain inquired quietly, leaning toward the reader.

The tarot reader responded with three words, "A long journey."

Her friends gasped, and looked at each other.

"That's exactly what the woman in the tub said!" Rain found herself shouting now too.

Theo held her tongue but had to admit it, she was perplexed. This was all too spooky.

While the chaos commenced with her friends who were emphatically asking the reader more and more questions like rapid, excited fire, Winny spoke quietly in Theo's ear, "I just figured it out," she soothed, putting an arm around Theo's waist giving her a squeeze, leaning in close as Theo felt the hum of electricity exuding from her. She liked the way Winny's voice soothed her ears. Winny leaned in and said, "You're an Aquarius."

Theo's eyes widened and she turned to face her friend, her hazel eyes looking into Winny's brown ones. *How the hell did she just figure that out? What were the odds she just guessed? One in, what, twelve? Wait, eleven, since she'd ruled out one sign for her already?*

Time stood still for a moment, the energy in the pottery studio faded and it was just the two of them, looking at each other. The moment felt like magic. Winny knew Theo so well, and they'd only known each other for a short time. Was it destiny?

Theo reeled. Everything in her life was changing so fast, including her outlook. But no, she wouldn't start believing in something like horoscopes or tarot cards. That was going too far. But it *was* odd, she had to admit. And now Winny's astute statement. All of it did make her feel like there could be something to it. And the tarot reader's statement about letting your truth flow. It made her feel like it was time to tell the truth about what she was running from.

The card reader continued to detail what it all meant, now that the fourth card was in the mix, but Theo wasn't listening.

She could only feel Winny's soft and soothing energy next to her and the moment they just shared. But then the reader took hold of Theo's hand, seeming to look into her soul. Theo noticed the creases etched around the woman's eyes left over from smiles and, perhaps, wisdom.

"You have a destiny awaiting you, Theo Hart," she said.

Theo didn't recall telling her, her name.

"Listen to it. To your destiny. Next time you see this roadrunner, ask it who is Oxannae?"

The Walk to the Mesa for the Second Time

They walked out of the pottery studio, toward the mesa, back to their plan of finding an alien. A few of them walked along holding wine and Jen a bottle of whiskey, toward their next big adventure, this time only slightly intoxicated and not tripping on acid. Theo's friends were talking emphatically about their experience with the tarot reader who, Theo had to admit, had been spot on with her reading. She wondered about her friends' readings, too.

Maria began talking, "My tarot reading was unequivocally and entirely correct, if you ask me. You know, it is all true what the tarot reader said."

"Well we do live in Truth or Consequences!" said Jen. "Probably at least some truth to it all, just hopefully no consequences."

Maria responded, "Hmm, consequences. You know, I made some mistakes recently and the tarot reader definitely picked up on that. I've got some trouble I might face. I too am running from something," Maria stated this esoterically, looking at Theo.

Maria was talking more than she normally did. She had drunk quite a few glasses of free bagged wine at the pottery studio but they'd never seen Maria drunk. Maybe she was more talkative when she was drunk.

Maria continued, "I do not think I can escape that truth. I too hope there are no consequences, but I do think once you acknowledge your truth and stop running from it or fighting it, things get better. There is no doubt that tarot reader was right, about all of it. About what she said about all of us. Especially about you, Theo."

Theo was taken off guard by this. She felt thrown off by the whole experience and was on edge about the idea of telling everyone what she was running from. She was a little ticked off at people pretending to know how hard her life had been, or knowing who she was more than she did. And Maria, alluding to something she was running from without elaborating, trying to equate their experiences without knowing, was frustrating. How could she or the tarot reader possibly know her life? This mental gymnastics resulted in the following outburst:

"How do you know that it's all true, huh, Maria? There's no science, there's no actual proof, it's all general. This tarot card stuff is complete BULLSHIT!"

Her friends gasped and held their collective breath. They hadn't seen Theo like this before and Theo felt a rush of color to her face, but remained stubborn. She knew they all believed in this hippy crap, but not her, no, she just wouldn't.

Maria slightly shrugged. "I just know it. Truth is just known where I come from."

"Oh yeah and where's that?" Theo was feeling flustered. Her

friends often acted like tarot cards and horoscopes were reality or that they knew anything about her past. Some of it she just couldn't get behind, and she felt her emotions heightening. "Do tell me, where's that, hmm? Where are you from?"

Before she could retract her statement, Maria said, quite matter-of-factly, "Gazibnon 3000."

Everyone stared. Maria seemed mortified she had said something, albeit true, though the rest of them wouldn't know what she meant.

Winny let out a laugh, easing the tension. She reached up to put her arm around Maria's shoulders and realizing, again, that her friend was too tall for that, settled on Maria's waist, pulling her in close. "That's an odd name for a place, are you an alien from outer space?"

The others laughed, which settled the tension even more, especially for Theo. What was her problem? Of course her friends would understand about her past. It was something she personally didn't regret, and she realized if she shared it with them, it would be a weight off her shoulders. As she opened her mouth to apologize for her outburst and begin to tell them her story, Maria made a strained laugh.

"An alien? Ha ha, that would be crazy, right? Ha ha. Aliens are not real," she said.

"Yes they are," muttered Rain.

"Speaking of aliens!" said Jen. "Should we continue on our *journey* to find that alien?! Get it?" Jen interjected her own sentence. "*Journey*, just like the tarot reader said to you, Theo?"

Theo felt a bubble of frustration again, but took a breath, and let it pass. Having realized her frustration was rooted in mustering courage to dredge up her past, and that doing so would release it, like the tarot reader had said, made her relax again. She looked forward to taking the weight off her shoulders but was just waiting … for the right time to do so. She remained just a little tense. A lot was on her mind.

They walked onward into the night. Silhouettes of spindly desert trees protruded through the dark velvety desert and seemed to lean in on them, the red earth scuffing her boots. They walked in silence, each lost in their own thoughts. She couldn't imagine that the desert itself would really heal her heartache. It definitely couldn't heal her past, and finding an alien certainly wouldn't. How ridiculous this whole thing was. Her thoughts flip-flopped and she reminded herself to keep an open mind. After all, finding these friendships out in the desert had already brought her more happiness than she had ever known back home. Perhaps the desert, in that way, already was healing her? But how would they react to her truth? *Who even am I?* Theo couldn't help asking herself these existential questions as she walked along.

She looked around to see if maybe she would see the talking roadrunner again. An alien certainly couldn't fix her, but if that wasn't ridiculous enough, maybe a magical talking roadrunner would. Although she was half joking with herself, the other half did want to see the talking roadrunner again. And it was odd that the tarot reader had pulled a roadrunner image. Was it just the acid that the bird talked to her that one night, or was there something to it?

Alas, no roadrunner, just blackness, stillness and silence.

"Let's go up to the mesa," said Rain, pointing to that mysterious hilltop.

Theo's gaze was drawn upward. She had forgotten how high up the mesa perched. There was a steep cliffside on one face that Theo unintentionally imagined how horrible it would be to slip and fall down something like that. It would be a devastating fall.

"No, um, let's uh," Maria cast about, "let's actually try going down to the river!" she said in a last-ditch effort to persuade her friends not to go on the mesa. She pointed toward the Rio Grande and started for it, practically pleading them to follow her, "Maybe there are aliens down there!"

She strode toward the valley but lost her balance, only just catching herself in a flurry of drunken movement. It was no good, the others continued hiking onward.

When they got to the top of the mesa, no signs of an alien were to be found and they were on the verge of giving up and deciding to go home, to their campground, when someone spoke.

"We could sit up here, make a little fire and wait," said Rain, "Maybe we'll see signs of something while we're up here. You know, wait it out?"

Maria looked uncomfortable again.

Blood, Fire and Freedom ...
and Visitors

The fire crackled and swished in the night breeze as they sat in the dirt, passing around a bottle of whiskey, waiting for something, anything, to happen. The air was still and comforting, the desert exuding its calming energy that Theo had come to expect, just what she needed.

They talked around the campfire, discussing plans for the band. They determined they would indeed do a tour of sorts for their band before reaching Red Rocks. Winny presented the idea of doing a show in Albuquerque, Santa Fe, Raton and then finally the festival in Red Rocks outside Denver. They figured their old rocker friend Jane could help them sort out the details. At this point, Jane was not only their role model, she was like their booking agent. The ladies daydreamed aloud of their hopes about the band but Theo couldn't help her angst. Her situation might deeply impact everyone. It was now or never. She needed to tell them her situation.

Theo took a deep breath and a plunge, "Hey, um, I need to

tell y'all something. It might, er, impact our tour plans."

Her friends leaned in closer, the air was quiet and the fire crackled.

Theo fidgeted with a rock in her hands as she sat cross-legged on the ground. She decided to come out and say it, what she was running from. Her friends would likely understand. So, she got straight to the point, "I had an abortion back home. I was six weeks pregnant from my abusive husband and I didn't think it was right for a child to grow up in that ... that sort of an environment. And, well, I had an experience one night at the hospital, as a nurse, which made me realize life is short, and my life matters too. So, I thought it was okay to avoid the growth of those tiny cells in my uterus and stop them from becoming a human. Like removing a seed from the soil before it grows into a tree, ya know?" she said, avoiding anyone's gaze.

Instead, she looked at a juniper tree lassoed to the cliff by its own roots and felt the same as the tree. She forged ahead, "So I decided I needed to find someone to give me an abortion. But, as you might know, it's illegal in my home state. And I didn't know anyone who could do it, except—" Theo paused, then resumed, "except for me. So, I did the abortion myself. I had to. And then I had to get out of my home state. And I had to do what was right for me." She exhaled. She felt as though she'd been holding onto that breath ever since the whole thing happened. She finally looked up.

Her friends looked onward at her with kind eyes.

"You did the right thing, Theo," Winny said, putting a hand on Theo's clasped hands. "Why didn't you tell us earlier? You know we support women's choice. What freedom does anyone have if they aren't allowed to control their own body? I don't think your abortion was a mistake."

"I don't either!" Theo blurted, realizing they might be missing the point of the story, realizing they didn't know the laws in her home state. "I *know* I did the right thing. It was really the only option. It's just, the thing is," she took a breath, "my husband, my ex, found out and reported me. In my state, abortion providers can go to jail for life, if convicted. And, even though I was the abortion patient, I was also the abortion provider. And, well, I was convicted … of a Class-A felony … of murder."

"What?!" exclaimed Jen. "It was only six weeks, that's barely the size of a pea! I have boogers more sentient than that!"

Winny glanced at Jen with a look like, *let her finish.*

"Right, right, well," Jen stammered, realizing she was perhaps being insensitive, "Just to clarify, I think it's a beautiful thing if you want to grow those cells into a baby, I'm not saying it isn't. It's a beautiful choice! And that's just it. It's a choice." She nodded, as did the others, then looked to Theo to continue her story.

Theo continued, "Exactly. I mean I look forward to having kids at some point, but, well, they deserve better than the life left for me back home and the life a child would have been forced to grow up in, ya know?" She focused her eye contact again on the ground and brushed the sand from her hand. "And hell, I deserve a good life too. *I'm* a human being …" She paused, looking out at the city lights below and trying to put it all into words. She took a breath, then resumed, "When I was convicted, I left the state. I ran … here. I don't know just how long I would spend in jail because maybe my sentence could get shorter, you know, with appeals, but, wow, can you imagine going to jail for just doing what is right for your own body and life?"

Theo felt the weight of her situation gather at her shoulders, her body posture slackening. The fear of what she could face weighed on her now, suddenly. But, it felt good, more than good, to get her truth off her chest and to talk to people she trusted. The truth was she knew she had done the right thing. She'd always known that. It was just … a lot.

Winny seemed to sense this and scooted closer, putting an arm around her, and looking at her with those kind, brown eyes.

Theo felt an overwhelming sense of relief and comfort at having her truth out there with her friends and in the healing hands of the desert of Truth or Consequences. The town and the surrounding landscape seemed to exude love and understanding. Though she wondered, what would be her consequence for having an abortion? Would it be jail time? Or freedom to live her own life, the life she was now embodying and seeking? If she hadn't had the abortion, she never would have left her home state and never would have met her new friends. She never would have felt the otherworldly joy she felt with these ladies and the joy of playing music, of finding herself out here in the Wild West. And there was something particularly special about the way she felt about Winny but she couldn't place it.

"What was the experience you had that made you think about how life is short?" Rain quietly asked.

"What? Oh," Theo started, "Well … One of my patients died. In childbirth. It was heart wrenching. It made me think about how, well, the life of the mother matters too. My life matters. It made me think about this whole crazy existence thing." She blew out her cheeks, not knowing how to put her feelings into words, what it all meant, but there was more to tell her friends, something which could impact their tour. So she said it. It was something she'd been worried about for a long time. "There's something else, too ... I think I'm being followed by someone. Someone who is trying to take me back to my state. Someone who might be dangerous."

"Who?! Your ex-husband?" asked Jen.

"Maybe," Theo breathed. "But he's not who I've seen watching me. I've seen someone else I think is following me. A stranger. I didn't officially divorce my husband, even though I call him my ex and, well, I didn't know how to get away other than to just leave. I certainly wouldn't put it past him to hire a private detective to find me and then, I don't know ... Then he would come get me himself and take me back to the South to serve jail time for what I did. Or he would hurt me. Or, or ... or kill me. I know it sounds crazy, but I'm just worried. I saw a man here in town watching me. He had a tattoo of an eye on the side of his head. And I saw him again at Guitar Mart in Albuquerque. Maybe he was sent here by my ex to come get me." The last poured out of her in a flood.

"Yikes," Jen said quietly, her gaze focused on the stick she was poking the fire with. "Do you think the tattoo eye is, like, meant to allude to, like, a 'Private Eye'?"

That thought hadn't even occurred to Theo and she was momentarily stumped.

Winny looked at Theo, intertwining her fingers in hers as they sat in the dirt and said, "It doesn't sound crazy. I dealt with something like that in the past, as you know. And you deserve to be free. We'll find a way to get you out of this mess. We'll keep you safe."

Theo realized she *did* feel safe. She felt safe, especially in Winny's eyes. At ease. And the fact that they had both been through something similar made Theo feel that much more connected to her. She wished they didn't have that in common, abuse, but, here they were. She grasped Winny's hand tighter.

"Have you considered contacting a civil rights agency?" Winny suggested pragmatically.

Theo sighed. "Maybe. I just don't know that it would do any good."

Her home state considered Theo a criminal and she was sure her ex-husband was trying to track her down through a private eye to make her pay for what she did. The ex, that's all she wanted to call him, had called her endlessly since she'd left. So had the courts and her home state and the police. The truth was, she was an outlaw, for controlling her body with her own nursing knowledge. And now, she feared for her life.

Winny tucked a hair behind Theo's ear and a spark of electricity shot up Theo's spine. Their faces got closer to one another, so close Theo could see her own upside down silhouette reflected in her friend's brown eyes. Theo noticed Winny glance down toward Theo's mouth as she parted her lips, just slightly. *Was Winny leaning in?* A flutter of butterflies rose in her chest.

Then, a flurry of movement caught Theo's eye and pulled her attention to the bushes.

It was the roadrunner. *Did the others see it too?* But before she could ask them, it was gone. Theo felt a relieved smile form across her lips. She took the sign of the roadrunner as a good one. It seemed to appear at transformative moments.

Winny appeared to be processing everything Theo had just laid out in front of them.

"You don't deserve this fear, Theo," she said.

Theo could see the emotion building behind Winny's brown eyes on her behalf and watched as Winny stood and began pacing around the fire.

"The way I see it, women have this natural and beautiful ability, and burden, to make a choice as to whether or not to bring life into this world. And it needs to remain a choice," Winny said, trying to summarize a complex and nuanced topic.

"Well said," affirmed Rain.

"Snaps!" said Jen.

Hearing her friends' encouragement, Winny continued and embarked on an on-brand monologue about pro-choice, society and the nature of femininity in everyday culture. "Society tells us to be more man-like. What does that even mean? More fierce, more strong, more violent? Fuck that, we need more womanhood! More nurturing, more loving, less war, more peace."

"Yeah!" affirmed Theo, pulling her attention to her friend again. She felt great admiration for Winny, and noticed how her voice moved like liquid.

"Where I come from," said Maria, who was visibly fairly intoxicated, her troubles seemingly forgotten, "We do not even remember what war is. We figured it out. We devised a system that works for everyone, even creatures and plants and animals. We devised a system that is similar to what you all would call utopia. Where I come from, there is no patriarchy, no capitalism, just pure blissful utopia and—"

The other ladies looked at her, their heads cocked inquisitively.

Maria cleared her throat, "You know, my town. We just uh—" she backpedaled nervously. "My town, we uh, we have socialism and whatnot and we just, you know, uh, our taxes go to taking care of people. That's what I mean."

Everyone seemed mostly satisfied with this answer but Theo was still unsure about Maria. "Where did you say you're from? Aren't you from Albuquerque?" she asked.

But Winny was already back on her monologue about society. "You know, I used to be afraid of my womanhood," she continued as she paced the fire, while her friends looked up at her from their terrestrial spots on the ground. "But let's not do that! Let's be unapologetically *woman*. Let's control our own bodies and choices. Let's laugh at society's menace toward us and let's piss in their pessimistic faces and make the world a better place like we know it can be. For everyone. Men included! We're women, we're sexy, we're smart, we're scary, fuck you! Our bodies are powerful and crazy, fuck you!"

In that moment, she reached up her skirt, into her own body and pulled out her menstrual cup and poured out her blood into the fire.

"Ewwwwww, Winny what the fuck!" said Jen, "You've really gone too far this time."

Maria could have sworn she'd seen humans do plenty of weird things in her research studying humans, but this was probably the weirdest.

Theo laughed appreciatively.

"I mean it though!!" Winny was exclaiming, "I want a woman president, I want a woman pilot. I want a woman teacher and doctor and I wanna watch movies made by women, I wanna go to strip clubs where strippers are happy and respected for their profession! I also want … Great goddess alive! I want *choice* and *freedom*. The right to decide about our bodies and lives. I want that right for you, Theo. And I want that right for all of you, us!" she said, with a drunken swoop of her hand toward her friends.

"Hear, hear!" said Jen.

Rain nodded emphatically. Maria did too.

"Well," started Jen, trying to shift the conversation back to the idea of the tour and show at Red Rocks. "If there is a private eye following you, and possibly your ex is on the way too, all the more reason to get the hell out of dodge, huh? Drive to Red Rocks?"

"But doesn't this mean I'm putting y'all at risk?" Theo inquired. "Ya know, basically harboring a fugitive?"

The group contemplated the idea but Winny scoffed, "Girl, you know you are our *ride or die*. We're here for you, thick and thin!"

"Hear, hear!" shouted Jen again, taking a sip of whiskey.

Rain again quietly nodded and Maria shrugged.

Theo beamed. These were her friends. Her crew. And they supported her through everything. She'd never before had that.

Maria's eyes were serious behind her glasses. "But the ex and the possible private detective … they will find out where we are going, will they not?"

No one apparently knew what to say to that.

Winny thought for a moment. "Maybe. But … I don't think it's right if they stop us from living our lives either. 'Specially not right to stop Theo from living hers. Isn't that the whole point? To have freedom? You decide, Theo, but I think it's better to get out of dodge AND live your life and your joy of playing music. Right?"

Theo thought for a moment. She knew Winny was a little biased, considering it was her dream to play music at Red Rocks and go on tour. But she did love playing music. And being with her friends, especially Winny.

Suddenly, Theo noticed a perceptible shift in the air. The night grew stiller and more palpably quiet than before. Crickets stopped chirping, the wind stopped breezing, and everything ground to a silent halt, like it had that first night they'd been on the mesa. She felt her stomach roll over.

There was a blaring, bright light. It illuminated the five of them atop the mesa. Was it the private detective? Or the police? Had they tracked her down?

But no, the light was above them, in the sky, like a beam shining down from the dark night sky. *No, it couldn't be,* Theo thought. She wasn't even tripping this time. She looked up. *That wasn't possible.* She squinted her eyes more, trying to look past the bright light at the object projecting it. *Could it be?*

Above them, was what appeared to be an enormous flying saucer.

New Mexico Lore

New Mexico has a well-documented history of alien, UFO and flying saucer sightings. Of course, there was the infamous Roswell incident where a rancher came across debris of what supposedly was a flying saucer. The term flying saucer was coined in 1947, that same year but prior to the Roswell incident. An amateur pilot, Kenneth Arnold, was flying near Mount Rainier in Washington and saw an unidentified flying object, similar to, reporters would later write, a saucer. But what the newspapers wrote wasn't entirely correct to what Arnold had described. He had meant to describe the *way the object flew*, like a saucer bouncing if you skipped it across water, not the way it *looked*. Nonetheless, the term stuck. Arnold said he had calculated the speed of the craft, which appeared to be going around 1,200MPH, faster than anything humanly possible at the time, before the sound barrier had ever been broken. In a 1947 newspaper story by the East Oregonian, Arnold was quoted as saying, 'Everyone says I'm nuts, and I guess I'd say it too if someone else reported those things. But I saw them and watched them closely.'

The Roswell situation in New Mexico in particular was later blown off as a weather balloon. But the rancher, William Ware 'Mack' Brazel, upon whose property the unidentified flying object landed, swore it wasn't. Brazel, and other witnesses, described the metal material as otherworldly and strange and that it would resume its shape no matter what you did to it, even if you took a sledgehammer to it. The rancher also described an unknown language inscribed upon it.

There was supposedly a second crash site in Roswell, where first responders arrived on the scene. One firefighter said he saw a disc-shaped object in the ground with non-human bodies lying near it. A sergeant who arrived later still was told not to look under the tarp where the bodies were, which he did, and claims to have seen aliens.

In 1950, in Farmington New Mexico, fifty independent people, some of whom were pilots, reported seeing silver flying discs on one particular day in broad daylight.

In 1957, two personnel at the Kirtland Airforce base in New Mexico were tracking a strange object on radar and with binoculars, that they described as a car standing vertically in the sky. They said the object could hover, change direction, and move strangely and quickly.

In 1964, in Socorro, New Mexico, a police officer, Lonnie Zamorra, responded to a call for what appeared to be some sort of crash up on a hillside. So he drove to the scene expecting to help victims of a car crash but instead saw a foreign object rising into the air, which then took off at a high speed.

These stories have added to the lore and the mystique of the desert in New Mexico, something most residents have largely ignored. Most tourists visit Roswell, not Truth or Consequences. Why would they? Not much was known about alien sightings in Truth or Consequences.

Until now.

There Theo was, grappling with what she saw before her. The bottom of the disc had glowing red lights in shapes she didn't recognize. The object was dark, metallic in color, quiet and still, and made absolutely no sound whatsoever.

The UFO hovered above them.

It spanned nearly the whole horizon, as far as Theo could see, stretching over them, its red lights pulsating. There was an odd stillness to the air, seemingly emitting from the dark disc and the beam of light stayed projected on them, making it hard to see anything but it. Theo looked at her friends to see if they were seeing what she was. They were all peering up at the disc, eyes wide. Maria just looked nervous. What appeared to be an oval door slid open and the air started to swirl. Theo's stomach did another flipflop. The world around her sounded like she was underwater.

For the first time in what felt like hours, there was sound; a low pitched, staccato-type sound but it was coming from somewhere to her right, not from up above. Then, movement followed along with the sound to her right and Theo slowly peeled her eyes away from the hovering disc and looked to see an object on the ground coming toward her. It was a dog. It was Bowzer. She registered the sound was Bowzer barking and he was running toward her.

Theo tried to shoo Bowzer away to try to keep him safe from the object, and wondered how he had gotten so far away from town in the first place. He just bounded closer to her. There was a shift in the air and she returned her gaze upward. The dark disc was gone.

All five ladies looked at each other, apparently dumbfounded.

"Let's get outta here," Winny whispered.

They gathered their belongings as quickly as they could, Bowzer now in tow, and made the trek down the mesa back toward town. No one said a word.

A Secret Door in a Bookshelf

Six Days 'til the Red Rocks Show

The next day, Theo woke up in Blissa. Her quiet, comfortable and safe, camper. She had a metallic taste in her mouth that she couldn't place. Was it drugs from last night? No, she and her friends hadn't taken any. An image came swimming back into view, one Theo feared she would never forget; a dark, foreboding disc in the air. *Had that been real?*

She rolled over and peered through the curtains, across the campground and over to the top of the mesa. It seemed looming and ominous. Different from how the mountain had felt before.

A sudden loud knocking at her door made her jump. She stumbled out of bed and swung the camper door open to an image of her four bedraggled friends peering in at her. Winny with her wild dark hair disheveled from sleep, or lack of sleep, Rain's kind, soft face, Jen looking tiny next to Rain, and Maria, tall and mysterious. Theo peered into the light through the camper door at her friends, trying to wipe the sleepiness from her eyes.

Winny held out a french press in her hand toward her. "Coffee?"

She invited them all into her cramped and quirky camper, all five, shoulder to shoulder, and taking a seat where they could. Winny sat next to Theo on her bed. They looked at each other for a brief moment and shyly smiled. Rain sat straight-backed and cross-legged at the breakfast bench, Jen sprawled out on the compact camper table and Maria sat silently on the only other bench.

They talked all morning about what they'd seen the previous night. This time all of them had definitely seen the same thing— most assuredly, a creepy unidentified object, they concluded. Rain had no doubt it was a UFO. Jen and Winny were still wondering if it was perhaps something the government was hiding that no one was supposed to know about, not a UFO, and Maria was emphatically backing Jen and Winny up; it was *not* a UFO, according to her, but maybe had something to do with the government. Then there was Theo. Theo had decided she was officially on Rain's side. It had definitely been a UFO. Or a UAP according to modern language. She had never been so sure of anything in her life. But she wasn't expending energy on trying to convince the others. She knew what she saw.

If it was a UFO, which Theo was convinced it was at this point, this changed everything. All night, Theo had been thinking about the strange object and about what Rain had said in the Airstream last night over spaghetti. Their spaghetti dinner now seemed so long ago. Like the whole world had transformed. Theo found herself dreaming about other worlds, both terrifying and hopeful. She wondered what life was like on other planets for aliens and why they would choose to come here. Rain's questions echoed in her mind, *Would they be visiting out of curiosity? Would they be peaceful? Or visiting with intent to harm?* These were the questions she found herself plagued by. Why did they hover over the mesa?

Morning rays of light turned into afternoon rays of light, streaming through the curtains. It was autumn, but the little camper warmed up in the heat. Theo caught a glimpse of something odd at Maria's sleeve seam by her hands. Something blurry. Like when there was a glitch in a photo or video that made a temporary double image. She could have sworn she saw—

"Well, what do we all think? Should we go on tour?" Jen asked, anxiously.

Theo's thoughts were transported to the moment Jen had asked that question last night, right before the giant black disc, and right before Bowzer galloped to their side.

> *Bowzer had run up the hillside to sit at Theo's feet. They'd made it down the mesa safely, none of them saying a word and Theo had walked to Mark's house, as it appeared Bowzer had gotten out. It was lucky Bowzer had stumbled upon them and wasn't lost in the desert all night. Or were they lucky Bowzer had found them? Theo wondered why the disc had disappeared right as the animal bounded toward them.*
>
> *"Bowzer!" Mark had said, crawling onto the ground to let his dog emphatically lick his face when Theo had brought him to his house.*
>
> *Bowzer certainly had been a little disheveled, with*

quite a few burrs stuck in his fur, but other than that, he was all right, despite having gotten out through the front yard the previous day.

"Where was he?" Mark had exclaimed.

"Up on the mesa," Theo responded and Mark's face had gone pale.

"The mesa?" he repeated, pointing across his pool to the mesa peering over the town.

"Erm, yeah ... "

"Was he okay?" Mark had said, nervously scratching Bowzer's ears to the pup's approval.

It was late, Theo was exhausted and terrified of what she had just seen but she had asked nonetheless, "Mark, what do you know about that mesa?"

Mark tried to change the subject, "Thanks for bringing Bowzer back. I was worried sick."

But Theo pushed, "Mark, I think ... I think we saw a UFO last night up on the mesa."

Mark had looked at her for a moment then, seemingly careful about how his response might be received, he said, "Yeah I've seen quite a few up there."

"Really?" Theo had not expected that.

He then invited her in for a decaf and they talked all evening about UFOs and aliens until the sun rose. She enjoyed Mark's company and felt oddly relieved about her experience after talking to him about his. Apparently, he'd seen two UFOs and several tall, lanky figures walking on top of the mesa back in 2013 and had blocked it out for a while but then recently remembered, and questioned himself *whether or not it had been real. They brainstormed together what such figures would be doing up there; perhaps gathering intel on how to take over the planet. Or maybe it was a portal up there. Or perhaps they were observing humans from higher ground, much like scientists would. Or, like professors, studying a different culture. Theo's mind had jumped to Maria, who was tall and often came across professorial in demeanor. But that was ridiculous.*

Whatever the beings were doing up there, Theo and Mark came to the conclusion that it must indeed be true that aliens were real and they were here, in Truth or Consequences. Theo's mind had melted into a cognitive dissonance accepting the idea that aliens did in fact exist and that it was disconcerting, yet, strangely reassuring, to know other beings were out there. She was now sure she had seen an alien her first night in town and that she had seen an alien aircraft last night with her own eyes. The alien was tall, slender and had been holding an object which exuded an eerie, albeit, calming energy. It was something Theo couldn't explain. And tonight, the dark disc was, well, otherworldly and ominous. But still, something was very different. This time, it was darker.

As the sun had started to rise, they parted ways and hugged. Mark smelled sweetly of cedar and patchouli and she held onto him. She didn't like the idea of parting ways, not with everything going on, not just yet. He was so reassuring somehow.

She thought for a brief moment, then said it before she could take it back, "Would you like to accompany me and

*the girls on our band tour?" She blinked at him in a
sleepy, post-trauma groggy stupor.*

*The invitation to Mark was out before she could stop
to take a moment to consider what the other girls might
think.*

*Mark had grinned sleepily, and replied genuinely, "I
would be delighted."*

Theo parted the curtains of her Blissa camper and looked up
at the mesa before responding to Jen's question. "Yes, I'd like to
do the band tour," Theo said, not sure when to bring up that
she'd invited Mark.

The ladies lounged for several more hours in her cramped
camper and Winny orchestrated travel logistics. They would
need to make a lot of calls today and book venues. The list Jane
had given them was short, so they'd need to get creative.

By 4 p.m. they had called everyone on Jane's list and not a
single venue was able to host them so last minute, not even for
the 'Queen of Chaos' as one of Jane Harper's former bandmates
residing in Santa Fe had called Jane: It just wasn't feasible.

Just when they were thinking the idea might not work, Rain,
in her quiet contemplation, put forth a harebrained idea, "Why
don't we just get driving and see what happens? You know, get
into the flow and see how it goes?"

Her idea was to spontaneously see what venues would want
to host them as they went, knowing that they should get going
as soon as possible, considering Theo potentially had people
following her. That, and the fact that they all wanted to get as far
away as possible from that UFO, which had caused them to

question the purpose of their own existence. What did the aliens want? This was now the second time they had seen them.

"The sooner we get out of dodge and away from aliens, the better," agreed Jen, who had now come to terms with the idea of aliens being real as well, and was fully on board with Rain's crazy idea.

Rational Winny, however, was still on the fence about the alien concept, clinging to the idea there was some sort of explanation, some sort of hope that there weren't scary otherworldly figures watching them, perhaps right now. Winny kept referring back to science and that there must be information they were missing. She felt there must be some logical reason, some reason they were all imagining it. After some convincing, she took Rain up on her idea to fly with the wind and take to the road without any prior booked venues and see what they could drum up on the way. Theo surmised that the prospect of going on tour with the band was just too exciting to ignore for Winny, which, luckily, went hand in hand with their great escape. This show would be a lot of exposure, and whoever was following her would likely figure out where she was after the show, but she decided to cross that bridge later. Priority number one: get moving.

"Well what're we waiting for!" shouted Jen, getting up from her seat in the Blissa camper so fast she bumped her head on the ceiling. Then, rubbing her half-mohawked head she made a bolt for the door.

But Winny brought her back to earth, "Wait, wait, wait! Some of us have jobs, you know? We'll need to try to swing it with our employers first," she said, nodding to Theo before returning her attention to Jen, adding, "You do too, Jen."

Theo had clearly almost forgotten that the rowdy Jen Hernandez too had a stable job being a server at one of the green chile restaurants in town where she would need them to acquiesce to her leaving, first.

Winny continued, "I've got to square everything away here at the campground before we go, and—" looking at Maria, she said, "I'm sure Maria's got to make some phone calls to her job in Albuquerque where she works as a ..." Winny's face scrunched into a puzzled expression. "What is it you do again?"

Maria's eyes shifted and she replied vaguely, "Yes, uh, yeah I better call my place of, er, employment, to, um, secure a temporary leave of absence from my position where I work at a job of employment in Albuquerque. The city where I live."

Winny tilted her head at Maria's now unsurprising oddity. Nonetheless, it was settled. They had made the decision to embark first thing tomorrow morning.

Theo opened her mouth to mention she'd invited Mark, but then closed it, chickening out.

Everyone was getting up to leave to return to their proper RV campers or motorhomes to make calls and arrangements, and she realized it was now or never.

"So, I-I ... invited-Mark-to-come-along-on-our-tour," Theo uttered, the words coming out in a single stream and nervously adjusted the brim of her hat, unsure what everyone would think.

To her surprise, most everyone was on board with it. *That was easy.* Maria said she liked the idea. In fact, her eyes lit up at the mention of bringing Mark. But Winny's expression was hard to place. Her eyes moved away from Theo's.

Jen shrugged. "Sure, why not take him, we have room for a sixth person if we take the Airstream."

"That old hunk of junk?" said Winny, pointing to the vehicle

Jen and Rain currently resided in. "Nah, let's take my Winnebago. It's more fuel efficient and should get us around just fine. It, uh, well, unfortunately only holds five people, but we should save gas. No need for a sixth person. If we take the Airstream, we'll lose time too. To be honest, I'm not even sure that old thing works, it's already broken down once," Winny said, apparently realizing she'd stumbled on a perfect reason not to take the Airstream and, therefore, to not take Mark along. "Plus, it'd be impossible to park. There's that too," she concluded.

Rain looked on, quietly listening, eating a spoonful of cold cranberries out of a can.

"Relax, it'll be fine on the road," Jen dismissed waving a hand in the air.

Winny wasn't entirely sure. She mused that the Airstream was, "less of a reliable mode of transportation than that tin can of cranberries." But nonetheless, she could tell everyone wanted to take the Airstream, in part because it could double as free lodging. So, they ultimately decided to take the Airstream. Additionally, from there on out, they affectionately called their Airstream the Tin Can from time to time.

That evening, they went to Jane and Bert's house and told them about their tour plan, if you could call it that. They also asked that, should anyone inquire specifically about Theo, not to give out any information.

They played music all night, shaking off the strange encounter with the UFO, and enjoying what would be their last evening in Truth or Consequences for some foreseeable time. Later, they sat around Jane and Bert Harper's kitchen table laughing and cracking jokes as they waited for a very late-night dinner to cook on the grill outside. Jen joked about how, walking into Bert's music shop had felt like walking into Ollivanders wand shop, a mysterious and magical place.

"Pff, magical place? You think that's magical? My studio is bitchin'," said Jane Harper.

"Well, can we check it out?" Jen asked.

They walked up a curving staircase to the second floor where a wall of books and a single warmly-lit reading chair stood in the corner by a window exposing the stars outside. Sitting on the shelves between the books were collected items like old photographs of Jane and Bert with long hair and tie-dye, vintage record albums and empty ceramic vases.

"Cozy!" Jen hummed approvingly, running her hands along the lightly stained oak.

"There's more!" said Jane, pulling one of the empty ceramic vases like a lever.

There was a *click* and a crease in the bookshelf creaked open, revealing a hidden door.

"Radical!" Jen oooed, and the other ladies stared in giddy, childish excitement.

"I've always wanted to walk through a hidden door in a bookshelf!" Theo enthused.

They walked into a room with a ceiling full of skylights exposing even more stars dotting the Truth or Consequences sky. Jane flipped a switch and a gentle lighting revealed walls lined with books, travel trinkets, heirlooms and more records in frames. Crystals and tarot cards galore, plants winding themselves serpent-like around the shelves. A historic-looking gramophone sat in the corner.

"I got it fixed up to play modern records," said Jane, pointing proudly to the gramophone and popped in an old jazz record.

Music crackled to life and Theo felt instantly cozy, mesmerized by how music could set an atmosphere.

"Ooo!" said Winny "I love these old cameras!" She took a polaroid camera off a shelf and tinkered with it. "May I?" she asked, then took a few photos of the group and sat down on a plush rug, setting the photos out to dry.

"I like to come up here and get lost in thought, contemplating the cosmos through these windows," said Jane, peering up at the night sky, her eyes aglow and seemingly lost in thought. "Luckily no alien encounters for me … yet."

Maria pursed her lips, then added, as though she couldn't help herself, "It is nice to contemplate the cosmos. You have no idea just how much is out there."

Jane's expression was perplexed. Then, for a moment, a flicker of light above the mesa caught her eye. Her eyes narrowed. Theo noticed too, her thoughts wandering to the alien they had seen that first night.

"What's in here?" Maria said, pointing to a giant clay jar on the coffee table in front of a couch nestled neatly into a nook.

"Check it out," Jane said.

Maria stuck her hand in and pulled out several neatly wrapped dark chocolates.

"Have one," Jane encouraged.

Maria did. You could tell she melted the moment it reached her tongue. "What is this?" she groaned. It seemed Maria was referring to the substance as though she'd never had chocolate before. But Jane clearly interpreted the question as what *type* of chocolate it was.

"It's my favorite. It's a French brand called Kaukah."

"Caca?" Jen repeated back to Jane. "You mean like shit in Spanish?"

Rain let out a laugh.

Theo looked over to Winny who was on her back on the plush rug now looking up through the skylights, while the others tested terrible pronunciations of the chocolate brand. She couldn't help but notice Winny's expression as she stared up at the stars: soft and subtle, the light hitting her brown eyes just right. She looked so relaxed, a slight smile on her face.

Theo thought about how hard Winny had been working to get the band going. How much she'd always wanted to be in a band. And now, that dream was materializing as they were about to head out on a, albeit very bizarre and unplanned, band tour. Was that what she was smiling about? Was that why she looked so content?

Theo walked over and laid down next to her on the plush rug. "Whatcha thinking about?"

To Theo's surprise, she replied, "You," with a smile.

Theo couldn't help it. She felt her face flush. "Me?"

"Yeah," Winny replied, turning to face Theo. "You've got this quiet sort of resilience that I find very impressive. And comforting, in this weird way. Ya know?"

Theo didn't know. She'd never gotten a compliment like that before. She noticed a soft and comfortable breath move Winny's chest up and then slowly back down. For a moment, Theo was transfixed by her face. Subtle freckles dotted her cheeks, the night sky behind her. She thought about how happy she looked that day dancing in the rain when their Airstream broke down.

A voice from down the stairs startled Theo's thoughts back into the room. It was Bert.

"Hey y'all! Burgers are done!"

"Yuuuus burgerrrrs," said Jen who was finishing a bite of chocolate. "Someday imma start a fancy hamburger joint called Her-Burgers and Fries," she said and practically hopped out of the room, mohawk shifting to the other side.

Rain put down the crystals she was holding and stopped the seeming chanting she was doing under her breath with them and followed Jen downstairs, Jane following suite, then Maria too, after snagging another piece of Kaukah.

Then it was just the two ladies, Theo and Winny. They looked at each other for a moment. Then, Winny got closer. She put her hand on Theo's hip. Theo felt a surge of warmth flare in her cheeks, but she felt excited. Butterflies. *What was this?*

Winny leaned in and kissed Theo.

Theo kissed back. If it were a cartoon, fireworks would have exploded in Theo's pupils. Or drawn hearts would have floated up from behind her head. Or a *Wowza* dotted in a jagged comic book thought bubble.

Winny gently pulled away to look at Theo, and both of them smiled.

"Hey, you lovebirds ready for dinner?!" said Jen, popping her head back through the hidden bookshelf door, knowingly ruining the moment with a wink, pointing down the stairs where dinner waited for them.

Before responding, Winny reached her arm up holding the polaroid and *click* took a photo of herself and Theo lying on the plush rug together, smiling.

Sabino Canyon

Five Days 'til the Red Rocks Show

The next day, Theo awoke in her tiny camper feeling lighter than she ever had, a stark contrast to how she'd woken up yesterday. The sun was just rising, illuminating the east corner of her camper, the light caressing this and that through the curtains. Theo thought about her kiss with Winny. How right it had felt. After dinner, when they had parted ways when they got back to camp, Theo could have sworn Winny paused, as if to invite her in to the Winnebego, but had instead gone in for a hug, a comfortable hug, the kind where you feel your muscles relax into the other person for what feels longer than the actual time is, and then that was it: They parted ways.

Theo felt confused but radiant, excited, and there was a warmth in her heart she hadn't felt in a long time, or … ever? What was going on? Did this mean she liked women? Theo hadn't given it much thought before, and found herself spinning, feeling confused but also … right. Her Southern belle mother would not approve, that was for sure. Nor would her military father. But, what did it matter what they thought? Theo hated that she found herself thinking about what her parents would think.

She made herself a cup of coffee in her tiny black-and-white-tiled camper kitchen, and sat on the steps watching the sun rising higher into the vast sky from the east, dots of sorbet-colored clouds gently lighting up the horizon. Theo packed a backpack of clothes and put her cello into its unceremonious cardboard box, vowing to get a cello case someday. She took time to be present. She was not sure when she would return to this place she had called home for several months. She liked it here. It felt sad. But she was looking forward to their band-tour adventure, and plus, she knew she had to get going. She had already stayed too long in one place. She would have to come get her Subaru though.

The ladies piled into the Excella Aistream and picked up Mark and Bowzer then took to the road in Jen's giant tin can, the big metal container gliding along the road.

"Wait, Jen, why are we going south? I thought we were heading north toward Red Rocks?" asked Winny.

"Change of plans, cowgirls! I talked with my old friend Topher in Tucson who is a bartender at this little hole in the wall called the Suave Saloon, and the band they originally booked all got terribly sick!" she stated joyfully.

"Well that sucks for them," said Theo.

"Yeah but it's great for us!" continued Jen, "Our first show on our tour. I can see the magazines now. *Face Orifice.*"

"Alien Strata," corrected Winny.

Maria gulped nervously.

"Do we have enough time? I mean, we still need to make it up to Denver?" said Theo, not familiar with the territory out here.

"Oh yeah, we sure do!" said Jen, her small body behind the

giant wheel making her look like a cartoon character.

"I don't know if that's such a good idea," said Maria, looking nervous and disheveled.

Arizona was prime alien territory. But she was overruled, and they continued driving.

"It'll be a quick turnaround cuz the show is tomorrow night. So we gotta get into Tucson, find somewhere to camp, and then play the very next day," Jen said.

Theo frankly liked the change of plans. All the better to change it up if indeed she were being followed.

The hours flew by. Dusty Southwestern scenes of patchy juniper among muddy earth and bright blue sky glided past the window as Theo daydreamed. There was something transfixing about this part of the planet. All five ladies, and Mark and Bowzer, seemingly daydreamed too, each lost in their own thoughts. Theo turned to observe her friends, wondering what they were all thinking.

Winny gazed out the window while tinkering on her acoustic Martin, the delightful music dotting the atmosphere, seemingly soundtracking their journey: A show at Red Rocks was no joke: Sure, they were just the openers, but such a high caliber venue meant a lot of exposure. Winny had always dreamed of a moment like this. Theo imagined what it would look like to see Winny featured on the cover of Rolling Stones sometime: *New artist spotlight: Winny Ampeg of Alien Strata: Haunting voice, intricate, reverb-y, melodic guitar.* She smiled and looked on as Winny picked the strings, her dark hair moving, as she swayed to the beat she was creating. Theo recognized the rhythm as a classical guitar riff in major tones.

Jen steered the Airstream like she was the captain of a boat, sailing across the cement-laden seas across the mirage swooping desertscape highway. She bobbed her head to Winny's music, maybe daydreaming about owning that fixer-upper home she'd always wanted, one with a garden in the back and a sexy husband in suspenders there with two dogs. Two dalmatian mixed lab siblings, one named Lola and the other Larry. Maybe she would quit her job as a server and meander the world in her Airstream, perhaps driving down through South America one day to visit her distant relatives in Chile. This was an idea Jen brought up from time to time.

Theo's eyes wandered over to Rain as she meditated, cross-legged on top of the queen bed in the back, allowing the environment to pass by through the low windows, her body swaying slightly to the movement of the vehicle and to Winny's music, light changing beneath her calm eyelids. Monk-like and peaceful.

Mark … daydreamed about Theo, Theo thought bashfully, and hikes with Bowzer, shuffling a deck of cards absentmindedly. Bowzer slept quietly on a couple blankets on the floor in the kitchen area, occasionally kicking his paw, as he likely thought about chasing a particularly chunky squirrel.

Maria. Theo's brow furrowed. This was a difficult lady to guess for.

$$\Delta\Delta\Delta$$

Theo didn't know it but Maria daydreamed about earning a Planetary Prize, (her species' version of a Nobel Prize) for her daring discoveries, and risky research while living among four crazy human ladies, one man and one dog. She hoped that, perhaps winning the Planetary Prize would help authorities look past her breaking interplanetary law.

In addition, Maria was pondering the oddity of the humans driving in their strange oil guzzlers. She hoped one day she could help them evolve to get rid of them. She had already helped her new human friends in some way at least. She had helped them on their journey to become musicians. She had quietly, and secretly, imparted musical knowledge and talent to them through telekinesis. The humans had no idea. This was her small way of helping. Maria hoped, if these ladies succeeded in gaining a platform through music, a group of people who could reach a larger audience, she could help impart knowledge to the greater human society on how to improve their planet. So far, she felt her plan was working.

△△△

Theo finished scanning the Airstream at her friends and her thoughts slid back to herself and, well, if she was being honest, she felt lost. She thought about her kiss last night with Winny. How right it felt. But what did it mean? She wasn't sure. But she knew she certainly was into Winny. And Mark. She looked at the two of them now, and each of them looked over at her as if on cue. So she looked away, back out the window.

Theo also thought about what would happen if she was caught by the private investigator she surmised was following her and taken back home. Or worse, what would happen if her ex-husband found her. She tried to shake that thought and mentally moved to the performance. She couldn't believe her music was well received by people. Sure, she knew the basics of cello, but never in her wildest dreams had she thought she'd be decent enough to play at Red Rocks. Something felt like all this was too easy. It seemed like she and her bandmates had gotten incredibly good at music, at an inhumanly fast pace. She also thought of the alien they'd seen on top of the mesa that night and the UFO. *Maybe aliens had something to do with it,* Theo chuckled to herself. *Maybe that's how they magically got so good at music so fast.* She shrugged off the funny idea, that was just too hilarious.

She moved on to what in the world she was going to do with her life. For the first time in, well, ever, she was happy. She was truly happy with her friends, living in a little camper named Blissa in a glamping campground in a tiny and obscure town called Truth or Consequences, New Mexico, with one person, Winny, who she felt she was falling in love with. Which also made her confused. She'd never before considered being into women. And yet, here she was. In a way, it kind of made sense. But she also kind of liked Mark. She tried her best to feel feelings for Mark, because allowing herself to feel for Winny felt too foreign, still. Right but foreign. Theo thought there was a decision that would need to take place at some point but she didn't want to think about that just yet.

Life was beautiful. It really was. She loved being in the desert with her new friends making music. It felt like living art. She imagined a painting hanging in a museum of the scene. A transcendental desert scene, she and her friends visible in a gray Excella Airstream popping out of the painting. But how long could it last? She would need to get a decent job soon, she couldn't work at a ceramics studio forever. They'd only given her time off because they couldn't afford her quitting. And she worried she couldn't outrun her problems forever. She tried to let go of her worries and settle into gratitude of the wild and joyful new life she had stumbled upon in the desert.

A bump in the road jostled Theo out of her thoughts.

"Pothole!" announced Jen, her petite arms wrapped around the steering wheel like a kid driving a school bus.

Theo peered out the back window and caught a glimpse of something silver in the light. Her heart sank. She had a sudden feeling they were being followed. Yet no car was in sight. *Probably just that weird feeling again.*

But Bowzer seemed to sense something too. He jerked out of sleep and clambered onto the queen bed in the back where Rain was jostled back into the present. She went to snuggle the dog and scratch his ears, but Bowzer paid no mind, focused instead out the window, seemingly frozen in concentration.

ΔΔΔ

The topography transformed before their eyes. Slowly but surely, as they drove closer to, and crossed into Arizona, into the Sonoran Desert. Saguaro cacti emerged, like marching men on a hillside, ready for battle. Or like dancers, frozen in time, prickly arms raised in different poses. Or like aliens, outstretching their arms toward the cosmos. Theo had never seen anything like them perched on a hillside like that.

The saguaro cactus, or Carnegiea Gigantea, was a rare creature. It only grew in the Sonoran Desert, a span of land stretching mostly in Mexico, and in the Southwest corner of Arizona, with a small sliver in California. It didn't grow anywhere else on the planet. These resilient, spiny chunky plants, on average, were forty feet tall with the tallest one ever measured reaching seventy-eight feet. When little, they fed off the kindness of other plants, they needed a nurse plant to grow next to and to shade them from the elements while they strove to reach ten years old. Usually, once they were past the age of ten, they could really start growing. Eventually, they overtook the nurse plant and absorbed more water. So the nurse plant inevitably withered away, but the saguaro remained, resilient, strong, and standing the test of time in the stark weather of the desert.

The saguaro had an impressive maze of roots that stretched just below the surface and absorbed much sought after water. Some of these Sonoran creatures lived to be 200 years old. Their quiet wisdom preceded them. To the Tohono O'Odham tribe, the saguaro were more than just plants, they were a different type of humanity. The saguaro were venerated as respected members of the tribe. Origin stories of the saguaro included a story of a young boy, some traditions said girl, who sank into the ground and emerged as the first saguaro. To this day, the O'Odham harvest the fruit of the saguaro in a semiannual ceremony, respecting and venerating the vibrant spiny plant.

Theo stared out at the cacti stretching their arms toward the sky all afternoon. She had no clue of their history, but respected and appreciated these foreign, to her, plants.

They ate lunch in a town called Tombstone, which, as Maria informed them, used to be a mining town. It played a pivotal role in transforming the state of Arizona into a bustling mining zone. It was also the site of a famous movie loosely based on a gunfight that took place between outlaws in the 1880s, a movie Theo had never cared to watch.

It was impressive how much Maria knew about history but when asked how she knew, she just shrugged.

$$\triangle\triangle\triangle$$

Maria couldn't tell her new human friends that she had been studying humans for nearly all of her 190 years of life on her planet. Her PhD in human studies was certainly coming in handy now for, if nothing else, impressing the humans she was illegally convening and cohabitating with when she exhibited her knowledge of human societies. She'd had a hard time convincing those on her planet that her studies were worthwhile. She felt they represented an important key to the past. Perhaps they were all connected at some point, somehow. Kind of how on Planet Earth it was discovered that Neanderthals and Homo sapiens lived at the same time and how they were perhaps more humanlike than previously thought. Or, perhaps, Maria was not giving these humans as much credit. Maybe they were more advanced than she thought.

Most Gazibnonians knew Earth was in peril and that the human inhabitants were, knowingly, destroying their own biodiversity, land, and water and fighting between themselves and between countries. Something they called *war*. That they were heating up their atmosphere to a boiling point where they and most lifeforms would not be able to survive, due to a sticky, pungent substance they called *oil*. Oil and other petroleum derivatives were used to fuel their vehicles, create their products of *plastic* and propelled their modernity forward. Maria and people on her planet knew how reductive this was, considering there were so many other possibilities and ways to create energy, productivity and progress but humans seemed to be bent on willfully ignoring the problem, pursuing such a future in the name of *power*.

Gazibnonians had it figured out: They did not have *cars, oil, power* or *war* or cultural and political institutions called *patriarchy*. How bizarre. But Maria was of the minority mindset on her planet that humans could be helped: That they weren't stupid. Power was what seemed to be the problem and it was in the hands of the few on Planet Earth. The ones with the excessive money. A class called *billionaires,* soon to be *trillionaires* controlled production. If they wanted to, they could help the planet. But they didn't.

Maria didn't want to *just* learn from human mistakes, she wanted to help. All humans. She knew she was breaking interplanetary law by interacting with these particularly wild-lady-humans but she hoped she might make a difference for them, perhaps plant some seeds of knowledge regarding how to create a world of paradise, or utopia (a word humans would use if they ever visited her planet), that she and her species took for granted on her own planet. She wanted to somehow relay that a better world was possible and achievable. But how? Were humans too far out of touch to prevent their own demise? Maria was hopeful that somehow, they could get themselves out of their self-preserved pickle. Perhaps with a little help from herself, an alien, they could improve. She just currently didn't know how. Yet. It was partly why she traveled with this unruly crew, the band known as Alien Strata—to get some sense of how humans in general thought, felt and interacted. So that one day, she could help them.

ΔΔΔ

That night in Tucson they stayed at a campground just outside of one of Jen's favorite old haunts, the Sabino Canyon. The canyon was impressive with its landscape of saguaro cacti and rushing creek from recent rains. The river was uncharacteristically high and fast. They were told by rangers not to go near it for that reason as flash flooding could be dangerous and to remember to wear clothes tonight, as temperatures were going to drop to an uncharacteristic low this November night.

Jen's bartender friend Topher and his friend Rick stopped by to play horseshoes under the bistro lights they strung from the Tin Can to a couple tall cacti. The two brought extra sweatshirts for everyone, as it was already getting very cold. Topher and Rick stood in contrast to one another, Topher with gorgeous dark skin, glasses, suspenders, and just the right amount of facial hair; Rick with pale, sunburned skin, a hole-y band shirt and hair styled like he was the singer of Sum 41.

Topher made a great shot and whooped. He and his friend Rick were winning.

"Oh sure," Jen was saying flirtatiously, "bring your game here and beat us all at it."

"We're not normally this good," Topher was saying, "we must have the game gurus in our favor."

When it was time to wash the camping dishes after dinner, it was Theo's turn to get more water from the campground pump.

She walked along the dirt road, swinging an empty bucket and humming one of Alien Strata's tunes, the darkness enveloping her, the meager flashlight from her phone a tiny beacon. It was surprising just how low the temperature had plummeted in the last hour, and she was regretting not snagging one of the extra sweatshirts the guys had brought. She pulled her thin flannel closer to her body, wishing she was wearing more layers than yoga leggings and a cotton shirt with a wolf, moon and cheesy cowboy on it that she had acquired in Tombstone. She shivered. The pump was on the opposite side of the campground and it took her a moment to find it. She glanced around the dark scene and couldn't help feeling anxious being alone, thoughts wandering to someone, such as her ex, or the private detective, or maybe aliens. Was that why she kept having the feeling of being watched? She scanned the road in the distance and the horizon for any sort of flying saucer and saw nothing. She cleared her throat and tried to shake the feeling, along with her shivers.

Finally, she found the water pump. It was near the river's edge and the sound of rushing water enveloped her mind as she pumped water into the bucket absentmindedly. She was tired. *Traveling really took it outta' ya*, she thought.

A glimmer of movement and her heart stopped.

She imagined the man she had seen staring at her from behind the books at the music shop in Albuquerque. Was it that guy? Then she imagined her ex-husband. Was it him?

Thankfully it was neither. It appeared to be a little critter making noise by the trees. A flurry of movement and Theo was surprised to see a roadrunner emerge from the mesquite trees, peering out at her. In fact, it had a marking resembling a wave. It looked like THE roadrunner she'd seen in Truth or Consequences, twice! Theo was dumbfounded. The roadrunner's wave marking was not moving this time, so that part must have been the acid, but there was still a wave marking. Curiosity burned like fire inside her. She was not one to be superstitious or believe in tarot, or anything of the sort, but it was beginning to intrigue her. The words of the tarot reader came to mind: *Next time you see this roadrunner. Ask the question, who is Oxannae?*

She took a cautious step toward it, not wanting to scare it away and looked around to make sure no one was watching.

The roadrunner stood, unfazed, tail raised, peering at her, blinking its beady eyes.

Theo crept closer and whispered, "Who is Oxannae?" She felt slightly ridiculous.

The sound of the river was strong.

The roadrunner tweaked its head, then turned to leave, jumping into the trees.

"No, no, don't go, little roadrunner. Who is Oxannae?" Theo whispered more assertively. She parted the tree branches, stepping toward where the roadrunner had been and found her foot falling farther than she anticipated, sending her tumbling down the ravine she did not realize was right there. The sound of the river rushed up to meet her, louder and louder as she tumbled through the dirt. Her phone launched out of her hands into the air, illuminating the cliffs and landing goddess-knew-where. Bye-bye phone. And then, with a sudden burst of cold, Theo felt herself fall into the rushing river, pulling her from the hillside.

The coldness of the water took her breath away.

Theo was not the best swimmer. She tumbled through rapids and rushing water left behind by the recent rains, gasping as she tried to grab rocks spinning past her.

She struggled and struggled. She went below the water several times, catching gulpfuls of sandy water in her mouth, reemerging time and again to spit it out, her eyes scanning the river bank once above the surface. *Oh god, oh god, am I going to die?* She grasped at the hillside and a tire halfway submerged came loose, sending her back into the pull of water. She tried again, this time grabbing onto a branch from a mesquite tree and successfully began holding on.

She pulled herself toward the river bank sopping wet, doing a pull up gesture and rolled one leg onto the dirt, then the other. She lay there on the ground for a few minutes catching her breath. *I made it,* she thought.

The rush of relief came and went as fast as it had arrived, when she stood up and had no idea where she was. Plus, she had lost her phone. Where was the campground? All she could see before her was a land laden with saguaro cactus shadows, rocks, and mesquite trees. The crickets chirped in song. It sounded like laughter to her. She shivered, now severely cold from being soaking wet and also from the uncommon coldness of this particular desert autumn night. She took a moment, and a deep breath, swallowed her pride, got her bearings and walked toward what she hoped was the campground.

Onward she went, trudging, unsure of where to go or what to do. She had frequently felt lost in her life, metaphorically, but now she well and truly was. She was unaware of just how much time was passing. Her teeth chattered and her body was so freezing it began to go numb. She started to feel dizzy and confused. Then warm. Her wet clothes suddenly felt very hot. She forgot where she was and stumbled a few times, feeling clumsy. Her muscles felt unusually stiff.

The sky began to pulsate different colors and music swam in her mind. *Am I tripping again?* she wondered, not sure what was going on. She took a breath. *Think. What are my symptoms?* She went through her symptoms, leaning on what she had learned in nursing school; these were symptoms of hypothermia. *Shit.* She hadn't realized it right away. Not an average day where one could get hypothermia in the desert.

Time was of the essence. The lights of the city took flight into the night sky, like fireflies. Like dandelion seeds taking to the wind. The music in her head was like a loud, but soothing lullaby, willing her to go to sleep. She thought of the music she and her new friends had created together and continued walking around a hillside, seeing dots of light. Must be Tucson. So she was indeed going in the right direction but they were far away. Where was the campground? She needed to think fast. She again felt woozy.

Silhouettes of saguaro cacti she had seen earlier in the night began to move gently along the landscape, like marching soldiers. They reminded Theo of a scene in a Mickey Mouse movie when the broomsticks come to life. The music to the old worn out VHS tape popped loudly into her head and she sat down, against her own savvy judgment, willing herself to just give up for now and keep walking tomorrow in the light. She was so tired.

Slowly, the shadows lengthened across the already dark landscape and crept in closer toward her. She felt overwhelmingly ill at ease, her skin crawling, wanting to jump out of her own moonlit-shadow. She felt the sensations of failure, stress and an overwhelming fear of her ex-husband and his abuse.

She was about to be swallowed whole by these cacti if she didn't get up and do something.

Fire

Theo paused and breathed, then shook herself and began walking again, her mind wandering to older times. She caught her toe on a stone and stumbled, her hand landing in a small barrel cactus. The needles stabbed into her palm and one particularly long spine punctured the side of her thumb. Theo winced and uttered a few Southern curse words. She was tired, lost and freezing cold, and now *this*. Her eyes welled suddenly with tears. Thoughts of the past crept up on her and the weight of her former self and previous life engulfed her like a cup trapping a spider. She decided to listen to the thoughts instead of fighting them and time swam.

The surgeon bumped into her from behind and her hand had landed on the needles about to be used, stabbing her hands and sending the just-sanitized-tray of medical equipment clattering to the floor, fraying her nerves further. Her pupils narrowed and focused on a task she usually felt she failed at; the task of adequately providing healing care to the people she was supposed to be helping. She was exhausted from long shifts and little support. She was tired, wired, and burnt out. How could she truly help people if she herself needed help? How could she heal people if she herself was not fully whole? And the needles. So many needles. Theo knew she was not the best at administrating drugs via needles and it made her nervous every time she had to stick someone with one. But it was more than that.

The day that particular woman, Shantelle, had died in childbirth, a woman who wasn't even her patient, the one in room 223, that day really stuck with Theo. She shouldn't have died. It wasn't fair. These feelings made Theo certain she couldn't be in a profession anymore where things like this happened. But she felt like a failure, like she had abandoned her higher purpose of helping people through their child labor.

Her face was wet with tears as she sat in the dark dirt, looking at her bloody cactused palm. More thoughts of failure seeped their way in.

Tears at the thought of being married to a man who was downright cruel. She remembered getting one last ride from him to work and the way the car door had echoed as she slammed it closed, planning on taking the bus out of town as soon as possible and then buying a new car to get away, before he realized she'd withdrawn the extra funds.

Theo felt the cactus needles pulsing in her palm and thumb.

Sometimes she blamed herself for it all. But she had to let go. If it was true as the title of a book suggested, 'The Body Keeps the Score' then it was time to release and let go of that score. Oddly enough, the abortion was the beginning of her freedom. The beginning of respecting her own life and living self. One day, she wanted to have children, but it needed to be the right time and with a person who would respect the children and her. She deserved good things.

She thought about her new friends and how they had changed their trajectories in life. How they had started again, particularly Winny. If Winny could do it, she could do it too. She picked herself up. No more needles. No more needless suffering.

She decided then and there to switch those neural pathways away from thoughts of failure and to focus the neurotransmitters firing in her brain to what she wanted to grow; a life of joy, like the life she felt with her friends. She still wanted to help people, somehow, but she realized she needed to forgive herself first. She wasn't helping anyone if she wasn't happy and healthy herself.

She slowly extracted each cactus barb, one by one, until she got to the one in her thumb, wincing as she pulled it back through and out of her skin and flicked it to the red earth. Blood pooled in her hand and she applied pressure.

She trudged onward, but lost her balance again, this time with her bloodied hand landing on some particularly dark rocks. But they were soft. They were charcoal. She was standing amid the debris of an illegal dumping site, the remains of which had clearly been burned. Shards of plastic and remnants of someone's belongings littered the landscape; old dishes, uncountable bags of trash, an old burned-up couch. Theo suddenly felt like she belonged there too. She felt like garbage. *Wait, wait, wait,* she thought to herself and, again, switched her mindset, running through her mantras. *That is the old mindset. I'm a new person, I deserve good things. I deserve to be happy. To control my own body, to have a job I actually like, to make music with friends. I deserve to be loved.* That one, she had to remind herself of again, practically shouting it in her brain, *I deserve to be loved!*

She picked herself up once more. It was time to shed her old self and let the desert set her free. *New life, new me.* But first she needed to find her way back to civilization before the early stages of hypothermia got worse.

An old gasoline tank lay next to a broken-down refrigerator. It gave Theo an idea. She would need to get someone's attention out here and she also needed to get warm. She could kill two birds with one stone, or 'feed two birds with one scone,' as Winny would phrase it.

She piled up a couple of garbage bags and doused them in gasoline. But how would she light them? She had seen how to make a friction fire on a TV show she adored where people survived in the wild for months but there was no way she could do that. Where in the world would she find matches or a lighter? As if in karmic answer, she saw a lighter lying right there on the ground next to where the gasoline tank had been. In fact, there were several. Someone had truly left everything behind. She tried one lighter, but it did not work. *Must have gotten drenched in the rain.* So she tried another. Nothing. She picked up a pink Barbie one, the last one, praying to the god-she-didn't-always-think-existed until moments like this, that the lighter would work, and … it didn't. She searched around in the dark for anything that caught her attention, sifting through old plastic melted plates and rags of burned clothes and then—she felt a little box in a scorched pocket of a jacket. It was a box of matches. *No way they wouldn't be drenched.* But maybe there was hope. She tried one, and it worked. It worked!

The little spark illuminated from the match head like a cherry on a cigarette and she flung it toward the pile which immediately engulfed in flames.

"Aaaaoooooooo!!" Theo howled, adding more nearby debris to the bonfire while warming her hands by it at a safe distance, careful not to warm herself up too fast. Plus, the burning trash did not smell fantastic. "Thank you!" she cried out. "Thank you, matches! Thank you, mountains! Thank you, stars! Thank you, fire!" she shouted to the quiet landscape, embracing her inner rowdy Jen. Her inner hippy-dippy Rain. Her kooky quirky Maria. Her wild-child Winny.

Oh, Winny. She adored the way Winny looked at her and she adored the way she felt when she was with her: safe, authentic, happy. She felt so right with Winny. Did that mean she was gay? But she also liked men, she was almost sure of it. So maybe bisexual? *Umm.* Either way, she realized something important. *I'm into women,* she thought.

"I'M INTO WOMEN!" she exclaimed aloud, her voice bursting, spinning around like she was on a mountain top, ready to sing *The Sound of Music,* instead of dancing in an illegal dumping site around a raging garbage fire. She added another coyote howl, "Aaaooooooooo!" for good measure.

She sat by the fire, hoping it would be enough for someone to find her soon. Time was creeping along and not in a good way. Theo held her breath. She could have sworn she saw movement to her left.

"Hello?" she said into the still night air. A single cricket chirped then stopped.

Again, she sensed movement. She stopped and listened. The saguaro cacti seemed to be encroaching upon her. They started to move inward toward her but gently, like a group of people dancing inward around a maypole, encircling her as though intertwining ribbons around her. Theo let go and embraced the hallucinations.

Slowly, the saguaro figures morphed into images of her friends. Jen with her jet-blonde-dyed grown-out mohawk, curly haired Rain and Maria's green eyes, peering into her human soul. But most importantly, Winny's brown eyes and confident grin.

"Theo!" the cacti shouted at her. "Theo, wake up!"

They tried jostling her with their pokey limbs and peered down at her. The cacti were not, in fact, cacti at all, they were her actual friends, looking at her, urging her to wake up.

Winny's eyes came swimming into view. "Winny?" Theo whispered. "You found me. You're going to save me. How did you find me? Was it the fire?"

"Yes, that and some crazy woman shouting 'I'M INTO WOMEN!'" Winny said with a smirk.

The rest of the night was a blur. She was in the hospital for most of it, but the doctors assured her and her friends she would be fine. They had gently warmed her up with heated compresses to the center of her body and a rescue blanket.

Theo had asked about the severe hallucinations, to which the doctor had responded, "Just a fleeting perk of hypothermia."

The Suave Saloon

Four Days 'til the Red Rocks Show

Back at the Sabino Canyon campground that morning, Theo slept late in her cozy Airstream bunk bed. They all spent a lazy day in the Tin Can watching old music videos and snuggling with Bowzer on the couch while snacking on cheese puffs and the occasional veggies and humus dip, as per Rain's request.

The band asked Theo over and over if she was ok and if she felt up to playing in the show that night, to which she repeatedly assured them she was a little tired, but other than that, fine.

"It's weird," she said, "but I feel lighter than ever."

That night, when they got to the venue, a dingy hole in the wall as Jen had aptly described it, Jen said hi to Topher behind the bar, and Winny immediately ordered tequila shots. Winny was clearly nervous. One of Topher's coworker bartenders with a mullet and seventies eye glasses came by with an entire tray of shots for the group. They downed them. It was time for a sound check.

They played a tune or two to a nearly empty room where only a few people were witness to their testing each instrument to check the sound levels; the sound woman who gave them the thumbs up, Jen's handsome friend Topher, and the mulleted bartender. Mark and Bowzer had gone for a walk. Alien Strata, feeling pretty good with their run-through, returned to the bar to smooth out their frayed nerves with a little more tequila.

Mullet Man came back over with more limes. "You ladies are all right," he said. Then, turning to Maria, "And you, tall lady, you're a decent drummer! Where'd you get all those arms to play all those drums?" he joked.

Maria laughed nervously, hoping he couldn't tell that she actually had several extra arms hidden in plain sight under her human suit. But Mullet Man didn't seem to be serious, so she laughed it off. In fact, was he hitting on her? Or was that just a bartender thing?

A few more patrons straggled into the bar and Rain asked quietly if they wanted to go outside and smoke a joint. Theo declined, but Jen, Topher, and Maria said yes and went outside. Mark and Winny stayed behind with Theo; Mark on Theo's left and Winny on her right. She was smack in the middle of both of them and realized this was the first time the three of them had been alone, ever.

"So, er, uh," Mark started, running his hands along the condensation on his pint glass, "What song are you all going to start with, 'Dance with the Desert'?"

"Nah," Winny replied frankly, looking across the bar past Theo to Mark. She took another sip of what this bar called, a *Suave Saloonerita*, a half-assed attempt at naming a margarita. "We're saving that song for last. Definitely our best one."

Theo beamed.

"Gotcha, gotcha. Good idea. I like that song too. It's really beautiful," replied Mark, looking at Theo.

Theo sat between the two of them, awkwardly sipping her drink.

"Yeah, it's a beautiful song. Very captivating," Winny said, looking at Theo and bumping Theo's knee as she crossed her legs.

Theo couldn't help but feel like they were talking about something or someone, else.

"Hey, you all're up," said Mr. Mullet Muscle Bartender Man, pointing toward the stage.

There were probably about twenty people, tops, in the dark room.

Winny's eyes widened. "Hold on, I gotta grab our crew!" she said and took double gulps of her *Saloonerita* before going outside to find the others.

Mark smiled at Theo. Theo smiled back. Mark started to say, "So, I was thinkin'—"

When Jen suddenly came swooping in and grabbed Theo by the shoulder, swirling her up and out of her barstool toward the stage. "Lessssss gooooo!"

Man, the lights were bright up on stage. Theo sat with her cello resting against her thigh and looked out toward what could barely be called an audience and still felt stage fright well up in her throat. This was a new venue. A *real* venue.

Winny walked up to the microphone while multitasking and adjusting her guitar strap around her shoulders to rest on her waist. Her smooth D'Angelico electric guitar seemed to glow under the lights. Winny's nerves seemed to have disappeared as she confidently approached the mic. She was cool, calm and collected. It was amazing to see. She effortlessly introduced the band as Alien Strata, (filling in for Fluid Mouth) and turned around to face her band. She smiled and mouthed the words, "We got this."

Theo breathed a sigh of relief. Seeing Winny's confident face and illuminated brown eyes were reassuring. Winny seemed to be in her zone, her happy place. Theo looked swiftly back toward Maria who looked slightly frightened, but ready. Rain looked spacey as ever behind her keyboard and Jen looked amped, posture straight and tall, hand and fingers across the four bass strings and gently readjusting her bleached hair. Once more, Winny at the front, poised and ethereal. *Here we go*, thought Theo.

Right on cue, Theo strummed her bow across the cello and then Maria kicked on the beat. Jen backed up on the bass with some heavier tones and Rain put down a couple chords. Then Winny brought in the guitar and vocals; it was seamless. First song down, five to go. The twenty people clapped haphazardly and a few more passersby walked into the dark bar.

Theo looked out across the audience. Jen's friend Topher was grinning at Jen, giving her the thumbs up. Theo's eyes passed along the dark crowd of hipsters, hippies, cowboys and seeming-bar-regulars, a couple of whom seemed entranced. Her eyes passed toward the sound woman whose gaze was focused on the sound board and then toward the bar, where Mullet Man Maestro was dealing out more drinks without taking his eyes off Maria. Theo caught eyes with Mark, who smiled. *Do we have groupies?* She thought with a laugh.

After a couple more songs, one of which Jen had written and which nearly started a circle pit, it was time for Theo's song. *Man, this was scary.* But then again, she'd already been through some scary situations. She cleared her throat and adjusted her cello while Winny introduced the next song into the mic.

Theo began to sweat. It was her turn to sing now while playing the cello. This was tough. She adjusted the mic toward her mouth, her thoughts drifting to ideas of failure. Thoughts of her failed career popped into her mind and unnerved her and she tried to focus on Winny's words. But Winny's voice faded off from Theo's mindset again as if muffled between her ears and the thought of her failed marriage came swimming in next, along with her violent-leaning ex-husband. If she didn't stay focused she would lose concentration and her rhythm.

Winny was now looking at Theo with an expectant expression. *Shit,* Theo had missed her cue. That's ok she could start again. She ran her bow along her strings and it sounded like dying cats. The crowd visibly recoiled as she apologized into the mic. *Oh god, she was messing it up.* More thoughts of failure. *It's ok, I got this, I got this.* Theo took a breath and reminded herself of how she found herself last night, unafraid, dancing around the illegal dumping site she set on fire, and chuckled. *New life, new me. You can always start again.*

She felt reassurance once more and put her bow on the strings again, this time assuredly and beautifully, and she began her vocals, to which her bandmates harmonized with too while bringing in their instruments. *Whew, it was working. It was sounding good.* The audience had clearly recovered from the first wrong note and Theo allowed herself to be lost in the moment of the music, not noticing the room had filled up with closer to fifty people.

At the end of the song, Theo opened her eyes and realized she had been so lost in the music she'd nearly forgotten where she was. But the audience loved it. They clapped and whistled and hooted.

Winny wrapped it up, "We're Alien Strata, thanks for coming out tonight! Tip your bartenders, vote, and be a good person n' all that shit!" She grinned and then turned around to face her band. She smiled at Theo in a way Theo hadn't seen yet. This was most definitely Winny's happy place. Theo liked seeing her that happy.

Afterward, a few people came up to them to compliment them on their music and ask a few gearhead-type questions. One guy with patches on a jean jacket vest couldn't believe Winny got that great reverb tone without a reverb pedal.

"Nope, no reverb pedal although some day I would like an Ocean's 11 Pedal, but no-go just yet. Just dialing in to the amp, and having good luck with a good sound tech," Winny said, wrapping up her guitar cable and pointing to the sound woman.

The band was riding high. They stayed at the Suave Saloon until 2 a.m., Theo and Winny talking for hours excitedly about how the show went before hunkering into the Tin Can for the night, which Topher had said they could keep parked in the lot out back. Everyone lounged in the comfort of the vehicle while coming down from the high of performing, except Jen who had gone over to Topher's studio apartment for the evening. Rain was asleep in the queen bed in the back, snuggling with Bowzer and Winny was chatting with Mark and Maria about music, space and time, clearly still feeling electric after the show. Theo tried to catch Winny's attention to see if she wanted to step outside for some quality time together, but Winny was so engrossed in talking. The two of them hadn't had time alone since their kiss and Theo was hoping it hadn't been just a fluke. But, she understood Winny's excitement after the show. It was hard to come down after having such high energy on stage. *What an amazing night,* she thought. *Never in a million years did I think I could do something like that, and yet, I did it.*

She stepped outside the Airstream and wrapped a sweatshirt around her. She sat, peering up at the stars from a lawn chair. The Suave Saloon was just enough outside the city that stars could be seen twinkling and winking down at her. Theo peered up at the Big Dipper and its piercing North Star, lost in thought. She then heard the creaking of the Airstream door and saw a diagonal cast of light streaming out onto the parking lot. It was Maria.

She took a seat next to Theo, joining her in staring quietly up at the stars. They sat in silence together for quite some time.

"You know how," started Theo, "everything seems so insignificant when you stare at the stars?"

Maria nodded.

"I feel like I've been underestimated my whole life. Like I'm just this little woman from the South with no brains and no talent and nothing to offer but creating babies and trying to be attractive. Like, I have nothing else going for me. Trouble is, sometimes I feel like that's all I am anyway."

Maria said nothing, just listened, as though her silence was wisdom.

"But last night when I was lost and sitting by that fire," Theo continued, "I had a jolting experience that, for lack of a better word, helped me come to understand myself and my journey. And tonight," breathed Theo, "I did something really special. I really did that. I thought I sucked at the cello and at singing but I practiced and I got better, set aside my fears and truly went for it. I don't know how or why but I did. It's like I drummed up this confidence and love for myself I didn't know was there and made something truly cool happen with music, something I'm proud of. And I feel this kind of," Theo searched for the word, looking into the sky and then down into the dirt, reaching down and sifting the sand between her fingers in thought, "I feel this kind of glimmer of understanding about myself and about the universe after playing music tonight. I feel as though I've pulled these feelings from inside me and turned them into art. Like I matter but also … not. And that's a good thing. Ya know?"

Maria nodded again in that way, all-knowing and yet innocent. Like someone who has landed in a different culture, observing, learning, and being. "I think I do know," she said quietly, "We are all so terribly insignificant and yet profoundly important at the same time."

"YES!" Theo said, feeling the relief at being understood. "Yes exactly."

They absorbed more of the night sky, silently together, soaking in its silence and its all-knowing mystery and blackness. The crickets chirped, toads nearby groaned, and the saguaros listened intently from a distance.

Theo breathed a sigh, feeling the exhaustion of the day setting in. "Well I'm going to head in. You?"

"I'm going to stay out here a little longer," said Maria and she stared out across the parking lot up at the sky.

Theo quietly walked back into the Airstream. Winny was asleep next to Bowzer and Rain on the queen bed, Mark was snoring loudly on the top bunk, and Theo figured she'd take the couch and leave Maria the lower bunk. She still wasn't sure how to handle things between herself, Winny, and Mark.

She fell asleep as soon as her head hit the pillow and slept hard.

Theo dreamed she was walking along Sabino Canyon at night, alone. Suddenly, Maria appeared, guiding the way toward the water, where they sat and stared at the stars. The stars began to shift, forming circles, and rotating into the shape of an eye. A center star illuminated green. In the dream, Theo was in awe.

A Dot in the Distance

Three Days 'til the Red Rocks Show

The next morning, Theo, the early riser as always, walked down the block to get coffee before anyone else was awake. She liked the quiet of morning. Despite only a few hours of sleep, she felt good. Like a weight had been lifted. She found herself looking into the past less and less, her walking thoughts more focused on the present and imagining an illuminated future.

She brought coffee for the coffee drinkers, tea for Rain, and some muffins and a chocolate croissant to put aside for Jen whenever she returned from Topher's. They all sleepily snacked on their breakfast and sipped on tea and coffee before getting ready to hit the road again. They had decided to go up through Phoenix and Sedona, then head east toward Albuquerque.

When Jen got back from Topher's house, her friend, as she called him, she said she'd had a fantastic night, and was glad that she had a *brann-spankin new IUD*, and they were ready to continue on their journey north.

"Let's rock," said Jen hungover-idly and turned the key in the ignition to head out.

But it choked and wouldn't turn over. Jen tried again. Nothing. Jen tried again. Still nothing.

The six of them peered over and down into the engine of the Airstream, clueless. Jen called Topher. He said he'd bring over a friend of his who was a mechanic, but not until the afternoon. So there they were going to have to stay for most of the day.

The morning turned into the afternoon while everyone sat in the hot Airstream, quietly looking at their phones and trying to recharge from the previous night, waiting on the mechanic. You can't beat free mechanic service, so they waited. Theo was disheveled not having a phone, knowing it was somewhere at the bottom of the river in Sabino Canyon. But Theo had to admit, it was at least a nice break from the unrelenting missed calls and messages.

Theo was getting hungry again and a little antsy. She didn't want to be staying in one place too long, she just had a feeling. "Hey, wasn't there a sandwich shop down the road?" she asked.

"YES, thank gawd, I'm starving," said Jen, not waiting for an offer and handing Theo some cash before plopping back down in the pullout dining chair. "Club sandwich, would ya please?"

Theo chuckled, made a mental note of what everyone wanted and walked back into the Suave Saloon parking lot. She made her way toward where she remembered the sandwich shop being.

"Wait up!" said a voice. It was Maria, her fiery wild hair lifting with the breeze. "I will come with you."

They walked quietly in the direction of the downtown area, the air buzzing with desert life, the Airstream falling further and further from view.

Maria looked at Theo, then away, then at Theo again. "I am

so sorry about the Airstream," she said.

"Oh, hey, it's not your fault," replied Theo, shrugging.

"No, I mean, it *is* my fault, and, well, I am sorry."

"How is it your fault?"

Maria looked like she had a secret that was ready to explode. "Remember when, uh, you said you were worried you were being followed?"

Theo stopped walking. "Yeah."

"Well, uh, I was worried about that too. As in, I was worried *I* was being followed. Which would mean *we* were being followed. And, well, I was right. And they must have tampered with our vehicle."

Theo was confused.

Maria turned to look at the Airstream, now a dot in the distance. She pointed at it but Theo didn't see any cars nor any pedestrians that might be following nearby. "No, not there," Maria said, then pointed further up, way up, Theo moving her gaze upward. "There," she said.

Right above the Airstream, a thousand or so feet in the air, was a giant UFO hovering silently.

The SandWitch Shop

"**H**OLY SHIT!" shrieked Theo. "Ok, um, things just got a little too weird. What … WHAT?!"

"Shhh, shh, calm down, I will explain everything," Maria said, worriedly.

"What is there to explain!" said Theo. "How did you know there was a UFO? And what do you mean 'they tampered' with our Airstream? And, and—" Theo recoiled, feeling like she didn't know who Maria was anymore. "What do you mean it's *your* fault?"

Maria was holding Theo by the shoulders, trying to make her head stop spinning. She took off her glasses and looked straight in Theo's face. "Like I said, I will explain everything, I promise."

Theo looked into Maria's eyes. For the first time, she noticed they were abnormally giant and green. Fluorescent green. Like that type of green that is illuminated under a blacklight. Like the green eyes she saw that night on the mesa. Like the green eye from her dream she'd had the night before.

"AHH!" shouted Theo, jumping back away from Maria.

All she could think of was documentaries on aliens and how

they performed experiments on people. Before she knew what she was doing, she took off running. As fast as she could toward the Airstream. She heard Maria's footsteps pounding the dirt behind her and suddenly, Maria appeared in front of her.

Theo yelped and quickly side-stepped Maria, grit and sand flying as she booked it past her. *Run away. Run away from those abnormally big green eyes.*

She suddenly felt a weight against her and within a millisecond, was tackled to the ground.

"Hold on, hold on!" Maria was shouting, "I promise I am not going to hurt you, please! Please just listen."

Theo rolled Maria off her. There was something desperate in her voice that made Theo sit up and still. She looked at the Airstream where her friends were, helplessly inside while a UFO levitated above them, then back at Maria. Those piercing green eyes. Her face had softened, and her abnormally large eyes were slanting into a pleading expression. Theo took a breath and said, "Ok. Go ahead. Tell me, what's going on? Are you, you a, a, uh—" Theo stammered.

But Maria finished her sentence for her, "An alien? Yeah, yeah, I am an alien." She shrugged. "I have my PhD in Human Studies, I am from the Planet Gazibnon, (like I accidentally told you all one day) and I am going to be in big trouble if you do not keep it down," she said, glancing over and up at the UFO. "Can you just keep your cool and walk to the sandwich shop with me?" she said, trying to help Theo to her feet. "I will explain everything."

Theo's face resembled an open-mouthed goldfish at all the information but she stood up, not quite believing what was happening. Meeting an alien, nay, befriending an alien, was not what she had intended when she drove out West.

The SandWitch Shop was a witch-themed sandwich lunch spot, with Wiccan symbols, crystals, plants and fake skulls dripping from the walls. The cashiers, seemingly begrudgingly, wore tall black witch hats. Theo rolled her eyes at yet more weird hippy stuff seemingly everywhere yet, now she was sitting across from an alien, eating a Cauldron Club Sandwich. *When in Rome …* she figured.

"Okay," Maria breathed. "I do not quite know where to begin."

"First of all, should we even be talking about how you're a, you know, *an alien*, in front of other people?" said Theo, glancing around at the other patrons guzzling sandwiches.

"Oh, that part is fine. When something is hidden in plain sight, humans seem to notice it even less," Maria replied. "Take, for example, my eyes. You had no clue how giant they are compared to yours, until I drew your attention to them, did you?"

Theo thought about that for a moment. "I guess that's true, they were there the whole time behind your glasses right in front of me, I just wasn't … well I just … I guess I didn't see them."

"Precisely," stated Maria. "That is how I am able to disguise myself. Well, for the most part. That and this human costume I have been wearing," she said, looking down at her body.

Theo didn't know what to ask about that. Did she even want to know? She thought suddenly about that silver flash that had caught her eye, like a glitch in a photo.

But Maria continued, "Part of the reason I am quite a good

drummer is because I *do* have extra arms. Six arms. They are just hidden underneath this human costume. But I like to bring them out and use them while we are playing music, mostly while no one is truly watching."

"Hmm, it *is* true, people never notice the drummer," said Theo, thinking about the last concert she'd gone to where the drummer was completely clouded in smoke from the fog machine.

"See what I mean?" said Maria. "Hidden in plain sight."

"Are you saying all drummers are aliens?"

"No, no, no, I'm just saying, I tend to hide well in plain view. And I happen to be a drummer on my own planet too."

"And you have a PhD in Human Sciences?" This was *so* interesting.

"Human *Studies*," corrected Maria. "Yes. And I am a professor too. I was conducting field research on what you all call, the mesa, when you ladies interrupted an experiment of mine—"

"What kind of experiment?" Theo interrupted, her eyes growing wide with worry, thoughts flicking to abductions and probes.

"Nothing like those documentaries you all watch," Maria said wryly. "No probing or anything like that. It is more like, well, you know when your species is studying another species? Like in a zoo? Or similar to," Maria snapped her fingers, and waved her hand trying to remember something, "What is her name? Jane Goodall! Similar to how Jane Goodall observed and conducted her research."

"You're Jane Goodall in this scenario and we humans are the apes?"

"*Mmhmm,* yes. You are all very interesting," concluded Maria, taking another bite of her Superstitious Salami Sub. "Your language is jolty and confusing though," she added, gesticulating animatedly while she talked. "Why do you guys have so many different ways of spelling things? I after E except after C? Pfff, that is not even true, give me a break."

"*That's* what you're concerned about?" Theo said, losing track of the conversation.

"Look, I study humans for a living. You all interrupted me that first night we met and the human-encounter caught me off guard. I was transfixed by this otherworldly experience, seeing humans so up close. Your states of awareness were seemingly in a different realm. A couple of you actually *saw* me. And that is rare. Human's do not normally see us. Because well—"

"The hidden in plain sight thing?" Theo said helpfully, nodding.

"Exactly. That and, well, we have special suits. And you all were very intriguing, talking about wanting to play music together and I thought that sounded fun. Music is transcendental on my planet too. So, well, I decided to put on an old human suit I had from a costume party—"

Theo tried to imagine what a costume party might be like on another planet, *Perhaps kind of like humans dressed as aliens at a Roswell convention but … in reverse.*

"And I took my ship over to that music shop, Guitar Mart, in Albuquerque to see what it was like to play drums among humans, and wow, it was fun! To play music and get lost in the ephemeral, universal state of sound among foreign species was a dream. That is when you guys stumbled on me, AGAIN, and I felt like the stars had aligned. I felt like it was meant to be. I wanted to be among you and see what it was like and to continue creating music with ... you. So I thought about it after you left and, damnit, I was going to do it, no matter the consequences! So, after flying overhead and noticing you all had broken down in your Airstream, I stole a truck and—*voilà*, as Winny would say ... I have to admit, you all know how to have fun."

The gush of information suddenly abated and Theo agreed, "The having-fun-thing is new to me too. But yeah, we do have fun don't we?"

"Yes, we do," said Maria, sighing and smiling.

"So, so ..." Theo was thinking. "So is that how you've been getting to and from Albuquerque and Truth or Consequences? In a flying spacecraft?"

Maria simply shrugged and nodded. "Yes, I have a little vehicle stashed aside on top of the mesa. I go up there and observe you all from afar when I am not with you. You know, taking notes, gathering data, etc. I was afraid you all were going to see my vehicle up there that night after the tarot cards, when Rain wanted to go find an alien, well, *me*. But then something interrupted ..." Maria trailed off.

Theo remembered exactly. A giant UFO, the one that had engulfed the entire visible dark sky that night. "That was your spaceship!?" she asked, bewildered. It had looked like the one that might still be above the Airstream.

"No, no, great goddess-creator, no, that was—is someone else's entirely, I do not even want to go into that yet," Maria responded with a look of concern as her glance darted out the window toward the Airstream.

Theo wondered what in the um ... universe was driving that

giant UFO. The idea left a pit of anxiety in her stomach. *If it wasn't Maria, who, or what, was it?*

"And maybe I was getting a little too carried away," Maria continued, not noticing Theo's fear. "With the band I mean. Having too much fun. Why did you all have to name our band *Alien Strata?* That is going to give me away! I mean *come on*, Alien on Earth?" She pointed at herself incredulously. "I am an alien on earth! It is against interplanetary law for aliens to interact with humans, much less cohabitate, and be *friends with* humans. I am, as humans would say, *screwed*, if they find out the full extent of my sabbatical trip here on Earth. And yet I still want to help humans. That is where I need your help."

"Why me?" Theo asked, so immersed in the conversation she'd forgotten her Cauldron Club although Maria had scarfed her own sandwich between confessions.

"Because of your heart, Theo. You have a good heart."

Theo had never been told this before. Mark had alluded to it when they first met but compliments made her uncomfortable. So she changed the subject, "So, um, so who, or what, is in the UFO above the Airstream right now, and what do they want?"

The bell to the door of The SandWitch Shop dinged. It was Jen and Winny.

Maria whirled around to face Theo again. "You cannot tell them I am an alien. You cannot tell them any of this! I am only telling you this so you can help me. Please! For me. Do not tell them anything. Until I can get a chance to properly explain and fix this mess."

Theo had so many questions. She didn't know what to do. Jen and Winny were approaching.

"Hey ladies!" Jen said, "We wondered what was taking so long!" She slid into the booth next to Maria.

Theo's face was frozen and Jen laughed. "Why do you look like you've seen a ghost, Theodora?"

Theo still said nothing.

"Hey, Jen, you wanna order or what?" said Winny.

"Yesss! Do you think they sell those hats?" Distracted, Jen scooted back out of the booth and headed to the counter with Winny.

Maria turned back to Theo, her big green eyes pleading again. "I promise, I mean no harm, I want to help you all, help you get to Denver and play music, some fame even, maybe, and help other humans too. Just give me a chance. But first I need you to help me by keeping this secret."

It felt weird to keep a secret like this from the others. Theo worried this kind of a secret could tear a band apart. But … Maria was an essential part of the band. They needed a drummer in order to even *be* a band. Theo knew how much it would mean to Winny to keep the band together. And it would be Winny's dream to reach some sort of fame. Plus, Maria needed help. She was her friend, alien or not.

Theo nodded. "Okay. But you've gotta tell me everything."

Maria looked visibly relieved. "Deal."

Otherworldly Creatures

There are many questions humans have when it comes to aliens. What do they look like? While most scientists and researchers cannot definitively say there could be life elsewhere, since there has been no proof yet, (clearly they haven't met Maria) they do acquiesce that there is a high likelihood, we just haven't seen it yet. They admit that there are hundreds of habitable planets in our galaxy alone. Scientists define habitable planets as those which sit in that comfortable zone between a sun or star where liquid water could reside on the surface. In this scenario, life is Goldilocks: Conditions can't be too cold or too hot, they have to be just right. But researchers also admit that even past this zone, for all we know, life could exist out there as well, just ... not the type of life we know or understand. Jupiter's moon Europa has a perfect potential for this, given that it has a saltwater ocean trapped beneath an icy exterior, which could possibly contain life. But the true existential question is: What if something *besides* life exists? That is a much larger, and truly unanswerable question.

The possibility of life elsewhere is both vague and hypothetical. Take, for example, the idea of alien appearance. Some researchers think aliens could glow red, blue or green, similar to coral reefs, as some organisms use pigments that absorb from UV rays to emit a colorful glow. Other astrophysicists hypothesize that otherworldly creatures would evolve to fly, as some planets contain dense planetary atmospheres. Others still, think that perhaps creatures elsewhere have evolved to live underground. But … the ideas human intellectuals have come up with don't compare to what really exists out there. Some scientists concede that if life did exist elsewhere in our galaxy or universe, it would likely be single-celled organisms. Far in outer space, this would prove difficult to study. However, examining signs of life left behind by microorganisms here on our own planet would help provide clues. Microbial residue in dried-up hot springs has been examined by experts to study the topic. And still others believe that alien sightings occur more frequently near hot springs—something about geothermal energy attracting more species foreign to our planet.

Despite human's hesitancy to regard aliens as real, it hasn't stopped them from trying to send signals into outer space so as to be noticed by life elsewhere. In the early 1800s an Astronomer from Austria, Joseph von Littrow, supposedly proposed digging expansive trenches in the Sahara in geometric patterns and setting them on fire, for the purpose of, essentially, saying, 'Hello Aliens, we are here!' The crater Littrow on the Moon is named in his honor.

Perhaps that is what other cultures, more ancient ones, were doing. What was the purpose of the mysterious Nazca Lines in Peru? Art for the gods, pleading for water? Or attempted communication with the 'heavens' or with aliens? Since humankind first learned to look up at the stars and see themselves so small, the question of our own existence has marinated in people's minds. Where philosophers have pondered a boundless universe, humans have always wondered whether or not we are alone. This question of life elsewhere has plagued the human mind, and toyed with our understanding of the meaning of life. What would change if humans met aliens?

ΔΔΔ

They all sat in the booth together, Winny animatedly talking about the difference between Taylor and Martin guitars.

Maria asked suddenly, "*Martian* guitars?" at which point Theo had to hold back laughter imagining little men from mars holding Martian guitars, whatever those looked like.

"No, no, *Martin* guitars," Winny clarified. "Martin guitars are the original, the OG of guitars. Been around since 1833 when it was started by a guy with the last name of, you guessed it, Martin. Taylors are incredible guitars too and they've become big in the industry, making their own signature guitar shapes. Taylors are especially badass because the company is decently sustainable. They grow their own Koa wood. I just like my Martin for its personal history."

"Yeah?" asked Theo. "Where'd you get your Martin?"

"My father gave it to me before he passed away. He was a good man. When I was a kid and I couldn't fall asleep, he would play guitar for me, kinda like reading a bedtime story, and well, it always worked. I'd fall right to sleep after that. I guess maybe that's partly why I like music so much. It revolves around some of the best memories I have."

Theo put a hand on Winny's. She wasn't close to her parents

by any means, in fact she hadn't spoken to them since she'd left, but at least they were both still around.

When they finished eating, Theo, Maria, Winny and Jen took two sandwiches to go, one for Mark and one for Rain, who were still in the Airstream, and a slice of pastrami for Bowzer. As they walked closer to the Tin Can, Theo noticed the UFO still there. She looked nervously at Jen and Winny. *How could they not see it? It was right there!* But Jen and Winny's eyes stayed even with the horizon. If they had even slanted their chins upward slightly, they might have noticed it. But they didn't.

The UFO looked like the one they had seen that night up on the mesa. It still gave Theo the heebie-jeebies and she pinched herself a couple more times to make sure she was not dreaming. She looked around to see any roadrunners. Maybe she was tripping on acid again. *Wasn't there something about LSD flashbacks? Something about it staying in your bloodstream or in your spinal fluid?* Theo didn't know, but she was pretty sure she hadn't taken any acid recently, not since their first stint up on the mesa which was what had seemed to start this whole mess. But this experience was different. This was in full daylight.

She looked over at Maria with her giant, bug-like green eyes behind her glasses, now so visible, and over to Jen and Winny who were chatting excitedly about ideas where they would play their next show once they got the Airstream up and running again. As they approached, the door opened and Mark walked outside. Bowzer came bounding outside too, toward the pastrami in Theo's hand.

Theo looked up and saw the UFO had disappeared.

"I think we should be good to go now, with the vehicle," whispered Maria out of the corner of her mouth. "I think I figured it out."

"Figured what out?" whispered Theo.

"What're you two whispering about?" chuckled Winny.

"Nothing!" said Theo, a little too loudly and unconvincingly and Winny looked perplexed.

"Should we try the vehicle again?" inquired Maria to the group.

Now that Theo noticed it, she realized Maria had a very formal way of talking. Like she was trying too hard to sound human.

"The mechanic hasn't even come yet," Jen said, shielding her face from the sun with one hand and fanning it with the other.

"I do not know, let us just try it," said Maria with feigned casualness.

They all got into the Airstream and, with the ease of butter melting on hot toast, the engine started.

The Metal Show in Snowflake, Arizona

They chugged along, heading north toward Sedona, Arizona. Rain had taken the wheel, and Winny was sitting at the fold-down table, talking on the phone with Jane Harper asking if she had any connections to venues there. Alas, she did not.

Theo found herself staring out at the transfixing saguaro cacti once more. Some were bright green, not quite as green as Maria's eyes, but it got her thinking. Knowing aliens existed changed everything. What else didn't she know about the world? Or the universe? Were these cacti secretly alive, like people? Were the Tohono O'Odham people right? Why had Maria chosen to tell *her*, of all people, her secret? Theo felt uncomfortable. She didn't like keeping something from the rest of the group.

She looked over at the others as she so often did. Quiet, meditative Rain behind the wheel, Jen scrolling on Instagram slouched over the kitchen table, and Mark playing solitaire across from her with Bowzer snoozing on the rug beside him. Winny staring out at the road in the passenger seat, no doubt daydreaming of Red Rocks. She liked this whole scene. But Maria being an alien had thrown a wrench into things. She didn't know what to think. Was Maria peaceful, or did she secretly mean harm? Or was she just a curious professor, like she had said? And was that UFO still following them? Theo looked out the back window, remembering her feeling of being followed. Had it been the UFO watching them?

The day cruised along and they arrived in Sedona just before nightfall. Time was of the essence if they were going to try to get another show booked somewhere. So they decided to split into twos, and each stop by a bar or venue Winny had googled that might want a live band, spur of the moment. Theo's heart instantly tugged towards going with Winny. But she also wanted to figure out more about this alien business and ask Maria who the aliens were that appeared to be following them. She worried the whole band could be in danger. Theo thought for a moment.

"I'll go with Maria," she volunteered.

This was met by inquisitive looks from both Winny and Mark.

"Okayyy, um I guess I'll go with Mark and Bowzer," said Winny as Jen and Rain marched off together.

They all split up around Sinagua Plaza, a cute small downtown area with impressive rock structures sprouting into the air in the close distance. Theo kept squinting toward the rocks to see if there were any more UFOs peeking around the corner, now constantly suspicious and was relieved to see that there were not … As far as she knew.

After some time trying to find venues with no luck, Maria and Theo found a spot on a bench next to some shops to take a seat and talk.

Theo contemplated which questions to start with. "So, um… how did the Airstream start working again?" She was starting with the easy questions first, working her way up to *What the hell is going on?*

Maria went on to explain the type of technology she and her people had on their planet. It was beyond Theo's comprehension. Something about harnessing physics and atoms, a substance they utilized from their planet and then replenished. Something completely renewable, sustainable and with zero emissions, nothing like oil. Maria said vehicles ran silently and seamlessly, effortlessly through the air, utilizing high speed air trains and following GPS flight patterns on their screens. Either way, transportation didn't disrupt life going on below.

"Oddly enough," she had added, "we call them air-streams."

There was no concrete and no roads on her planet, just plants and trees and clean air. Theo tried to imagine what a paradise like this looked like, but her only frame of reference was the opening credits to *Futurama*. Maria said it was kind of like that, but with no traffic.

"So, how did the Airstream start working today after the SandWitch Shop?" asked Theo, reiterating her question.

"Oh, the beings in the UFO do not really like dogs," Maria responded flippantly, waving her hand casually in the air.

Theo was perplexed by this answer. "And that's why they left that night on the mesa too, when Bowzer came bounding toward them?"

"Yes, they are more cat people," said Maria.

Bizarre, thought Theo. "More importantly, who, or what is in the UFO and what do they want with us? Or with you?"

Maria opened her mouth to answer but someone walking toward them holding a phone politely interrupted them, "S'cuse me, but are either of you in a band?"

Theo had seen this guy somewhere. And then it dawned on her. "You're that guy who finds musicians in the real world on Instagram!"

"Yeah, that's me." The guy with the phone smiled.

Winny had shared his page with Theo on Instagram and said it would be her dream to get featured on the page. Bands featured on there went viral. This would make Winny so happy.

"Our band is called Alien Strata," the words were out of her mouth before she realized it probably wasn't a good idea, considering they had a real incognito alien in their band who had some secret and didn't want to be exposed for the alien she was. Plus, Theo was supposed to be flying under the radar too.

Maria looked nervous sitting next to her and Theo looked guilty, exposing their band to the world with this guy. But … they were going to perform at Red Rocks, the word was going to get out at some point.

"I found a song of yours on Google," the guy was saying, "Looks like it was someone filming your set last night at a bar called the Suave Saloon. Cool. Mind if I share it?"

Theo nodded and then shook her head, no, they didn't mind. She thought of Winny and not Maria. Before she knew it, the guy was saying *thanks*, gave her his business card and walked away. The encounter was over in a blink of an eye. Did they just go viral? Did he hear anything about their conversation ahead of time about the UFO?

Theo was quite sleep deprived and wasn't sure what to make

of the whole interaction but before either of them could say anything more, Winny and Mark came swimming into view from further down the street, Bowzer bounding ahead, as usual.

"Was that the music Instagram guy?!" Winny was asking, ecstatic.

Theo nodded.

"Did you give him some of our music to share?" Winny squeaked.

Theo nodded again.

Winny jumped into her lap and gave her a big hug and giant kiss on the cheek. Theo beamed. "You're amazing, Theo!"

Theo noticed Winny smelled like lilacs. She loved lilacs. Mark was looking at the two of them, bewildered, then over at Maria.

"So uh, did you guys find a venue for tonight in Sedona?" Theo blurted.

"No dice," Mark said, pouring some water into a portable bowl for Bowzer. "But we did get a tip for a house show just outside a town called …" Mark had to glance at the flyer again, "Snowflake, Arizona."

"Snowflake, Arizona?" Theo ridiculed. "Pff, is it home to a bunch of sensitive hippies?"

Winny raised her eyebrows. Theo was still adjusting to being a hippy or hipster or, whatever it was she was blossoming into while out in the West. Rain then appeared out of nowhere, startling them all, as though she'd been standing there the whole time.

She jumped in to explain the name, "Snowflake, Arizona. They get a bunch of snow there. It's in northern Arizona, you know, high desert and whatnot? But we can't go there."

"Why not?" Mark asked while he scratched Bowzer's ears.

"That's where it happened to Travis Walton," Rain responded, matter of factly, smoothing a crease in her flower print dress.

"Uuuum, Rain, who is Travis Walton?" Winny asked.

"He got abducted by aliens in 1975 and went missing for five days. Yeah, no, we can't go to Snowflake, Arizona."

Winny looked from face to face. "Buuuut, it's a show. And we don't have anything else lined up." Winny's mind was clearly only on playing another show.

Theo looked at one of the flyers. It listed several bands, most of which had illegible metal-band-looking writing. Like mustard zigzagging across a slice of bread. "Looks like a metal show," she said.

"Yeah, it does," Rain despondently replied, looking at the flier. "I'm afraid Jen's going to love it."

ΔΔΔ

"I LOVE IT! Let's DO IT!" Jen howled.

Jen was fully committed to the idea when they met back up at the Airstream for a homemade meal of boxed Mac and Cheese. "My first ever show was an Iron Maidens show, ya know, that all-female cover band of Iron Maiden? My parents put those big honkin' headphones over my tiny baby ears and I think that's when the love of metal seeped into my bones. I was hooked from a young age. I can't possibly pass up an opportunity to PLAY in a metal show. C'mon!"

They discussed the pros and cons. One con was they definitely weren't a metal band. Indie country and metal aren't necessarily two

172

genres you think of together. But Jen was determined. And so was Winny. They were willing to risk the alien encounter thing. Maria was not pleased. But Jen was particularly persuasive.

"We have that one song that's more heavy! Ya know, the one I wrote that almost started a circle pit that one time? What if we just played that one song?" She was practically begging the group.

"I'm sorry Jen, what if it's not safe?" Theo was saying. "I mean, it's at someone's house. And metal people can be pretty intense. Drugs and satanic symbols and all that stuff ... I just don't think it's a good idea. Annnnd, you know, the risk of aliens? Let's not."

Twenty minutes later they were on their way to the house show.

They showed up to a dilapidated ranch-style home. The lawn was littered with beer cans and a group of people huddled by the front door smoking cigarettes and sucking vape pens.

Oh boy, thought Theo. *I'm too old for this.* But they loaded their gear into the living room where a band was already playing and people were thrashing about.

Theo couldn't stand the vocals. Very guttural.

"That's gotta hurt the vocal cords, huh?" said Winny whispering in her ear.

Theo nodded, soaking in Winny's energy so close to her, then jolting upon hearing another Bowzer-like growl from the singer. It was going to be an interesting night.

They went to the kitchen where they were offered PBRs, and to Theo's surprise, everyone was very welcoming and kind, but she was again reminded of how much older she was than everyone. And she was wearing way too much color for this crowd. The six of them stood out like a collective sore thumb, even Jen who tended to wear a fair amount of black. But Jen was clearly loving every minute of it, bobbing her head to the distorted guitar and screamo vocals.

Theo wondered how this crowd was going to take their music.

Turned out, they loved it. They especially were *mindblown* as one starry-eyed, Hot Topic-donning teenager put it, with Maria's drumming skills during their faster songs. Apparently, she'd never seen such impressive drumming.

"Looked like she had extra arms!" she'd gushed.

Oh man, if they only knew, thought Theo.

One of the youngsters said they'd seen Alien Strata on Instagram. *So their post did go viral. This was going to get interesting.*

After their part of the performance, some new fans wanted to chat Winny up, they loved her vocals and reverby guitar. Winny was clearly loving the adoration they were getting about their music and Theo was hoping to get some quality time again with her but to no avail. She also tried to pull Maria aside and ask her more questions about her planet and why she was here, specifically with them but the young crowd couldn't get enough of her in particular. They seemed to look up at this tall, lanky, green-eyed woman with starry eyes, asking questions about drumming and bands that inspired her. Maria was listing off band names none of them had ever heard before, which was no surprise, considering they were bands from another planet.

Theo couldn't believe that none of them saw it—the alienness. Yes, she hadn't either. Not at first. But she had thought something was weird about Maria. She wished she could talk to

Winny about it. Or Mark. She looked around for both of them but they were now off somewhere in the house party.

Theo resigned herself to patting Bowzer on the head in the corner, who panted contentedly, seemingly not bothered by the loud music or the mass of people around them. No one seemed to want to chat her up about her cello.

Rain breezed over and gave her a nudge with her shoulder. "Having fun, m'lady?"

Theo nodded, "Mmhmm." She thought about asking how she'd played tonight but was afraid of the answer. So instead, she asked about another topic that concerned her. "Hey, Rain, you seem to know a lot about aliens. Um, how concerned should we be? About them, I mean?"

"About being in Snowflake, Arizona where someone was abducted in the seventies?"

"Yeah, that, and ... also, just in general," Theo added, vaguely.

"Well if you're talking about Travis Walton, the guy who was abducted once, he was terrified. For years he thought they were experimenting on him and whatnot. The whole experience basically ruined his life."

Great, thought Theo, looking over at Maria, who was now leaning down toward her adoring fans, signing autographs.

"But," Rain stared off into the party of dancing people, the noise making it hard to hear the two women talking. "In later years he started to think that maybe the aliens had abducted him because they accidentally got him with their laser beams n' stuff, which was harmful, and so they took him aboard to help him. He now likes to think that maybe alien life elsewhere has evolved past violence, war, aggression and all that stuff. He said, something like, 'I do not believe aliens are bad. I believe that extremely technologically advanced civilizations evolve out of what we call evil.' Basically saying, aliens evolved to be better than humans are to each other."

Theo's posture straightened, again glancing over at Maria who was now assisting a fan with a selfie, stretching out one of her long arms, like a selfie stick, to snap a photo. "He said that?"

"Yeah, yeah," Rain continued, "But, there are plenty of other people who have been abducted who don't feel that way at all. In fact, they have nightmares the rest of their life and, you know, the whole experience was horrifying."

Again, with the ruining-of-life-thing. Theo's shoulders slumped involuntarily. "I'm going to get a little fresh air," she breathed, and Rain gave Theo a big pat on the back before heading back into the mosh pit, nearly losing her Birkenstocks.

Theo slipped away, out the door toward the Airstream. She pulled a ladder down from the back and climbed on top of the giant tin-tube of a vehicle, listening to the muffled noise from the party and the crickets chirping. It felt nice to be out in the desert air again, alone. She looked across the quiet dirt road toward the horizon at the moon. It sat between telephone wires like a single music note between lines on sheet music. She pondered what to do.

Footsteps. Someone was coming. Someone was wrangling the ladder, trying to come up.

It was Mark. And he was looking a little *loosey goosey* from liquid encouragement.

Uh oh. Theo was only slightly concerned he might fall off the side, wobbling up that ladder but he sat down next to her.

"Hi," he said, with a flushed smile.

Theo had the feeling he was going to try to kiss her up here. On paper, it would be a romantic moment. But as much as Theo tried she just wasn't feeling it. It was suddenly so simple, she realized. She adored Mark, he was an amazing guy. But not like that. She adored him as a friend. Whereas … she liked Winny. No, she *loved* Winny. There, she'd thought it. Theo realized she was in love with a girl. *Huh.* She thought. *Wasn't expecting that when I drove out West.*

"Theo, I want to tell you something," Mark was saying, a slight stutter.

"Listen, Mark, I need to tell you something too," she said.

"Let me go first," he said, clearly mustering the courage to say something important to her.

But Theo didn't want to hurt his feelings. "No, let me go first. I'm sorry I—"

And they both said what they had to say at the same time.

"I'm in love with someone else!" Theo blurted.

"I made out with Maria!" Mark shouted.

Theo paused, absorbing what she had just heard and then, "Ya madeoutwithanalien?!" She said it so quickly it was unintelligible.

"What?" he asked.

"Nothing, nothing," corrected Theo, clearing her throat and disguising her accidental disgust. "I said you, uh, *ehem*, you made out with a Canadian?"

"Maria's from Canada? That would explain some of the things she says that I don't understand," said Mark, looking up and lost in wobbly thought. "Like when she said she was from Gazibnon. That must be somewhere in Quebec. Yep, in fact I've heard of Gazibnon. Yeah it's a province in Quebec," he said self-assuredly, thinking he was explaining something to her. Theo nodded. Gazibnon was indeed *not* a place in Quebec.

"Anyway, Theo, I'm sorry. I know we had a cool thing going, but I have to admit. I have feelings for Maria."

"Okay! No problem, I understand," Theo rushed, not wanting to know the details. *How does an alien kiss?* Theo tried to dismiss the odd thought, grateful instead that Mark had not heard her confession in light of his own.

"It happened last night while you were asleep," he continued, ignoring Theo's body language, "I woke up to Jen's snoring and so I went outside. Maria was there, looking otherworldly in her lawn chair, staring out at the stars and we got to talking. She just seems to know so much about space and planets and intergalactic travel, I couldn't help myself. I was transfixed by her intellect. So we kissed. But I won't continue without your blessing," Mark finished saying with a slight hiccup.

Theo paused and smiled. "You've got it, bud," she stated, patting him on the back as they stared out at the desert together, silhouettes of saguaro cactus looking out at them. "And I wish y'all the best with it," she added genuinely, curious to see how this was going to go.

Mark climbed back down the ladder to head back into the house party and Theo sat there pondering life. She laughed a little to herself. How weird it all was.

As she sat there, she felt a pair of eyes on her. *Damn that feeling of being watched!* and looked back over toward the house. A few people stood in the light of the porch smoking or vaping, chatting in classic party mode, but one figure, further in the dark, seemed to be peering out at her, a single small red dot of light pulsating from his puffs of a cigarette. The man was in shadow, but she could see he was clean-cut and could just barely make out that distinctive eye tattoo. It was the same guy she saw looking at her at Guitar Mart in Albuquerque and the same one who'd stared at her from a mechanic's shop in Truth or Consequences.

Theo's heart welled in her chest in fear. *Who was he? Was he a private investigator sent to spy on her?* Whoever he was, he was tossing out his cigarette and walking toward her. Theo had to think fast. She needed to clamber down from the Airstream and make a run for it. Her instincts told her to. Or at least to run into the party and find her friends. *Quick!* He was approaching the ladder, getting closer and closer. *Shit, too late to clamber down ...* She would need to jump. Theo looked down at the eleven-some feet below her. She could break an ankle. *Nope, that won't work.* Panic started to set in.

And then, Theo felt an odd sensation. A stillness settled on the air. Just like the time she was up on the mesa and saw that alien. Well, saw Maria, as it had turned out to be, a fact Theo was still grappling with. *Was Maria around?* She couldn't see her. *Can I even really trust Maria?* Noise near the ladder. Someone was clambering up. Why was this man following her? Time to act fast. Maybe if she jumped and rolled she would make the jump. That's what she would do. She'd seen rock climbers and parkour athletes do that. She would have to do it. *Here we go, one two—*

Theo felt the odd sensation increase. And then, it happened so fast; the quiet enveloped her, the crickets ceased to chirp, and her ears went silent, as though she had popped in her noise-canceling EarPods. Or as if she'd jumped into water. Sounds of the party fell distant, muffled.

The man reached the top of the Airstream and took a step toward her but Theo suddenly felt her vision swirl, the saguaro cacti below swooping into a circle, her vision completely blurred. Her stomach flipped as though she were on a Gravitron amusement park ride, the one from the nineties that spun you in a circle while you clung to the wall for dear life.

Green streaks of light swirled across her vision as she felt her body go *up, up, up* and she saw images of the blurred Airstream, the man below her becoming a distant dot. She caught one tiny glimpse of the aircraft, the UFO, she was being beamed up into. It was triangular and small, not like the enormous circular disc they had seen that night on the mesa and not like the one that hovered earlier that day above the Airstream. It occurred to her oddly that this particular UFO reminded her of a Ouija board piece, the planchette, full with a circular bulbous window. Her heart swelled as she was beamed into the craft.

Then, the world went black.

The Planchette

It was dark. Theo heard distant chattering in a language she didn't know. *Oh great, I'm seriously in an alien aircraft with aliens talking gibberish near me. Green men, experiments, oh man, oh man.* Theo was incredulous, almost embarrassed, about her circumstance, but not yet afraid.

It was so dark she thought her eyes were closed. But they weren't. It was still pitch black. And whispers of a foreign language were audible, trickling into her eardrums. That's when the fear set in. *How am I going to get the hell out of here if I can't see anything?* Then she noticed something else or more like, *felt* something else. She was lightheaded *and* lightweight. Nearly weightless. Whatever surface she was sitting on was velvet to the touch, and she was apparently levitating above the ground. Her senses felt obsolete, beyond intuition; the way a drone instrument sounds in a sci-fi movie.

Then, a soft light illuminated in a corner, then a few more, enough to give her a sense of perspective, of where she was. Sure enough, Theo saw she was sitting—levitating, in a velvet red armchair. It was surprisingly comfortable. As she hovered in her armchair, she tried to take in the scene as quickly as she could, to figure out how to get out of there. There were expansive bookshelves encircling a dome-shaped wall, defying gravity staying in their shelves. There were warm lamps and soft pillow chairs and rugs. If Theo didn't know better, she would have said it was cozy. A row of what appeared to be cabinets and some sort of cooking device sat in one corner. Come to think of it, the way the craft was arranged made her think of a foreign, fancy RV or technologically advanced Airstream.

On a table sat an open notebook, a pencil, and a mug, soft steam wafting from it, as though someone's writing had been interrupted by her arrival in the triangular craft. And there were windows; sweeping windows that stretched over across the ceiling in the dome of the craft, toward a center bulbous skylight, what Theo had pictured as the window of the Ouija board planchette, making the stars visible. Through one window, Theo could see Earth twinkling below them. Her heart launched into her throat at the sight of how far away they were and she scanned the room again. A spiral staircase appeared to go both up and down. She tried to run toward it but found she could hardly move. She was, instead, drifting through the air, like in a dream where you're trying to run but can't.

Theo felt awkward in the air, flailing her arms about in an attempt to get closer to the staircase. *What use were stairs anyway, when there was no gravity?* Then it occurred to her that whoever was driving or flying this thing must spend a fair amount of time on Earth. Or another planet with gravity, why else have a staircase? The way the craft was arranged made her think of the Airstream. Do aliens travel across the solar system? Are UFOs just alien RVs, drifting along and seeing the sites of other planets in the universe? She imagined aliens in sunglasses and aloha shirts, holding cocktails and seeing the sights much the way humans would.

Theo had somehow managed to float over to the staircase and looked up to what appeared to be a spectator deck with armchairs, then down to perhaps another room laden with ornate rugs. Just as she was going to try to make a run for it, or, rather, a float-for-it, down the stairs, a door slid open seamlessly.

Theo caught a glimpse of what looked like a futuristic cockpit, a room with a windshield and blinking lights, but no buttons. Maria and someone else, or, better yet, *something* else, emerged through the door, before it silently slid shut. *What was it?* The thing, it reminded her of something but she couldn't place what.

"You are here!" Maria said exasperated, worried, as she approached Theo looked like a deer in headlights at the top of the spiral staircase.

There was something near Maria on the table by the notebook that now illuminated, capturing Theo's attention. A glowing orb. It was similar to the one she had seen the alien, no, *Maria*, holding up on the mesa that night. What was it?

"You should not see this, not yet. You have much to learn before you go back," Maria said. She seemed very agitated.

With that, Maria waved a hand over Theo's eyes and the world went black once more.

The Break Down
Desert Show

Two Days 'til the Red Rocks Show

The next day passed uneventfully, it seemed. The cacti of Arizona turn to juniper and chamisa once more as they crossed back into New Mexico, making their way to Albuquerque. They had spent the morning trying to figure out a show to play in Albuquerque and toyed with the idea of playing a show at Winny's place, Bar None, but three people were opposed to the idea.

One, Winny was opposed, because she did not want to stay too long in the town where her ex-abuser still resided. She only stopped by once in a while to ensure things were running smoothly at the business she managed. Otherwise, she worked on the administration remotely, doing bills and schedules etc. Two, Theo was opposed, because she did not want to put Winny in an uncomfortable position like that and three, Jen was opposed, because, 'Our audience will think we sound bad if they don't drink.' But Rain, Maria, and Mark thought it would be a good idea and Bowzer seemingly liked the idea, since he appeared to bark in approval. Democracy being what it was, they had ultimately decided to go for it and the planning for the show was coming together nicely.

Theo stretched out in one of the bunk beds in the Airstream, watching the world go by and trying to relax. Habitually, with her eyes on the window, she watched the landscape distractedly. The yellow dotted road lines flashed as they appeared and disappeared on the tarmac. Lost in thought, she had the vague, disconcerting feeling of a dream she couldn't remember from last night. She had a persistent sense of levitating, being somewhere with less gravity and the feeling had stuck with her all day, perplexingly. The very real memory of levitating in a cozy UFO craft had clearly escaped her.

She wondered about the man she had seen last night who had climbed the Airstream. It scared her. At this point, she was convinced he had been a private eye out to get her. But what had happened? She just remembered seeing a glimpse of him reach the top of the Airstream and that was it. Was the ex-husband not far away then? She finally told the band and her friends just how scared she was and Winny had put a hand on her knee in that reassuring way that only she could. She'd then told her adamantly they would all help keep her safe, she could count on it. They wouldn't let whoever it was catch up with them, and they'd departed early in the morning at 5 a.m. because of it. The trouble was, Theo couldn't remember what had happened after the man had approached her, or how she'd gotten away. That was troubling. Gaps in her memory kept seeming to happen and she didn't think she'd had all that much to drink last night.

She flipped over and turned her attention to Winny who was

hurriedly texting the people managing the non-alcoholic bar in her stead about getting a set together for them to play tonight.

Theo watched Winny and couldn't help smiling. She was so passionate about music. When she was in music mode, or planning mode, her eyebrows furrowed in concentration. Theo loved that. She loved the freckles on her face and her dark straight black hair. The way her tattoos dotted her olive skin and her thin, wistful lips. She wanted to kiss those lips more. Theo imagined how it would feel to lie in this bunk bed with her right now, her warmth and energy melding into hers. But that would be uncomfortable for the others, wouldn't it? Especially since she and Mark had recently had a spark. It was awkward. For Theo at least. She didn't know how to navigate all this. But then again, Mark and Maria maybe had a thing going? *But Maria was an alien! How was that going to work?* Theo shook the thought from her mind and returned to daydreaming about the idea of Winny snuggling up by her side in the bunk bed.

"Hey, Winny?" Theo said quietly but she didn't notice, just kept texting. Theo cleared her throat, "Winny?" she said again, a little louder.

Winny looked up, brown eyes focusing. "Hmm?" she said.

Theo thought about asking her if she wanted to join her in the bunk bed and watch the scenery slide by. But then she chickened out. "How's the show planning for tonight going?" she asked instead.

"Great!" Winny exclaimed, eyes brightening, "We have another band whose going to play before us, a local band called Dystopia Amora, I guess they're electro-pop grunge who covers only love songs." She shrugged. "And another band to open for us called

TracheotoME, emphasis on the *me*, a swing dance funk group with a guy who plays the accordion and also sings monologues."

Theo was perplexed by not just the names of these bands but also the bizarre genres. "Will our band fit in?"

"Oh sure!" said Winny. "Plus, we've got a couple bands opening for us, so technically we're the headliners! And my bar manager said she posted a flyer about the show tonight on Instagram and it already has over 9,000 likes! We really gotta get a social media account going," she added, thinking out loud. "Anyway, it looks like it'll be a packed show!"

Winny's palpable excitement was impossible to ignore and the other inhabitants of the Tin Can were now listening too.

"Hell yeah!" Jen shouted, crumbs exploding from her mouth from the pantry snacks she was consuming.

Rain beamed from behind the wheel and Maria smiled nervously. Mark grabbed Bowzer's paws to make the medium dog dance to the news to which Bowzer stuck out his tongue, panting in approval.

"And it's all thanks to you, Theo. You made it happen," Winny said with a content expression.

"Me?" Theo said, genuinely surprised. "What did I do?"

"You got the cello, you said you'd be in a band with us, which got us to take it seriously. You talked with Bert which got us the bass, which got us to meet Jane who booked the Red Rocks show for us. You wrote the 'Dance with the Desert song'—"

"Which I wrote inspired by you—" intercepted Theo.

"We should write a metal cover of our song, and call it *Dance with the Devil*," interrupted Jen.

"—and you talked to the Instagram guy to make us go viral. You did it, Theo."

Theo felt her cheeks fill with warmth, feeling uncomfortable with the spotlight and sheepish she was being given credit for something she felt she didn't deserve. But, perhaps, she had found her place in the band. Even if she wasn't that good at her instrument, she was at least good at spurring things on. Good at keeping the band going in her quiet sort of way. "I really don't deserve that much credit," she said.

Winny scoffed.

"No, seriously!" illuminated Theo. "It was all you, Winny. You had the idea to make a band, you're the passionate one about it. We'd be nothing without a frontwoman and leader like you. I didn't do anything. And really, it's all of you. You all are the talented ones," she said pointing to her friends in the Airstream.

"Well, it's true, it's definitely a team effort," Winny acquiesced, "but you should really give yourself more credit."

Her eyes were now beaming at Theo. Even from a few feet away, Theo up in the top bunk, and Winny down below in a chair by the window, Theo could almost feel like Winny's warm body was right next to her. How she longed for that. If only they could have time alone.

Then a loud *POP* noise sounded, followed by a *clunk, clunk, clunk.*

"Shit!" sputtered Rain uncharacteristically. "We just ran over something big."

"Dammit, Rain, is it flat tire?!" asked Jen.

"Don't look at me, it was an accident!" said Rain. "I've only ever slashed one tire before, and that was Theo's tire. And that was for the benefit of the band!"

"That's true. I should have given you credit for the band coming together a moment ago in my lil' speech," said Winny jokingly, extending an arm over Rain's shoulder in the driver's seat.

"Guys, seriously though, is it a flat tire?" asked Jen rhetorically, knowing indeed it was.

The group looked to Maria.

"Do not look at me! To my dismay, I am unable to fix this one," she said and shrugged.

They pulled over to the side of the road to an absolutely shattered front tire. The heat pounded down on them. Mark and Bowzer walked back along the road to check for roadkill. Bowzer peed several times along the way in affable expectation of nothing. Which there was.

Then, dusty hours passed as they tried to hitchhike a ride to a gas station, or to a tire shop, while Jen was cursing herself for not having a spare on hand. Everyone was in a down mood and it was looking like they were going to miss their show in Albuquerque. This would have been their biggest one yet. They had a lot of fans now that were counting on them.

Time ticked on and no one would pick them up. They made numerous calls to towing companies nearby but most of them said the wait would be hours, maybe not even until tomorrow. Ideas were floated around like leaving and getting a ride into town with one of the other bands. But they didn't want to abandon their beloved Tin Can. Who knew what would happen to it out here?

"What the actual FUCK are we going to do about this!" Jen shouted, more at the sky than anything else. "FUUUUUCK," she shouted, dramatically. "And I'm getting fuckin' hot out here."

People were getting grumpy. No decisions were being made and they were still stuck in the desert with a flat tire. Coyotes could be heard in the distance, and the crickets were starting to come out. The sounds were luminescent, if sounds could be, and the songs of wildlife seemed to echo across the landscape, and around the tall red cliffs they had broken down near. The coyotes softened, then erupted once more and the ladies all tuned in to listen. Theo often wondered if the desert life was laughing at her. It might have been the hot setting sun, but she was feeling a little loopy. Theo, in a momentary, almost hallucinogenic state, observed that the blobs of juniper trees protruded from the dirt, as if poking their heads up from the earth, listening. They looked like spectators watching them as the lights from the Airstream began to illuminate the steadily darkening ground.

Theo wiggled her head out of her daydream. "I have an idea. And it's a crazy one," said Theo, scuffing the dry earth with her boots, unsure what the crew would think. "What if we had the show out here?"

"Pff, what? Are you crazy!" Jen said. "Make people drive two hours out into the middle of nowhere outside some town called Gallup for a show out here! Where would we get power?"

"I guess those are all things we'd have to figure out," wondered Theo aloud.

"I adore the idea," Rain soothed, in her usual gentle way. "What a beautiful place to celebrate the Earth and bring the joy of music to people's eardrums." She picked up a handful of dirt and rubbed it between her palms before letting it fall. "I bet the music would ricochet off those cliffs over there just a little and provide some acoustic ambience."

"Yeah!" Theo was saying, "The sound of those coyotes really carried."

Jen was tilting her head up toward the cliffs her friends were talking about. "Ya know, maybe I like the idea too. We could call the show something fun, like "The Break Down Show.""

"I like it!" Winny whooped. "It's kinda like a play on music too. We could do a lot of music breakdowns for this particular set."

"Yeah, like when they say in music 'break it down!'" added Maria, looking enthused.

"True," Winny continued, "And we could call it the Break Down Show but also maybe add a word about these majestic surroundings."

"Ooo, divine!" chimed in Rain. "Maybe we could call it something like, The Break-Down- Divine-Desert-Goddesses-of-Music-and-Transcendental-Earth-Space Show."

Theo smirked. *So classic Rain.* Winny seeming to be thinking the same said, "That's nice, but what if we kept it simple? Like, The Break Down Desert Show."

It was a hit. Everyone agreed.

"If only we had time to make T-shirts!" Jen proclaimed.

ΔΔΔ

In just a few hours, cars began rolling in and parking along the side of the road. They just kept coming. They parked along the side of the slow highway, slightly on a tilt, headlights illuminating the hillside, then turning dark as passengers piled out to head toward the illuminated Airstream.

Winny had asked her employees from Bar None to bring out a generator, several boxes full of string lights they had in the back after a festival, and the PA system, mixer and speakers, plus a gig bar of colorful can lights.

The stage was just the ground in front of the Airstream, with tall stacked speakers and a PA but to Theo, the sight was magical. The silhouettes of the cliffs outside Gallup seemed to watch over them and the crowd of people speckling out onto the dry yellow earth in front of them was a sight to behold. This was a LOT of people. And they were here just for them. Well, them and also to see the bands *Dystopia Amora* and *TracheotoME*. It felt like a cool community. Again, she felt it was something to be proud of.

Dystopia Amora sang songs about a not-too-distant future where 'robots rotted in the ground, crushed by their own heart's inability of love' and the frontman for TracheotoME sang about his trip to the dentist while playing the accordion. Then, Alien Strata did their thing and had people dancing in the dirt, swinging to the music. Some people slow danced like they do in country Western movies to their slow song. Some people shouted trying to drunkenly sing along to their fast songs. It was a cool night.

People who attended expressed that it was fun having the show out in the middle of nowhere next to their broken-down Airstream. If anything, it helped their odd prestige, said one attendee. Or, as another fan put it, it bumped up their 'folksy alien desert vibe.'

Theo noticed Maria pursing her lips with a noncommittal "Mmm!" when she heard this.

They played music late into the night until police officers drove up and said they would need to have a public performance permit to play or to shut it down. So everyone left. Luckily, one of Winny's coworkers had brought a tire in for them which they planned to replace first thing in the morning during daylight hours. Maria, of course, was well equipped to replace it, given she appeared to know everything.

When most everyone had left and it was just the band reminiscing on what a magical scene the show had been, Theo felt her mood perceptibly lighten, happy from the night. The sensation was like being in less gravity. Suddenly, her thoughts were transported to the dream she'd had last night, no, the *memory,* she realized, she had of what happened last night.

She was levitating in a red armchair in a craft hovering above the Earth. Windows lined the walls, and part of a domed ceiling and floor. Maria was there, looking into her eyes and talking in a language to someone nearby that she couldn't understand. There was a glowing orb hovering above a table and books everywhere.

Images of Maria and the other figure, walking along a corridor of windows, the stars visible and Maria holding the glowing orb, floating above her hands, telling Theo something terrible, something very bad that was going to happen. Explaining. But what? It was all a blur.

The band members were all looking at her.

"Huh?" said Theo, swimming out of her reverie.

"I said, do you agree, Theo? Should we leave at 9 a.m. tomorrow?" said Jen, seemingly finishing a conversation they'd been having while Theo was lost in thought. "I swear, girl, sometimes you're on another planet."

"Oh yeah, yeah sure, 9 a.m. sounds good," Theo said, then thought for a moment. It was something she had been wondering about with regards to Maria. Should they be concerned that they were traveling with an alien? An alien with secrets? Theo had grown so fond of her bandmates, she did not wish any harm to befall them. Would it come back to haunt her if she didn't tell them about Maria? Maria certainly was mysterious. But she had grown to love Maria too, alien or not. But … what if Maria was dangerous?

"You guys, I have something to tell you." Theo paused, taking everything into consideration. Then she decided to say it, "Maria is an alien."

Six Arms

"**M**aria is an alien. She took me in her spaceship, a triangle-shaped UFO, different from the one we saw on the mesa, and, and I can't remember any of it, but she explained something bad. And she has some sort of secret she's keeping from you, from us." Theo said.

The band members and Mark and Bowzer looked at Theo like she was crazy. Maria's eyes were shifty.

"Remember that alien we saw up on the mesa?" Theo continued.

"Yeah, that was Maria," stated Rain, finishing Theo's thought casually and calmly, to everyone's surprise, especially Theo's.

"You knew?!" asked Theo, dumbfounded.

"Yeah, I've known this whole time. Look how giant her green eyes are," she stated, pointing to Maria's glowing green, oval and sparkling eyes behind her glasses. "Those aren't human. And she said she's from Gazibnon."

"Is it a planet full of gazebos or what?" Jen quipped.

"And I'm pretty sure she's got extra arms she brings out while she's playing the drums," Rain added, ignoring Jen. "Remember when I said I thought maybe an alien could help heal your broken heart, Theo?"

Theo thought back to the night her friends had comforted her about her broken heart and how they decided to go looking for an alien again up on the mesa. The night they saw a UFO for the first time. She nodded, answering Rain's question.

"Yeah, I thought Maria might offer some guidance. She knows nearly everything about the universe, I take it." Rain said, matter-of-factly.

"Why didn't you say anything?" asked Theo fidgeting with her long braid.

"It's all hidden in plain sight. When people are ready, they'll see the truth," Rain responded.

The others, Winny, Jen and Mark, were just staring from Theo, to Rain to Maria, mouths open.

"Ahh!" Jen exclaimed, pointing to Maria's eyes. "I see them now! Those things're huge! But, but, it's not … possible," she stammered, trying to understand.

"This is crazy talk," said Mark, trying to laugh it off. "You guys, c'mon, don't be mean to Maria. She's from Canada! She's not an alien. Gazibnon is a province in Canada."

Maria paused, took a deep breath and looked out across the landscape, before appearing to come to a decision. "It is true. I cannot lie. Let me show you a piece of who I am and what I look like."

Then, with the majority of the party in suspense with plasticine looks of blank wonder, she then rolled up her sleeves, and, one at a time, six extra arms fanned out abnormally from her elbows and into the air, like spindly pick-up sticks with webbed hands at the end. They each moved in a kaleidoscopic way. It was like nothing any of them had ever seen before. The arms reminded Theo of cacti reaching up toward the sky. Maria's skin began to vibrate a glossy, bright green and seemed to be emanating different hues like a jelly fish before settling on green again, kind of like the way the earth vibrated different colors when Theo was tripping.

Everyone's mouths were agape like the figure in Evard Munch's painting, 'The Scream' as they tried to absorb the image of Maria's multiple arms and rainbow skin. Mark appeared especially perplexed, clearly in disbelief.

"But, but, we kissed!" he stammered.

"Yeah, you did not notice my extra tongue?"

Mark put a hand over his mouth, part disgust, part disbelief, part intrigue.

Jen couldn't help laughing. "Now THAT'S weird."

It was taking Theo a moment to recover from the shock of seeing aspects of Maria's true form. She looked on at her friend, a little intimidated now. How did you recover from seeing an alien's features in such a way? It was so strange. But Theo was comforted when she saw Maria's kind oval eyes. She was ready to know what the hell was going on.

"I'm sorry I told them about you, Maria. I'm just worried. What does it mean? Are we safe? I just wanna know," Theo began, feeling the need for all the secrets to be out in the open, "Why have you been traveling with us and playing in the band with us? What secrets are you hiding and … what the hell is following us in that UFO over there!" she added, just noticing an enormous, ominous disc floating above the cliffside, like the one they'd seen on the mesa.

They all followed her gaze. Everyone looked out at the UFO emerging from the cliffside and gasped. Theo could tell it was all too much for them. This was a lot for anyone to take in. Winny especially looked shocked. She didn't say anything, just stood there, arms at her sides, and an expression Theo couldn't place. What would this mean for Winny's dreams of making it big with music? Would this crush her dreams? Did this mean the alien, Maria, would have to leave the band? Most importantly, were they in danger? Had she done the right thing exposing Maria? Theo's head filled with questions and she had to struggle to remind herself she was doing it to keep them safe, because she deeply cared about everyone, Maria included. Her heart held them all.

Seeing the UFO in the distance, advancing closer and closer, and now seeing Maria's slightly terrifying extra arms (and tongue) was all very disconcerting. Maria could be dangerous. She took a few steps closer to everyone and everyone took a few steps back.

Her green eyes had a different look in them just now and she looked upward and gave a wave of one of her many arms. A second UFO appeared in a silent flash, a triangular planchette of a craft.

In an instant, they were beamed in light, and Theo felt the exuding sound she'd heard before, a low hum, those green streaks of light circled her vision and she felt that familiar swirling sensation. *Up, up, up*, all six of them and Bowzer went, off the desert floor and upward into the floating craft.

Time, Knowledge
and Velvet Chairs

Time is an interesting concept. It can feel subjective. Sometimes it moves fast, sometimes slow. Sometimes there are gaps in memory. All six people and Bowzer, were in the dark for an indeterminable time. Theo heard a foreign language being spoken. Then, a glowing light came on. She felt that same odd sensation of levitating and knew exactly where she was and the memory swam into focus. She was in the same floating triangle she had been abducted into the night she had sat on top of the Airstream. A soothing sound permeated the air from the now-familiar orb. The sound reminded her of the first time she'd seen it, the night she saw Maria, lulling, like slumber; she could almost hear lyrics. Theo wanted to listen to the sound forever but she couldn't, she needed to know what was going on. Maria had abducted them into this flying contraption and an escape could be necessary.

She looked around. Her friends were levitating in similar, different colored velvet armchairs. They looked oddly comfortable, given that they were all in a UFO. Maria was floating too, on a cushion in the middle, her extra alien arms and changing-color-skin looking otherworldly and comfortable, with one leg crossed over the other, dignified and professorial. Yet it was all so strange.

"Please let me explain everything," Maria began, "I realized I could not explain out there in the open where someone or the other UFO could see us. Plus, this orb helps with understanding. So I took you all up here, out of sight into my own ship, the Planchette, which has been hovering out of sight, traveling with us this whole time."

Theo thought of those feelings she'd had in the Airstream of being watched, Bowzer had seen something too. Had it been the UFO the entire time?

"*Ehem*," a foreign voice from the corner, someone nearby, cleared their throat.

"S'cuse me. I mean, I had to take you up into my *brother's* ship," Maria corrected. "Though these are all my books," she continued, "He has been secretly caravanning with us during our road trip. Our ships are silent, and fast which can help with camouflage."

The brother looked imploringly at them all, ready to be introduced. He looked familiar, but it was dark and, out of context, Theo couldn't place him.

"This is my brother and intern, Oxannae," said Maria.

He nodded a how-do-you-do.

Theo gasped. It was the name of the person the tarot reader had told her to ask the Roadrunner. Why?

"He is working on my dissertation with me about humans. And, well, we are both *screwed* if the Interplanetary Committee finds out we have been interacting with you all," Maria said.

The band members looked dumbfounded.

Interplanetary Committee? Theo repeated the title in her head. *What?*

Jen and Winny especially, the more practical of the group, were still trying to get their bearings and looking around the ship in bewilderment. Rain, perhaps not oddly, looked very at home, running her hands along the arm of her velvet blue armchair, whereas Mark looked positively terrified.

Theo was trying to find the right questions to ask, and thought again about the name Oxannae. "How, what, um … ok." She took a breath, steadying herself. "First of all, your brother, Oxannae, hasn't been interacting with us, just you, right?"

"Well, no, that is not exactly true," Maria began, placating with outstretched multiple hands. "You know that odd looking, um, *clean-cut* guy you saw at the mechanic's shop, and then at Guitar Mart in Albuquerque, and then again the other night at the party?"

Theo looked on, wide-eyed. *That's why he looked familiar.* The man turned his head as if part of his introduction, making the tattoo eye on the side of his head clear to everyone. *What's going on?*

"Yep," Maria continued, "that was my brother, Oxannae, being, shall we say, less than discreet. We both have been wearing uncomfortable human suits. He is not a private detective, he is not a private eye, though he does have three eyes …"

"Where is the real third eye?" asked Rain, leaning in close.

Maria didn't answer this question, and instead, continued, "The point is, he has not been sent to follow you by your ex. He's with me. He has also been trying to study you closely. And, well, he had the *brilliant*," Maria said in air quotes, "idea of getting close to you and trying to talk to you. So he has been watching you all too."

"Well *you* did, why can't I?" Oxannae said, pointing at Maria, "If you're getting taken down by the Interplanetary Committee, then I might as well too. We're family. And I might as well get to know these creatures while I'm at it. Not fair if only you get to study them up close and even get to interact with them and not me."

Theo had the distinct impression Oxannae was the rebellious-type, looking for adventure. She thought the leather jacket he was wearing was a bit much. Seemingly younger than the rest of them, probably in his early twenties, he'd likely had a lot of fun that night partying with humans at the house show in Snowflake, Arizona where they'd played music.

"Yes, Nae, but I did not want you facing dire consequences like me. And, well, especially not before I got to explain to my friends what's going on." Maria added, looking at Theo, "The other night at that house party, my little brother was on his way to tell you all our secrets before I could and I didn't want you to hear it from him first. So, I beamed you up into the ship."

"So what *are* your secrets?" Theo said. She was growing a little impatient But the soothing sound surrounded her ears once again, calming her. Putting her at ease. *Where was it coming from? Was it that orb, somewhere?*

"Look, I can't tell you everything, or where that ethereal sound is coming from," she said, seemingly reading Theo's mind. "Not yet, it would literally blow your brains out. It is too much information for humans to comprehend. But I can tell you that myself and Nae—Oxannae, are in trouble. The UFO that has been following us, you know, the giant one floating above the Airstream that day I took you to the SandWitch Shop, and the one we all saw on the mesa a few nights ago? That is the Interplanetary Committee. They investigate to see if alien researchers have committed any interplanetary crimes, like interacting with humans. They then take alien researchers in front of a review board, and if found guilty, well … The consequences are … something I would rather not discuss at this juncture."

"Why did they show up that night on the mesa? Were they there to investigate?" asked Jen.

"Yes. They were there to find me," Maria summarized.

Theo thought for a moment. "Is that why you didn't want us to go up there? Because the Interplanetary Committee could be there?"

"Yes, Theo, you are correct. They had been tracking my activities and discovered my research on the mesa, peering down at you all through my ship's ocular lens."

"Like a microscope for aliens," Rain surmised wisely.

The thought made Theo feel like they were mice or amoeba being studied in a lab.

"They are trying to build a case against myself and Oxannae," Maria went on. "Right now, we are facing charges of interaction with humans and becoming friends with humans, but they do not yet know that you all know we are aliens." Theo's head was spinning but Maria continued, "Our sentences will be much more severe if they find out that you know and that *we* know that *you* know."

This was a lot.

Maria curiously added, "We face a lot more than something like jail time if we are convicted. Much, much worse."

"So, why don't you just leave, then?" snapped Jen, clearly feeling betrayed and confused. "We didn't ask you to study us like animals!"

It was not in Jen's character to snap like this and Maria looked heartbroken. Theo wondered what consequence Maria and Oxannae would face. And she couldn't help but feel badly for Maria. After all, she was their friend, not just an alien, or some stranger. And it sounded like she needed help. As if to support this, Jen looked ashamed at her own brash reaction. However, Jen's point too, about the weirdness of being studied like animals, was well taken by Theo.

Maria walked over to the cabinets as if to take a pause and pulled out six multicolored mugs before filling them with a liquid. Some of it lingered in the air in the less-gravity atmosphere, but Maria somehow ushered the droplets into the mugs too, then brought them over, her six arms coming in handy.

"Chai tea?" she said.

Theo wasn't sure how the liquid stayed in the cups but everyone took one. She sipped. It was the best chai tea she'd ever tasted. Bowzer bounded, floated, through the air toward Maria, licking her alien face and her skin turned from green to a warm orange as she smiled, then back to green again. Theo wondered if Maria's skin changed color with her mood.

"I have something for you, too," Maria stated as she floated to an upper cabinet and pulled out a dog treat for Bowzer, his tail wagging.

"So why did the Interplanetary Committee suddenly leave that night, anyway?" continued Rain crossing her legs into a pretzel as she hovered in her velvet chair. "Right when Bowzer came up to us, the UFO just disappeared. Why did they leave?"

Bowzer's ears perked up at the mention of his name.

"Oh yeah, that." Maria made a gesture of brushing it off. "They just do not really like dogs."

Theo was still amazed at this answer.

"Pure evil," Jen said reaching over and patting Bowzer on the head reassuringly.

"Wait, so—" Winny began. It was the first time she had spoken since arriving, and her pragmatic brain appeared to have trouble digesting it all. Nonetheless, she had connected two interesting similarities. "So the Interplanetary Committee is kinda like a bunch of cops?"

"In a way, yes," responded Maria.

"And you and your brother, Oxannae, are being followed by the cops … and so is Theo. You're both on the run from the law."

"Well, I guess I'm not, since …" Theo trailed off. The eye tattoo man was not who she had thought he might be. "I guess I'm not being followed by the police, since it was actually Maria's brother." She realized suddenly she was relieved.

"Well, sure, that was Oxannae, but unfortunately, Theo, cops are indeed trying to find you," Maria said and Theo gulped. "They are just more discreet than my brother. The police, the human police, well, private investigators, I believe from the South, have been undercover following you for weeks, you just had no clue. They have been following your every move. Watching you eat.

Watching you get dressed. Watching you practice cello. They just don't have jurisdiction to arrest you, they were only gathering intel for your ex. So they have been waiting and watching."

This was a creepy feeling. More creepy than the UFO ship they were sitting in. More scary than facing and talking with aliens. People, of her own species, were following her every move, invading her privacy, and also trying to control her body. It was so unnatural, unnerving, more unnatural and unnerving than the aliens sitting in front of her! She didn't know what to say. "How do you know all this?" she spluttered.

Maria lowered her green-eyed gaze to Theo. "I have been observing. Observing you all from afar. But not in the way the investigators were. From a distance, not private human things but to learn about your culture, to try to help make your world better. To try to make my own planet better too. Knowledge is power. The more we all know about each other, the more empathy we all have. And I believe we can help each other improve our societies, together. Achieve peace, balance and harmony in the universe, *and all that jazz*, as you humans would say."

With this, Maria seemed satisfied. Like she was acing a test of understanding humans. Perhaps living with and befriending them really was helping her get to know them better.

Here was an interesting juxtaposition, Theo thought: two groups of people were watching her, for two entirely different purposes. One was studying her and her friends, to understand them better, to create empathy, peace, harmony and understanding, yadda yadda. The other was tracking her in order to try to control her body, not to understand her perspective or reasons at all, but for the purpose of punishment. The alien observation, she realized, made her feel empowered and motivated. The human observation took from her, making her feel deprived, fearful, controlled. It shouldn't be this way, but it was. It was making her head spin. "Why didn't you tell me this?" she asked, her voice small.

"I am a researcher," Maria concluded, folding her many hands into her lap. "I aim to not influence the species that I am researching. But of course, I have very much broken that research rule. I am telling you now."

"Is my ex-husband now following me too?" Theo asked, afraid of the answer.

Maria looked at her. "That I do not know. Chocolate?" She offered, holding out a bar of what appeared to be dark chocolate.

Theo looked up, perplexed. Bowzer looked at it, hungrily.

"No, not for you Bowzer. I may be an alien, but I know chocolate is not for dogs," Maria said fondly, tugging one of his ears. Holding out the chocolate, she added, seemingly eager to inform her human friends her knowledge of Planet Earth, "I have learned that chocolate, a human snack, greatly enjoyed by the female human species, is desirable particularly in times of duress." Maria's big eyes were kind and empathetic.

Maria was clearly an advanced species and so was her brother. She seemed to know everything about humans. And an infinite amount about the universe and intergalactic travel, as Mark had observed. Her planet seemed far more advanced than theirs and Theo realized she could stand to learn a lot about Planet Gazibnon. Maybe getting to know these aliens really was a good idea, and, like Maria had said, a way to improve both their societies. Knowledge was indeed power. But only potential power.

They all sat for a moment, chewing chocolate, digesting the information together and hovering above the Earth in the cozy craft. Maria and her brother Oxannae took the opportunity to talk to each other in their native language. The foreign language Theo had been hearing.

"Wait, are you aliens speaking Spanish?" Jen exclaimed, regaining some of her unapologetic exuberance.

Maria looked at Jen inquisitively. "I thought you did not know how to speak Spanish."

"Well, I know some," Jen shrugged.

"It is a language very similar to human Spanish, yes," Oxannae said.

Wow, thought Theo. *I guess they aren't that foreign after all.* Maybe their species wasn't that different, considering their languages were so similar. She felt there was a lesson to be learned here. She floated over to the domed windows to look down at the small round circle of Earth. Seeing her home planet so far away gave her the sense of just how fragile it was. All those people, humanity, fit on that tiny dot that was now floating silently in the blackness of space while she and her friends floated in a UFO above it. It was beautiful.

"So I have a question," said Mark, finally.

Mark hadn't said anything at all yet until this point and reminded Theo of the way female characters were often portrayed in a male-dominated movies: there, but not doing much of anything important.

It was his turn to get in on the conversation now that he had settled slightly, getting over the idea that he had, indeed, made out with an alien. "How did you guys learn English so quickly?"

Maria batted her alien eyelashes. "My dear, aren't you sensing a theme? With years of study. We worked hard to learn a lot." She blew him a kiss.

Mark looked intrigued and impressed with his crush's intellect. "I'm more turned on than ever."

Theo looked over at the group. She was happy for the two of them. Mark was a kind and caring person. And so was Maria. They seemed to genuinely like each other. A human and an alien made an odd pair, but it seemed to work for them. She gazed at Winny, the woman she adored, with an expression as if to say, *What an experience, huh?*

Winny smiled back, knowingly.

"Ok, so now we've got more information," said Rain, getting back to the task at hand, "and now we all know you are here to help humanity and for us to help you too. I'm all for it. It reminds me of my eco-activist days. I felt such a purpose and connection to our planet. But what do we do? How do we help?"

Maria floated like an astronaut past the bookshelves and over to the domed window where Theo stood, looking down at Earth below, alongside her. "That is the question," she said, trailing off. "Have you all ever heard of the story of the ape on earth that learned sign language to deliver her last words to humanity?"

"Hold on, hold on my dear," Mark interjected, "You know sign language too?"

Maria smiled. "Sign language is actually the language of the universe, give or take. Most species out in the vastness of space have bodies, and so can communicate by conveying visual movements. Most species in space have different vocal chords, or bodily mechanisms for sounds, which makes for a beautiful array of music, or language, as you humans call it, but also exceptionally difficult to communicate. It is difficult to create similar sounds when different species have such varying means of *producing* sound. So, sign language is the most transferable language between us all. More universal. Just like how animals on your planet can communicate with sign language. Nearly everyone in the universe can communicate with sign language. After all, silence is music too."

Theo felt her already stretched mind doing a series of gymnastic splits. Were these the literal, aforementioned secrets Maria had been referring to? She held onto her forehead, feeling a headache emerging, and grasping onto it like it would indeed otherwise propel from her body.

Maria continued her story, facing the window, staring out at the vastness of space, as the others looked over at her, still levitating above their seats and sipping their chai teas. "There was a gorilla named Koko who was taught sign language on your planet whose famous words were recorded." As Maria quoted the gorilla, she did the words in sign language to match: "'I am Gorilla, I am flowers, animals. I am nature. Man Koko love. Earth Koko love. But man stupid. Stupid! Koko sorry. Koko cry. Time hurry! Fix Earth! Hurry! Protect Earth. Nature see you. Thank you.'"

The group was silent, pondering. Rain had a tear in her eye she briskly wiped away.

"Wow, that's beautiful. I think I saw that in a social media video. Is it true?" asked Jen.

"No, it is not," said Maria. "The video was edited."

Theo tweaked her head. "Guess you can't believe everything from social media, or from what people tell you."

"Well, not really. *Kind of,*" Maria corrected herself. "Koko was taught those specific sign language words quite a few years before her death as a Public Service Announcement to the world, so it is unclear if Koko the gorilla really felt that way or was just told to say the words, not knowing what they meant."

Theo felt she was on a roller coaster ride with this conversation.

"That's the story you're telling?" Oxannae rolled his eyes at his bigger sister, like a rebellious human teenager.

"Social media can be so misleading," scoffed Jen, tossing her floating mohawk aside. She was now looking at the titles of the books in the shelves.

"But the point of the story remains clear," Maria summarized, taking a sip of her chai and turning to face the group, her expression serious, her skin pulsing from green to dark blue. "It is time to protect the planet. So what if Koko did not say it from her own heart! Who knows, maybe she meant it? We will never know. But the humans creating the PSA and teaching Koko the words knew it to be true. It is time to take care of your home, the only beautiful home you have. I want to try to help you achieve what Koko (maybe) hoped for: Harmony and balance with your planet. But it is not easy. And people on my planet need convincing that you are even worth saving."

"Yuh, our people don't care about you. I don't know why my sister does, either, frankly," Oxannae commented, while he moved to the table in the back of the room, and propped his feet above it, hovering. "But I didn't wanna turn down a vacation to Earth. This place is weird. But yeah, my people don't want you interfering with our utopia. Frankly, don't mess with us. Got it? Don't ever come to our planet."

Wow, temper, thought Theo. She wondered again why the

tarot reader had said to ask the roadrunner who Oxannae was. She wasn't a big fan of this volatile little alien so far, but, as much of her trip had taught her, she was trying to be open-minded.

Maria continued where her brother had left off as she joined the group in the circle of arm chairs, "Oxannae is unfortunately correct. We are not to interact with the 'enemy,' referring to you, humans. Hence, the illegality of mine and Nae's actions while being here, with all of you. We need to educate Gazibnonians that you all are not that different from us, create empathy."

There it was. Maria's personal mission.

Theo felt the coldness of space through the window and looked again at Earth. She felt an overwhelming desire to protect it.

This was also a feeling known as the 'Overview Effect' and coined by an astronaut in the eighties to describe what many astronauts felt when looking at our small blob of Earth floating in space. It was a mental shift in an astronaut's cosmic perspective to describe a sense of awe for our home planet and the understanding of its fragility.

The group sat in silence for a moment until Rain broke it, her blue button eyes earnest and curious. "And what do we do about this band tour we are on?"

Theo had practically forgotten about the tour, what with all the information they had just received. It didn't seem nearly as important as it did before.

"And what do we do about Theo being followed by the actual private investigator?" Rain asked again, "And uh, did you ever answer the main question? What are we going to do to help humanity and Earth?"

"Pfff," Oxannae voiced from the corner, his head leaning back on his hands. "She didn't answer anything. She does that."

Rain offered advice, "Let your energy be used to build, not destroy."

"Precisely," Maria replied, as though Rain had answered any sort of question, despite the clear fact she had not. "I have a plan and it involves using a secret tool."

Theo wondered what this secret tool was.

Jen turned to her flowery friend Rain anticlimactically. "Where did you hear that phrase?"

"Read it in the tea leaves," Rain responded.

Harebrained Plans

They were up all night, possibly for three weeks. Theo was very confused about how time worked in Maria and Oxannae's Planchette, as they talked about how to help humanity from the impending doom of climate crisis. It was a seemingly insurmountable task, they concluded over and over again, much of which had something to do with that glowing orb. Was that Maria's secret tool? Theo was fuzzy on the details and it seemed that residing inside the UFO messed with her human mind. But she did know somehow that Maria thought she, Theo, was special in some way and that she could help. Something about her heart.

Ultimately, after much time and consideration on the topic of trying to avoid the human catastrophic road to demise, they felt they were too ill-equipped, still, to formulate a plan. They decided they would figure everything out after their Red Rocks show and first would need to handle Theo's problem with being followed. Winny, often the practical one, except when it paradoxically came to her obsession with horoscopes and tarot, again recommended getting a good civil rights lawyer and fighting the case. But Theo didn't want to go through the legal system again. So instead, they formulated yet another harebrained plan. They would meet Winny's friend in Denver who had access to fake IDs. From there, they would need to create a new identity for Theo and get themselves out of dodge. Theo had chuckled appreciatively at her sweetheart's ability to swing from practical to impractical so seamlessly. She adored it. They would execute their harebrained plan after the Red Rocks show. And Oxannae would man the spaceship, follow everyone in the Airstream, and keep it hidden, but available. It would be the perfect quick getaway if needed.

So, back they returned to the Airstream, and back on the road.

It appeared time had resumed to normal and they had only been away for one night in the UFO, or so they thought.

The Airstream was fired up with purpose, this time with Maria's—no, Oxannae's UFO, the Planchette, in tow, ready to appear at the call of a whistle. Now it was eight of them: Theo, Winny, Maria, Jen, Rain, Mark, Bowzer, and Oxannae in the UFO out of sight. As they headed towards a gas station, Maria mentioned her planet had no use for oil considering they had some sort of substance that powered their trains and vehicles that was completely renewable. Everyone in the band wanted to know what the substance was, and asked if they could get some in backstock for use on Earth. But Maria had insisted the technology on Earth already existed to make and do the same.

"So you're saying, we just gotta put our heads together more. That, and get the greedy billionaires who are not interested in anything that doesn't turn a profit, *interested* in this free, sustainable technology."

"Precisely," affirmed Maria.

"Got it. Yeah, that'll be easy. That's what those capitalist pigs like most. Stuff that helps the earth that DOESN'T generate money for them. Yeah, that'll be easy," Jen remarked sarcastically.

"If Planet Gazibnon can successfully get away from capitalism and patriarchy, and other systems of oppression, Earth can too," Maria had stated matter of fact.

So they drove on in their 1980s Excella Airstream.

Weather was coming in across the barren landscape. A seasonally early snow was drifting down toward the dirt and the roads were becoming slick. They decided to blow through Albuquerque, Winny almost insisted, so as not to revisit old memories there, and headed north.

The Reel Room

One Day 'til the Red Rocks Show

They took a break for the night in a town named Raton, or *mouse* in Spanish, named for the nearby mountain infested with mice when settlers arrived with the railroad in the late 1800s, a town Winny said she imagined would have spaghetti Western festivals with twangy guitar musicians and sci-fi-sounding theramins playing.

Theo and Winny took a stroll, just the two of them, leaving the rest of the crew at the restaurant where everyone ate for dinner. Finally, they had a moment together. They walked along the downtown strip of old buildings with colorful trim and other early 1900s features, past an old theater jammed between two buildings with a small marquee displaying movies that were on the way. In big letters it stated, 'Spaghetti Western Festival, November 9th' which was today. Theo gave Winny a playful punch at noticing she had been exactly right about the town, and they sat down on a bench, allowing the slowly falling flakes of snow to coat them, the sun just tucking away past the hillside for its nightly snooze. The snow trickled down, illuminated by a few streetlights that set it aglow. Theo felt drained. Tired. Exhausted. It had been a wild trip.

And yet, her soul felt more alive than it ever had these past several months. She had learned so much, not just about herself, but about music and the universe. Her head still felt the way it did when she was in the spacecraft, like it would explode. She felt grateful and excited, but also terrified and confused about what lay down the road for her. How would she get away from the criminal charges? The uncertainty felt unrelenting, even with the help of an intergalactic species. Even *they* didn't know how to help her. And all she did was be human. Nothing to say about the existential crisis they faced as a planet.

Winny looked into Theo's eyes, maybe sensing the strife behind them.

"I'm worn slap out," is all Theo could muster saying.

"Hmm?" Winny raised an eyebrow.

"Exhausted," Theo reiterated, realizing Winny didn't know the Southern phrase.

Winny nodded. "I know," she said and they sat in musical silence, feeling the desert snow gently fall on their skin.

Theo shivered a little and Winny brought her in closer. She began to cry and Winny just held her. They held each other for what felt like a long time. The snow sparkled on the pavement, glistening and the light from the streetlamps glowed under overcast clouds. No cars drove by. Even the light dusting of snow blanketed the streets, softening sounds and a slight wind breathed past them, then relaxed into silence again.

Music is universal. So is silence. Music and silence transcend across time and space. What is sound but particles exploding together violently in such a way that they vibrate and create a sound. At the dawn of time, the Big Bang occurred, and likely made a *Big Bang* sound. But perhaps the Big Bang *was* a sound. Perhaps from sound exuded all of existence. Does that mean sound is the source of all life? First there was silence, then there was sound. Perhaps they are equal, but different.

Theo sat on the snowy bench with Winny and pondered the idea of sound, and how it entered the ear. She had once learned that music, or sound, was pitches in sound waves, floating across space and hitting one's eardrum, one's delicately, naturally-constructed cochlea, teeny tiny hammers pounding, vibrating, to create a conceptual understanding of sound. Sound entered the external acoustic meatus, or the opening in the ear, and hit the tympanic membrane, which then fired the malleus and spiraled through the cochlea, made up of tiny sensitive hairs and a delicate balance of liquid, (which, if thrown off by even the tiniest amount, could cause severe vertigo) which then activated the cochlear nerve to send signals to the brain about what the sound reaching the ear instruments actually meant.

One might think Theo learned this in nursing school but no, she'd learned it from a drummer. Not Maria, but a friend she knew from high school who had sustained a traumatic brain injury and been a patient of Theo's during her residency, when she was working with all types of patients before settling on obstetrics. Her high school friend was obsessed with sound, and how it turned into music and would sit in her hospital bed informing Theo, her then-nurse, of her passion for sound.

The brain injury threatened her friend's passion, hell, her ability to communicate, but she was resilient. Through determination and help from experts, she retrained her brain to function again properly, and was again able to return to her life as a musician. Theo thought about this and the importance of sound and wondered what her friend was up to these days. Hopefully, living her dream as a musician. Winny certainly was, at least for now.

Theo looked at Winny, clearly lost in thought. Was she thinking about the Red Rocks show and what it would mean? Musicianship was a special thing. More than people gave it credit for, Theo was learning. It was meaningful, and yet paradoxically meaningless at the same time. *Wow*, Theo thought. I'm talking in conceptual and contradictory terms. *Am I turning into Maria?* She chuckled to herself softly.

"What?" Winny asked, turning to face Theo and brushing snow from her face.

"Nothing," Theo said, unable to explain the entire train of thought she'd just had. She felt different after spending time on Maria's UFO, like being in there had somehow made her feel smarter. Like she had absorbed something indescribably good from osmosis just being on that spaceship. She thought about that glowing, gentle humming orb. Maybe that ability to absorb information and the goodness she felt had something to do with the glowing orb, somehow. She had gone over to it, had felt it pulling her in, like she was one with the universe, one with everything. This … so-much feeling, however, was not possible to put into words for Winny. So instead she said, "Isn't it funny how, somehow being in that spaceship around that orb was really beautiful and helped us, kind of, absorb information?"

"I was thinking the same thing!" Winny stated serendipitously.

Theo smiled, "And that now we're just, like, sitting, thinking about it out here, not caring that it's snowing?"

Winny smiled warmly, her freckles creasing at the smile lines. "I like it," she said, squeezing Theo's hand, kissing her.

It was romantic, and lovely and Theo wished she could live in the moment forever. She felt electric that their kiss the night behind the secret bookshelf door had not been just a fluke. "I like so much that you're passionate about music," she said, clumsily, but wanting to express her love for Winny.

Winny's eyes lit up. "I've always loved music," she said, looking the way Theo felt—as though she couldn't put it all into words. "When I was in college, before I dropped out, I was roaming around the library and I came across this Smithsonian book about the history of music and there was this tiny, tiny blurb about what is considered to be the first image of a musician. It's on a painted wall in a cave called the Trois Frères, in Ariège, France dating back to 13,000 BCE. I thought it was just the coolest thing. Here was the first piece of history of someone playing an instrument. What would it be like to see something like that? But the general public are not allowed to go see it, since the paintings are so fragile and plus it was in, you know, France, a *little* far away from Portland, Oregon."

Theo nodded.

"Then, one semester, I was in an archaeology class and our professor was some top archaeology-guy and he organized a trip for ten students to go with him to go see *the* Trois Frères caves. We all had to apply and write an essay about why we wanted to go. I thought, this is my chance! I've never had luck with these kinds of things, you know, scholarships or the lottery or anything like that but I figured I would apply. So I wrote about wanting to see that image of the first musician because of my passion for music, and sure enough, out of a hundred-some essays, I was chosen for the trip."

"That's amazing, Winny! What was it like? Winning that trip?" Theo had no doubt Winny would have won over any teacher when talking about music, she had a way of explaining its power in a way that was entrancing.

"It was incredible," Winny enthused, "I couldn't believe I'd basically won a free trip to France to go see these caves and see the first image ever of a musician, the first visible history of someone creating music!" Winny brushed snowflakes off her skirt and snuggled closer to Theo for warmth, continuing her story, "When we got there, everyone was focused on the image in the cave called *The Sorcerer*, which was in a cavern called the Sanctuary. It was cool too, don't get me wrong: It was an image of a horned animal, humanlike, and shows what people thought was a great spirit or a master of animals and they thought maybe showed the practice of magic taking place there, and ceremonies too. But what I wanted to see was the musician one, called *The Small Sorcerer* who appeared to be playing a nose-flute."

A nose-flute?" chuckled Theo.

Winny laughed too, holding up an invisible flute to her nose. "Yep, a nose-flute. It was the first image of an instrument. So anyway, I was walking through the cave and it was dead, dead, silent because I was further from the group and all I could hear was this soft humming sound."

Theo immediately thought about the glowing orb and it made her thoughts stray further. *Was the orb sound, the sound piece from the Big Bang? The foundational particle, concept of existence? Or perhaps a by-product of existence?* She felt her head pounding again and as though they were both talking like professors, as though she'd gained a lot more knowledge ever since being in that ship. *Was that why Maria had to take us up into her ship? Because somehow, being up there, around that orb, made us understand better?*

Either way, Maria had a way of explaining and teaching things where it just made sense. And yet, what they had learned on the ship had just created more questions. Wasn't that the tricky thing about knowledge, though? Sometimes, like Rain had said, 'You don't know what you don't know,' and sometimes, learning more just showed you how much you still didn't know. Or, in other words, when you learned something new, you just had more questions than before. Theo wondered if she was high and whether or not any of this was making any sense. But, she was enjoying the intellectual exercise and made a mental note to ask Maria ... more questions, later.

Winny continued her story, "And then it was just me, alone, staring at this image of the first musician. It had this crazy feeling of power to it. Hawaiian's have a word *mana*, which means, power and spirit, or supernatural power, or ..." She looked around at the glistening snow. "Universal life force. And well, I feel like that's the best way to describe it." Her brown eyes turned to Theo's hazel ones and they held each other in a gaze for a moment.

"Yo, gal pals," Jen said, approaching their bench-turned-oasis.

She was walking toward them with Maria, now with her extra arms hidden back in her human suit, and Mark, who were holding hands. Mark seemed unfazed that the woman he was into was an alien. Rain and Bowzer approached too, bringing up the rear, their footsteps softened by the snow.

"Guess what?" Jen asked and the two lovebirds cocked their heads at her. "I booked us all an old hotel for the night! Figured we could use a break from the Tin Can," she said, nodding her head in the direction of the Airstream. "I was looking up some places while we finished at the restaurant and saw this cute and affordable apartment above some old theater where they play old Westerns."

Theo and Winny looked at each other and smiled.

ΔΔΔ

That night, they all bought tickets to *They Call Me Trinity*, an old Enzo Barboni seventies spaghetti Western, and relaxed in old creaky folding chairs in the theater, guzzling popcorn to the black and white screen. Winny put a hand on Theo's knee and left it there. The warmth of her hand seemed to transcend up Theo's body with a zing of arousal but the movie continued and the others didn't seem to notice Theo's touched leg.

Winny slowly slid her hand up Theo's thigh and gently squeezed it while she stared straight at the screen, a mischievous smile on her face. Theo's heart began to beat faster.

Winny whispered in her ear. "I noticed a closet in the lobby. Join me there?"

Theo's heart lifted and Winny carefully made her way out of the row of seats and headed for the door. Theo waited an endless minute, then followed.

She pushed the theater door aside where Winny was waiting, pulling her into a kiss, into what they thought was the closet, but was a room with the gold engraving on the door that said, Reel Room. The room was dark with only the flashing light from the screen through the window. It was vacant. They smiled, shrugged at each other at the surroundings, if nothing else it was even better than a closet, and Winny pulled her in close, grabbing and kissing her, running her hands along Theo's body. Theo was so excited.

They lay down together, two lovers in a Reel Room.

Reaching Red Rocks:
A Long Journey

Day of the Red Rocks Show

The next morning, Theo awoke in a comfortable bed soaked in sun. The rooms walls were old brick and it took Theo a moment to remember where she was; in an apartment above a quirky old theater in Raton. Rays of light bounced off Winny's peaceful sleeping face and Theo couldn't believe her luck. Winny was the kindest, most loving and certainly incredible lover she had ever had. Theo felt light as a feather. The passion in the Reel Room and then again later that night in this bed was beyond anything she had experienced. *Wow,* she thought to herself.

Suddenly, the door burst open and Jen jumped onto their bed and so did Bowzer. The pup began licking Winny's slowly waking face, to which Winny said, "Errrrrmm."

"Wake up, sleepy heads! It's Red Rocks show day!" Jen hooted.

ΔΔΔ

Theo stared at the ceiling, waiting for Winny to get out of the shower and then she would hop in there too, before they would embark for their big day at Red Rocks. Theo could still feel Winny's warm, tattooed arms around her. She felt the soothing sense of oxytocin still humming in her cells. *I want to do something romantic for her,* Theo thought. She ran through ideas for surprises or gifts or gestures but couldn't come up with anything. Then, after settling on an idea that would be at least vaguely romantic, she thought, she slid out of bed and walked down the hallway in her underwear, deciding to surprise Winny in the shower.

She tiptoed down the hallway so as not to let her friends see her in her tank top and tighty-whities. She could hear their murmured voices nearby in the kitchen, no doubt sipping their coffee and so figured she was in the clear.

She walked towards the bathroom and could hear music blaring, along with Winny's accompanying singing in the shower. Theo smiled, thinking about how music enveloped Winny. Before she went to open the door, she plucked a blossom from a geranium plant stationed by the window, then slipped into the bathroom.

Music surrounded Theo. It echoed off the walls, Winny's halfway punk-rock shouting accompanying it. The shower curtain was an orange scene of a desert, two towering cliffs on either side that reminded her of the canyon near Truth or Consequences with the mesa. Green cacti reached towards the bathroom ceiling and ground down towards the black and white tiles of the floor. The steam from the shower rose up like a vape cloud from a comic book employee on his way to work.

Winny's nude figure was just visible behind the desert-scene shower curtain as she danced to her music and her own singing.

Goddess, I love her, Theo thought, stopping for a moment. She couldn't imagine loving anyone more and felt as though her heart were growing outside her body, outside her humanely, earthly form. She realized, in that moment, that Winny was the love of her life.

Winny reached for the bottle of shampoo and caught a glimpse of Theo standing there, flower in hand in her tighty-whities and screamed in surprise. The shampoo bottle went through her hands, launching across the room and, with a *thunk,* hit Theo square between the eyes.

Winny immediately started to laugh, that big, confident laugh, in her relief that it was just Theo, "You scared the shit outa me, babe!' she bellowed with laughter.

Theo laughed and rubbed her forehead where the shampoo bottle had hit her. "Sorry I scared you! I wanted to surprise you with, uh, this flower!" She adorably and pathetically held it out toward Winny.

Winny smiled and reached through the shower curtain, grabbing hold of the geranium blossom, before pulling Theo into the shower with her, sheer tank-top and underwear and all, for a big, shower-drenched kiss. The flower melted between them.

A bit later, they crept back to their bedroom for their clothes, before sneaking back into the bathroom to dance to the music in the steam, while they helped each other get dressed. Theo couldn't imagine a happier moment in her life.

ΔΔΔ

The day flowed, as they puttered along in the Tin Can tour van, a vague glimmer of a new moon sliver visible in the blue sky. Some of them animatedly played Taboo, while Jen and Rain sat at the front, managing the radio station, putting on a podcast about American culture, which spurred an engrossing political conversation between the two of them about oil and billionaires.

"All I'm saying is—" Jen was saying, trying to summarize her point, "if billionaires would use the money and their resources to actually do good in the world, I feel like we could get a lot done, a lot faster."

Rain nodded. "Very true. And many oil executives and the oil industry itself deceived us. They knew about the scientific reports that showed how harmful oil use was for our planet and purposefully hid it from us for years!"

Theo had not been paying attention to the game, instead, listening intently to the conversation.

"Yeah!" Jen affirmed, who seemed to like it when Rain got more animated than her usual calm self. She met her friend's enthusiasm. "They completely deceived us!"

"The problem is the power is in the hands of the few," Maria chimed in.

"Yes!" Jen exclaimed. "Also, we the public kind of knew too, right? I mean, we should have been fighting more for our planet this whole time." She sighed, not sure where to take the conversation from there.

"Yeah, we deceived ourselves too," Rain surmised. After a moment she added, "But, there have been instances where we, ya know, the people, did make good things happen. Like when we banned aerosols and the hole in the ozone closed. That was no small problem we fixed."

Time went by and the group listened to the various bands they would hear at the festival. The fresh coating of snow on the desert looked like donut frosting as they listened to bands like the Sweeping Sallys, Mistake Bangs, and the occasional song from Hungry for a Lobotomy, as per Jen's heavy music request. Rain in particular grimaced through the metal songs with a supportive smile. Winny and Theo couldn't stop grinning at each other, while Jen headbanged and the others listened obediently. Bowzer's ears rotated backward at the metal, resuming repose, tongue out at all the other sound selections.

Theo and Winny sat on the couch together, hand in hand, giddy, like two high schoolers in love. Winny adjusted an out-of-place hair around Theo's ear and ran her hand along her long braid.

"Tell me, Theodora, what is something which brings you true joy?"

"That's easy," beamed Theo. "You."

Winny smiled her sideways smirk, "You bring me joy, too. But what else?"

"Our friends."

"What else?"

Theo had to think a little more. "I remember running track in high school. I really liked that. And, let's see … Before I got into my career as a nurse, I worked at a screen-printing shop."

"Yeah?" Winny looked intrigued and sat up, propping her elbow on the back of the couch in attention, listening to Theo.

"Yeah, I liked doing that. We blared loud music in there all day and I worked these screen-printing machines, sometimes got ink all over my apron and well, I just really enjoyed the vibe."

Winny furrowed her brow. "Why don't you go back to doing something like that?"

"Well, I still want to do something where I'm helping people. That's why I got into obstetric nursing."

Winny nodded, lost in thought at that response.

"What brings you joy?" Theo asked.

"I really like managing Bar None from afar," Winny responded.

Theo laughed a little. "I love that! You're so nuanced. At first it seems ironic because, my babe, you seem to enjoy your share of spirits."

Winny laughed too. "That's the thing! I do. But I also like promoting something which brings others joy too; a way for non-alcohol drinkers to find community and enjoyment being out on the town."

Theo hadn't thought of it that way before and liked the idea.

Winny jumped back to the topic they had started with, a thought seemingly occurring to her. "Ya know, Theo, there are other ways to help people, even within nursing, even within obstetrics. Have you ever thought of being a midwife? Or a doula?"

Theo had not, but the idea sparked a wisp of exuberance, of lightness to her mind.

They continued their drive, Bowzer bouncing along on top of Jen in the front seat, Rain concentrating on the road from behind her oversized sunglasses. Maria, her alien-ness now exposed, was able to point out her awe of the planet like the impressed and perplexed tourist that she was. She said she was boggled by the beauty of the starkly sprawling green hillsides outside Walsenburg, Colorado, an otherwise unassuming and fairly boring-looking place.

The sun extended its rays, causing shadows to lengthen across the sandpaper landscape. It awed Maria, who said she couldn't wait to tell her friends of her earthly experience. Everything was such a stark contrast to her planet.

On passing windmills, their pinwheel wings gracefully propelling the air, giant in the sky like dinosaurs, Maria commented on their gently drifting circles, "These generate energy," she said, perhaps assuming no one else in the group had a clue what they were, which—considering there were so few types of renewable energy in use on the planet Earth—was understandable. "We have a plethora of them on our planet."

Theo loved to imagine what Maria's planet was like. Every once in a while they would get tidbits about life on Planet Gazibnon while driving; the air travel for sustainable transportation, no fuel, nothing but that mysterious sustainable substance. Apparently, there were sprawling trees the size of the tallest buildings on Earth, where skyscrapers like Slinkies wound around them, instead of vice versa. There were two phrases Theo had heard Maria continually say, 'Construction not destruction' and 'Nature above nihilism,' and she chewed on these ideas like a gritty steak. Maria said there were floating islands of foliage thousands of feet in the air and that people would take tiny flying saucers up to floating mountains with waterfalls and rainbows like humans would take road trips. Theo was rapt.

The planet apparently did not have many variable climates, whether or not you were north or south. No deserts or ice caps, just flat foliage-dense land, like a rainforest, and then mountainous floating islands. Theo liked Earth's variable climate though and wondered if there truly was no place like it. Nonetheless, Gazibnon sounded like paradise. But it wasn't just the beautiful and bizarre-sounding planet that appealed to Theo, it was also their social systems. Apparently, on Gazibnon, they had a universal basic income, meaning everyone got a basic salary whether they worked or not. That meant there was no poverty. Gazibnonians who wanted to work made more money but with a rational catch: You could only make enough to cover three lifetimes of happy living at most. That was plenty as Maria had stated but not excess; anything past that was considered hoarding from the general people.

"The system," Maria was saying, "describes what most people on Earth would call socialism—"

"Dun, dun, dun," Jen joked.

"—which is only partly true, but Gazibnonian societies have an even better system than socialism, (one that has never turned into communism) it is just that, Earthlings cannot conceptualize a place where all humans are treated decently monetarily, so you cannot comprehend how good you could possibly have it, or how many better systems than socialism there are out there."

Theo was learning a lot and expanding her mind on the possibilities that could exist on her own planet. It sounded better than Canada but she couldn't help wondering, *Was it really like that?*

"Hey, Maria, tell us more about the people of Gazibnon," Rain asked, her eyes in the rearview mirror on Maria.

"What would you like to know?" asked Maria, as she sat at the dining table in the Airstream pulling a little uncomfortably at her human suit. Her extra arms were safely tucked away, while playing Cribbage with Mark who was clearly losing.

"Tell us more about aliens!" Jen shouted, nearly propelling from her seat and leaving a flurry of chip dust in her wake. "What are they like?"

"Well there are all sorts of us. Gazibnonians are not the only aliens. We are all diverse, from diverse planets, ya know? Like how humans are all different. And how different species on Earth are different."

Theo's mind was already spinning. "So then, what are some examples of what aliens look like?" she inquired.

Maria continued, "Some of us look like praying mantises."

"Argh, praying mantises?!" exclaimed Jen, unable to disguise her disgust.

Judging by Mark's wide eyes, he looked surprised too.

Maria continued, "Yeah, did you ever see a documentary where a man was out hunting in the woods, saw a spaceship that covered the sky and said he looked into the windshield and saw what could only be closely described as a praying mantis at the wheel?"

Rain was the only one who nodded vigorously and slightly fearfully.

"Yeah, that was real. I have studied human activity for almost a century and that guy certainly saw an inhabitant of a planet in my neighborhood." She nodding sagely. "Also, aliens can sometimes look like flamingos." The groups' eyes widened, perplexed but Maria continued, unfazed, "Who else, let's seeeeee ... Let's see. Oh! And some are opaque or *see-through*, as you would say."

"Like ghosts?" Jen questioned.

"Ghosts *are* aliens. They are just visiting your planet, you know, relaxing, checking it out and accidentally getting caught in sight by some of you."

"Radical," Jen said, stuffing a few more potato chips in her mouth.

"Wait," Theo said, her head feeling like it was ready to fall off its axis. "So, if ghosts are aliens visiting us, what about something like … Sasquatch?"

"Aliens," responded Maria.

"Bigfoot?" Jen asked through a mouthful of snacks.

"Same as Sasquatch, more or less, but yes, aliens."

"The Loch Ness Monster?" Mark asked, afraid of the answer.

"Aliens."

They went on asking questions like this with almost every answer being the same. Everyone but Maria sat in stunned silence for nearly an hour after that.

After a day of travel, they arrived in Morrison, Colorado, just outside Denver, for their show at Red Rocks and the *Alt-Cuntry-Festival: The West's Best Feminist Country Music Fest.* They even had a little time left over before the show to recharge. They browsed the little town, popping into a couple of shops. Jen came out of one holding out matching Red Rocks shirts that said: Red-y to Rock. They had all rolled their eyes and laughed, but put them on for the remainder of the day.

They drove up into the parking lot where the Red Rocks amphitheater was and parked where the bands were meant to park. Among the giant tour buses, their Airstream didn't look so giant anymore. They walked up the ascending slant between rocks into the amphitheater to gawk at the gorgeous scene before the show. Theo had never seen a place like it. The strata was bright, earthy red, and protruded into the sky like crystals, the seats ready for spectators to witness the glory of sound. Otherworldly, like a stadium on Mars. The pre-show music emanating from the speakers echoed iridescently and bounced off the rocks. They all breathed in the scene, time slipping by.

Theo wasn't sure what to expect from the attendees of the music fest, but found herself a little surprised that everyone looked so hipster and hippy, even metalheadish. For some reason, she'd thought it was going to be a lot of cowboy hats, and sure, there were a couple, but this was not the country type of style she knew from back in the South. No, this was liberal, South*west* country.

One fan recognized them, and they were amazed as a few others did too, even asking for autographs. It was surreal. Especially for Winny. Theo loved to see the look of happiness on her face. There were booths of woman-fronted businesses and artists, with men and women walking around, exploring the festival tents and what vendors had to offer. The support and peace-and-love-type of atmosphere was palpable.

"Like a hippy concert complete with a supportive, loving community," Rain had noted.

Theo wondered if this was a little like Maria's planet.

Jen stood in line for an enormous set of earrings that playfully swung from her ears and Rain waited to buy yet another flower muumuu. *Classic Rain.*

While they made their purchases, Theo, Winny and Maria went to the next booth over and perused a shop that sold festival paraphernalia but also, oddly, various plants and loose-leaf teas. They looked closely at the loose-leaf jars and all the names of tea

Theo had never heard of. It might be because she had smoked a joint with the group shortly prior, but she felt like she was in a magical shop full of jars used for casting spells and fixing ailments via incantations. An older woman with beautiful, long, thick silvery-white hair and red lipstick which popped bright against her olive skin, emerged from behind the desk holding a tray of small potted plants. She must not have seen the ladies standing there as she yelped, the plants launching off the tray.

"Sorry we startled you!" Theo said as she bent down to help pick up her plants, Winny and Maria helping.

"Oh, not to worry, my dear," the lady reassured them. "My! I like your hat," she said suddenly, her eyes crinkling. She looked at Theo and pointed to the symbol on the side. "Silphium seed."

Theo stopped stacking the plants back on the tray. "What's that?"

"You don't know? Surely *you* must know," the white-haired woman said, nodding to Maria.

Maria stopped assembling the plants back on the tray and stood up to leave. "I don't know what you're talking about," she said and walked away.

Theo thought this was odd, but was distracted by the woman's bubbling chatter.

She suggested that she try on a few other hats in her store. "You know," she began, "No hat will protect you from what's happened to your head."

"Huh?"

"I said, why don't you try this hat on instead," the silver-haired woman stated again.

Theo tried on a few, and left wearing a new one—this time, a hat sporting the Alt-Cuntry-Fest logo.

Jen and Rain joined them at the top of the stadium stairs in front of the row of booths, bags swinging, and together, they made their way back to the Airstream to join the others.

Once there, all six friends reclined, recharging before the show while Oxannae, Maria's brother, safely hid nearby in his triangular UFO. The band changed out of their tourist shirts and into their usual attire, getting ready. Theo had been thinking a lot about the orb but had decided to wait to ask Maria about it. It was too much to take on more information, especially right before playing a show. She wanted all her brain power to play the best damn show they could muster, especially since it appeared they had already achieved some small-time fame. *How did we get any fame already?*

They waited, and waited in the eighties' Airstream to perform.

Finally, it was time for the show, and they went backstage at Red Rocks. They sat out of sight, listening to the crowd humming, backstage in one of the coolest places Theo could have imagined. Where there normally would be a wall was a protruding set of red rocks, reaching up to the ceiling. The backstage had been built directly into the rocks, like a cave. It made Theo think about Winny's description of her magical experience in the Trois Frères caves.

They were going to be the first to play, the openers for the Alt-Cuntry Festival of that year and Theo felt the pressure. They all waited, their stage-fright-nerves jittering in their bloodstreams. She was nervous as hell and held onto her cello like a buoy in choppy seas. *That was a huge crowd out there.* She began to sweat. *Don't mess up, don't mess up, don't mess up,* she chanted in her head.

She closed her eyes and reminded herself of who she had become over the last few months. The troubles she had persevered through, the friendships she had formed with these ladies, aliens, men, a dog, the internal strength she had come to consider an integral part of herself now, and the knowledge she had gained about fledgling pieces of existence and the universe. *You can do this*, she told herself. *You got this.*

Winny sidled up next to Theo, smooth D'Angelico guitar held to her torso with her Western-flair strap. She whispered confidently in her ear, "You got this," and kissed her sweetly on the cheek.

Theo felt calmness sink into her stomach. *Ok, I got this. Relax, and enjoy the music.*

Everyone else in the band must have looked nervous too because Winny turned to face them all and started to give them a brief pre-show pep talk. Mark, Bowzer and Oxannae were also there for support and encouragement. Plus, they wanted to see the show! It was a once-in-a-lifetime opportunity to be in the cave-like backstage at Red Rocks, part building, part rock, which Maria said was architecturally similar to places on her planet. They peeked out at a sea of music aficionados rising upward toward the horizon above them.

"Hey, we've been through quite a journey together," Winny was saying, grabbing a complimentary drink from the table nearby and motioning for the others to take a glass.

Each person did and gently sipped, listening to their fearless leader, Winny.

"Just like that woman in the hot springs we met, way back when, said, and the tarot reader for Theo's reading said too.

We've experienced hardship, water, fire, and a long journey." Then, looking at Theo, she said, "I feel you rolling your eyes, babe. I know you think that lady in the hot springs was kooky, and that tarot cards and horoscopes and whatnot are all a bunch of *woo-woo*. But it all means something to me. I *do* think there's something to it. And you have to admit, you do too. Perhaps, at least in how you interpret it. Back me up on this, Maria," she said, only half joking, earnest.

Maria nodded in firm agreement.

Maria was supposed to know almost everything in the universe and she agreed?

Jen shouted, "Hear, hear, sister!"

Theo thought for a moment, then smiled. "I'm open to learning more. You know that, Win," she said and kissed her on the cheek.

Winny smiled warmly, returning her lover's radiant look, before resuming her speech. "We've been through hardship. All of our pasts are rough. Let's not let the past consume us, let's let the present liberate us. We've been through water, when we sat in the hot springs together for the first time and when it poured rain when our Airstream broke down and I shouted the lyrics to 'Time After Time.'" Winny and Theo smiled at each other.

"And we faced water when Theo nearly drowned in that river," Jen interjected, stating an uncomfortable fact.

"Yes, that's true too," Winny continued, "We've been through fire, when Theo signaled us, dancing around a garbage fire and professed her love of being a lesbian," to which the group chuckled. "And finally, it certainly has been a long journey, just like the Tarot reader and the hot springs woman said it would be: A spontaneous journey to get here, all the way to Red Rocks Amphitheater in Colorado from way down yonder in Truth or Consequences, New Mexico. And hot damn if we haven't learned some truth, and seen the consequences of our human actions if we don't *do* something for our planet, like Koko the ape *kind of* said." She took a breath, continuing her speech, "It's the truth that existence as we know it on this planet won't be able to continue, if we don't get a handle on this climate *shit*. We need to help each other find harmony on this living breathing ball of an organism we call a planet, floating through space. And maybe, just *maybe*, with the help of some friends, human and nonhuman, we can pull our shit together. Here's hoping that music can bring us all a little closer and make the world just that much more of a better place." She concluded her speech, raising her glass fondly to her bandmates and friends, "So, cheers! To music, to us and our journey and to our planet!"

"Cheers!" they all agreed.

One helluva speech, thought Theo, beaming at her best friend and lover. They all cheers-ed in the air and sipped their drinks. Theo was feeling amped up and inspired by Winny and so, although public speaking was never her thing, she decided to give it a go with a speech of her own. "I just want to say," she began, "before I met y'all, especially you, Winny, I never knew how sweet life could taste."

Jen raised an eyebrow. "Are you talking about something else?"

"What? No!" Theo stammered, "Get your head out of the gutter, Jen. No, I mean, I never knew how amazing friendship would feel. It's like warm, glowing orbs of light—"

"Ehem," Jen smirked.

"No! No, I mean, ya know, with you all, I have so much joy, it's like eating a peach on a summer's day."

"Okay, now you're just *trying* to be dirty!" Jen laughed.

"I give up," Theo laughed. "You know what I mean. I love all of our friendships, and I-I-I-" Theo was about to say it, about to say it in front of everyone: That she loved Winny. Winny looked at Theo, her brown eyes imploring. Theo continued, "I am so happy with you, Winny. You make me so happy." *Shit, I chickened out.*

But still, at least she'd said something. Something of how she felt about Winny.

Everyone cheered and whooped at Theo's terrible speech.

"Good speech! I only wish you'd said it in private," Jen joked.

With that, they took to the stage and peered out at all the eyes and ears drawn to them, the clapping and excitement audible. It was pretty packed. Not packed yet like it would be for Aurelia Olsen, but still pretty packed. And Theo felt proud. One set of eyes, however, stood out particularly. Across the crowd, toward the middle of the seats was a pair of man's eyes she'd hoped she'd never see again.

It was her ex-husband.

Theo's heart plummeted into her gut. *No, not yet. Not now. Not in front of this whole crowd.* Images of her past came launching into her psyche. Things she didn't want to remember. Things that scared her and made her knees weak. She looked around at her support system. At Winny standing confidently at the microphone, saying something to the crowd, unaware of the man watching Theo so intently. She looked over at Jen, shoulders back, hand at the ready on her four bass strings. She looked at Rain, still a smiling space-case at the keys and then back at Maria on drums who, guessing by the expression on her face, had noticed something was off in Theo's. She looked over to Mark, Oxannae, and even Bowzer backstage for some sort of guidance. *Now fucking what?* She turned around again to face the audience and noticed Winny looking at her eagerly as if to say, *You ready?*

Theo took a breath and put up a mental wall, telling herself, *Just play. Just play.* So she nodded to Winny. Winny smiled and Theo felt the world melt away again for a moment. *Here we go.* The music started up, they were playing their opening song. It was upbeat, vibrant, the sounds reverberating around the space so beautifully it felt otherworldly. At that moment, Theo reveled in the joy of playing their own music in such a space, the sounds bouncing off the rocks and breathing spirally through her cochlea, giving her a zing of serotonin.

The euphoria departed seemingly just as it had arrived when she saw the man she'd never wanted to see again moving determinedly past standing spectators, sidestepping until he reached the descending stairs. Her heart raced. *What was he doing? Was he approaching the stage?*

Theo missed a note with her bow, but with a jolt, resumed, hoping it was not noticeable.

There was a shift in Winny's posture. She had noticed something was off, just through Theo's sound, and Theo could feel the energy of momentary empathy from her.

She tried to not let this man distract her. That's what he wanted. For her to fail. She would not let him win. She continued playing, trying to resume her newfound confidence, something that had been so foreign before. But he continued to approach the stage.

Something else caught Theo's eye. A black dot was emerging in the sky, getting closer and closer. It was a UFO. The giant one they'd seen on the mesa before. Theo strummed her cello back and forth, and glanced furtively at Maria whose arms continued to move rhythmically on the drums, despite the growing size of the dot in the sky. Theo saw the shape clearly illuminated in the reflection of Maria's giant green eyes.

This is unreal, she thought and resisted the urge to pinch herself as she had so often wanted to do over the past few months, not knowing if something was indeed real, whether the good kind of unreal or the bad. In this case, she knew it was real and it was not looking good. This moment was no dream, this was real life, right? It was time to act. But … *What do I do?*

Her ex stepped closer and closer, one by one, down the steps approaching the stage.

The object in the sky grew bigger until it nearly eclipsed the entire sky, silently.

Silence was music too, she heard Maria's voice say in her mind. *But how did no one else notice the enormous craft hovering above them iridescently? Was this the people Maria feared? Had they arrived? What would they do to her? To them?* No one in the crowd had noticed, their eyes were fixed on the stage and, something Maria had said stood out in Theo's mind, the UFO was hidden in plain sight. It was time to act, to do something, but she felt frozen.

Winny had seen the UFO too, and looked at the others, not knowing what to do either, except continue to play, to sing, hopefully not drawing alarm from the large crowd.

The ex was now just a few steps from the stage. *What did he think he was going to do?* He raised something up to his line of vision swiftly, eyes dead on Theo, before the security up front or the ladies on stage could register fast enough what it was. A gun. *He has a gun!*

Time seemed to slow, the music jolted to a halting and cacophonous stop.

The crowd erupted in screams, both at the man with the gun and the black disc hovering ominously above them, now very visible, darkening the sky. It all happened in a millisecond. Theo pulled her cello in front of her face, stupidly and helplessly to try to block the bullet just as Winny launched her body protectively into Theo's line of vision at the same time as Maria tried to protect them both.

A bang erupted and then, a confusing swirling feeling, and her stomach lurched in circles as she felt herself being propelled upward into the sky. Chaos and noise seemed to encircle her all at once and she felt herself being pulled into the sky with Maria, the two of them going *up, up, up.* She saw, helpless, a birds-eye view of Winny lying on the stage, coughing, blood pooling at her torso, her movements beginning to slow.

Theo screamed at the sight of Winny down below. She felt helpless swirling upward, upward toward the dark disc in the sky, watching the chaos of the crowd swell and disperse, like ants under a laser-pointing microscope. It all felt so real and so far away.

All Theo could feel was the pain of seeing Winny lying there in a pool of blood.

Darkness blotted out Theo's world as she was swallowed up into the ship.

The Glowing Orb

The world was again dark and quiet. In the blackness, her attention was drawn to a dull but persistent pain she had not realized had been throbbing between her temples. Come to think of it, her head hurt nearly constantly the past several months. There were times she noticed it and times she didn't but it felt like a humming pain that was always there. Like tinnitus. She winced and opened her eyes again to the darkness that surrounded her. This was the third time she had been amongst this kind of darkness and quietness. She waited for a soft light to pop on, and for the gentle steady harmony of the glowing orb she had come to expect while in Oxannae and Maria's cozy ship. But this was not Maria and Oxannae's ship. That comfortable moment did not arrive.

Instead, there was just silence and darkness.

Theo wept, alone in the dark, not knowing what was happening, and fearing the worst about Winny. An arm reached out to comfort her. She could tell it was Maria before a light inevitably did come on. But it was different from before. There were no comfortable velvet armchairs to levitate in, no. This ship was cold, metal, and silent. A giant barren room. There were figures in front of her she could barely discern, but they were there, sitting, floating, staring. She could not see their faces nor distantly interpret their figures. They were something Theo could not comprehend. A different species entirely. Some had several arms, some had several eyes like spiders, but all different in shapes and sizes. Most had enormous, bulbous eyes like Maria's. They scared Theo.

Fear took hold until Maria's voice next to her said, "It is ok. It will be ok."

Time passed so bizarrely in that room and Theo's grief was so palpable, she did not know where she was, who she was, or what was happening. Was it a day, or three weeks? The next thing she knew, she and Maria were in a different room, a small, closet-sized enclosure with one tiny, airplane-sized window.

Theo raised her chin up from her chest, not realizing it had been resting there in slumber. Maria's bold green eyes were looking at her and she felt a glimmer of reassurance. "Maria? Where are we?" She paused and looked around at the sterile environment. Despite being in a spacecraft, it gave her the feeling of the hospital she'd worked in; fluorescent, tumescent, pulsing with lights beaming down on her. She did not like it and wanted out. Then came a sinking thought, *Winny.*

She could not bear the thought of a world without Winny.

"What's going on? Is Winny ok?" she asked.

Maria looked at Theo, her large bug-like eyes compressing into concern behind her glasses. "I do not know. I think so! But … I do not know. There is a chance, to save her I mean. To save us. But there is not much time. They thought they were just getting me, but they pulled you in too, into this craft. I am sorry you have been roped in like this."

"Wait, what's going to happen to you, now that the Interplanetary Committee has you? You never said what would happen."

Maria seemed to be mustering up the courage to say, "Well, I haven't been convicted yet … But if I am, which I suspect I will be, given that they probably have all the evidence they need that I have been illegally interacting and befriending humans AND that the humans know I am an alien … then …"

Theo waited for the response, concerned for her friend.

"So, well… You know how humans fear aliens performing experiments on them?"

Theo nodded.

"That is what they would do to me. Ostensibly I would be a lab rat for the rest of my life."

"Why?!" implored Theo.

"Well, to study me of course. To try to understand what is wrong with me that I would want to interact and befriend humans."

Theo couldn't believe it. Humans were living creatures too. *There's nothing wrong with befriending us, she thought.* "What can we do? How are we going to get out of here?" The walls started to feel very heavy.

"I am not sure," Maria began. "But there is hope. We have one tool left. They did not see me stash it in my pocket before they pulled us up."

She pulled something from her pocket and into her palm and began to open her hand. A tiny glowing orb, which grew bigger and bigger until it was the size of a football. Theo recognized it as *the* orb. The one she had so often thought about.

It began to hum that transcendental sound she had come to know and … love? It glistened reflectively in Maria's alien eyes and Theo could have sworn she heard a glimmer of a song she knew, a song she knew well. It was her and Winny's song, from dancing in the rain. 'Time After Time.' *Why was that orb singing that song?* Theo's heart dropped again down into her gut, as the image of Winny lying in blood on the stage reemerged in her mind. She had a feeling it would be burned onto her eyelids for a long time.

Theo looked at the glowing orb, thinking. She tried to put the pieces of the puzzle together. *What was this thing?* Whenever she was around it, she felt its pull. Like it was ready to suck her in like a black hole, pull her in. And, at the same time, she felt oddly smarter around it. "What is that glowing orb?" she asked.

"I think you have some ideas," Maria tilted her head knowingly.

"Is it … Well, in some senses, I feel like it could pull me into another dimension. And in others, I feel like it, somehow …" Theo felt slightly ridiculous telling Maria her theories. "Somehow, as if it knows things."

Maria smiled. "*Bingo*. It is both. For one, this orb is a tool, more like an instrument that I have been working on for many years. It assists me jumping between worlds, a teleportation device, if you will."

Theo thought for a moment. "Like a portkey. Or a stargate. Or, or, that device in *Contact* that took Jodie Foster through black holes to that other planet." Theo tried to make sense of it by conjuring any fantasy and sci-fi elements she could think of. How strange that this device was *real,* though. Her head hurt thinking about it. And thinking about Winny.

"Precisely," Maria continued, "and, in order to transport people and beings through it, it must contain knowledge of the universe. So yes, Theo, you are correct, it also knows things. In fact, it contains all the knowledge of the known universe. I wanted to gift it to humans to help you overcome climate catastrophe. To help our people and your people transport between our planets to better understand each other."

This was difficult to understand. A transportation device containing all the knowledge of the universe? *That was just crazy.* Theo couldn't help feeling that Maria was naive to think this could truly help humans. All the knowledge of the universe? Wasn't that like the Internet? Theo felt like people would just use it to watch silly cat videos.

Maria continued, "The orb presents itself as a light and glowing sound because sound transports and informs. Sound, in the form of words, educates. Sound, in the form of music and feelings, transports. I just harnessed this natural technology in order to use it as a powerful tool. I harnessed the sounds from the Big Bang and put it into this device. The sound, it is soothing yet ominous, is it not?"

Theo nodded, thinking about the way it had made her feel when she'd first seen it and the way its presence permeated her being.

"I was hoping this device could help our people understand each other better by allowing us to see each other's worlds."

"How does it work?" asked Theo, trying hard to concentrate. She had to concentrate because she had to get back to Winny. She had a feeling this orb would help her get back to Winny.

"Well, when utilizing this orb-tool properly in one of the few energy zones on Earth that promote the existence of a portal, one can walk through into another world. It is a connection between minds and physical connection between my planet and yours."

Theo thought for a moment. "And the top of the mesa in Truth or Consequences is one of these portal zones you're talking about?"

Maria nodded. "Yes. And, I was hoping, combined with this orb and your heart," she patted her own chest, exclaiming, "your compassion, we could help people understand how to save Planet Earth, and make them actually *want* and have the compassion to do so. But," Maria exhaled deeply, her green skin turning a dark shade of indigo, "alas, it does not work. I was hoping I could bring my people to your planet as tourists to see how not all humans are bad. And, I was hoping to bring humans to Planet Gazibnon to see for themselves what a beautiful utopian world can look like. But, this device only works for me in its current stage. And, I am not sure how to help humans utilize all the knowledge of the universe sufficiently."

Theo thought again back to the silly cat videos and how phones were like the orb in the way that they brought all the knowledge of the universe into one's palm in one glowing rectangular brick, and yet humans didn't know how to use it to help themselves. The device could transport us through worlds, yet humans would choose to use it for entertainment and sometimes, she had to think it, to divide themselves against one another.

Maria was still talking, "But this," she said, signaling the floating orb above her palm, "as it turns out, this is my greatest failure. I am a fraud. I do not know what I am doing. I do not know how to help humans or Earth. I have failed."

Theo could feel the weight of Maria's own personal disappointment in herself and her failed project in her career in the air between them, Maria's sense of self dissolving. She could certainly relate; she had once lost herself in what she thought was failure in her career but if there was one thing this trip had taught her, it was that you couldn't be too hard on yourself and you had to let go of the past. "Maria, this portal orb-thing is amazing but I think you're right," she said, putting a kind hand on her friend's shoulder. "It doesn't work that way. People can't just magically see how to fix the way they feel about the planet. They need to be taught how to do it. And," she began, staring at the all-knowing-glowing-transportation orb powered by the sounds of existence, "and that takes time. But it's amazing you've tried and you shouldn't give up! I think people already have the knowledge, for the most part, on how to save their planet from complete collapse, and I think most people have the compassion and desire to do so, but frankly, I also think the problem truly is … that power is in the hands of the few." She took a moment to think about what she wanted to say. *This was tough*!

Maria didn't rush her, just allowed her to explain.

Theo continued, "I can only speak for where I'm from in America, but I believe the problem is universal; we … well, we allowed ourselves to be deceived by powerful people because," she faltered again. *Why* did *this repeatedly happen?* "Because, we lost heart and I guess, we stopped thinking that was important. So, louder, harder, heartless people began controlling our country behind the scenes. And so, well, we've deceived ourselves, too. We forgot to focus on what truly matters. Our Earth, our one and only home."

Theo looked across the room, out of the sliver of window where the dot of her home planet was visible from the space cell they were confined in. Little Earth looked so fragile, so vulnerable. And it was being devoured by itself. *Us. Humans. Unlike Maria's utopian planet.* The thought gave Theo an idea.

She turned and looked at Maria's giant oval eyes. "We've deceived ourselves but we can move past our mistakes. We can actually make things better. It *is* possible to heal our planet. You know why?" Theo asked.

Maria looked into Theo's eyes. "Why?"

"Because we have a secret tool, a secret instrument. And it is not your glowing orb-portal thingy there. It's you, Maria."

"Huh?"

"You have knowledge about your planet and how you all made it a Shangri-la where people are happy and in harmony with nature and their planet."

"Yeah, but our planet is much different from yours."

"But, still! That is the missing link. We've been needing to see an example of a place that's done it, that's avoided environmental collapse. Lead by example! We have the *knowledge* of how to avoid collapse and we have the *compassion* to make it happen, but we are missing *hope*, the *example,* that we *can* make a harmonious planet happen. Your planet and *you* as our teacher is exactly that. We need someone who says, 'Look, this planet is doing it, we can do it too.' You have to teach us how y'all did it! *You're* a professor."

"But I do not know if humans are ready yet to know me, an alien, or to know the full extent of aliens and other planets. I have not even told you half of it, of what the universe is like. Plus, we

253

are stuck here," Maria glanced around the sterile room.

"Well, that part we will definitely have to figure out," acknowledged Theo defeatedly. *Winny. Oh god, Winny.*

Maria continued, "And I am just one person, well, one *alien*."

Theo felt it strange that the tables had turned. Now it was her trying to boost Maria's self-confidence, trying to persuade Maria to resume her goal of helping humanity. She saw through the star-laden window at the vast and seemingly emptiness of space. The stars winked at her, shining specks in the expansive blackness—wise, twinkling, luculent and yet ephemeral in the scheme of the universe. She thought back to that night she and Maria had sat outside the Tin Can together, staring up at the stars together in Arizona. "I remember what you said to me once, 'We are all so terribly insignificant and yet profoundly important at the same time.' That is you and me. We got this. Together, we can make a difference."

Maria listened, taking it all in.

"In fact," Theo continued, pausing to think even further back to that first night on the mesa. "I now remember that's what you said to us that night we met you, that night we didn't know it was you. You said, 'You are profoundly important.' You must believe in the ability we have as individuals to make a difference."

Maria thought long and hard for a second. "Yes, that is exactly it. Look, I cannot do it without you, Theo. You have the heart, the ability to show others the importance of stuff like this. If I am going to try to do something like this, to help humanity, to teach humanity how to avoid environmental collapse, and instead, how to create utopia on Earth, I need you. You are open-minded and you want to believe in something better. That is rare. But … most important of all, you have a big, compassionate heart."

Theo thought about that for a minute. Her heart. Right now, her heart felt shattered into a million pieces. *Was Winny okay?* If she was dead, Theo didn't know what she would do or how she would ever go on. She'd never had a love like that, a love that transcended time and space and within the blink of an eye, that love was robbed from her. Potentially forever. And it was all her fault. The ex had been after her, not Winny. She shook her head, changing her mind seemingly only moments after just trying to convince Maria that she herself could do it. "I can't do it, Maria. Without Winny, my heart is nothing."

Tears began to well in the corners of her eyes and she turned her face before Maria could see her cry. She held the bridge of her nose to prevent more tears, thinking about the one person that mattered to her most in the world, any world. The person who mattered most to her in this universe, was possibly gone. Forever. Her heart ached to be back down there, to swoop Winny off that bloodied stage and whisk her away to the hospital, or even work on her injuries herself if she had to: Anything to save her.

Theo stood there by the window silently, forgetting all about the hopeful conversation with Maria. She felt deflated and her posture slumped downward like it had used to so often.

Maria looked imploringly at Theo, unsure how to comfort her human friend.

She reached out and put one of her six arms around Theo's shoulder, her skin rippling different hues, peering down at the tiny Earth dot as it floated silently in the blackness. "Well," Maria said, "we are just going to have to find and save Winny then, aren't we?"

End of Book One

ΔΔΔ

Book Club Questions:

1. What are the aspects that create utopia on Maria's planet? Do you think such a perfect world could exist? Why or why not?

2. What do you think is the symbolism of the roadrunner and why does it show up at certain points in the story?

3. Why do you think time is often strange for Theo throughout the book?

4. There are themes about friendship, the magic of the desert, self-discovery, truth and consequences, and reality vs the bizarre. Can you name some examples of these?

Acknowledgments

Thank you to all the ladies out there who are telling their stories and to the environmentalists fighting the good fight for our one and only home. To my friends, so much love. To Agatha Whitechapel, my phenomenal, witty and wise editor. To Delaney Cummins, for creating an out of this world cover. To my mommers, my first editor and endlessly helpful red marker-er and my dad for telling me, 'You can really write.' My brother for believing 'You got this' and my partner, Nick for all his support and interest in hearing all my crazy ideas whilst we, at one point, stayed in an RV.

Thank you Elise for your incredible encouragement! You motivated me like crazy! And Sydney for being my rock-solid bestie and preliminary reader, and to Pablo's coffee shop for the best people and vibes, a place where I felt alive and comfortable to tell the quirkiest of stories into my laptop over cups of chai.